P9-DEV-471

Dover Thrift Study Edition

# King Lear

WILLIAM SHAKESPEARE

DOVER PUBLICATIONS, INC.
Mineola, New York

*Copyright*



*Bibliographical Note*

This Dover edition, first published in 2011, contains the unabridged text of *King Lear,* as published in Volume XVII of *The Caxton Edition of the Complete Works of William Shakepeare,* Caxton Publishing Company, London, n.d., plus literary analysis and perspectives from *MAXnotes® for King Lear,* published in 1995 by Research & Education Association, Inc., Piscataway, New Jersey. The explanatory footnotes to the play were prepared specially for the present edition.

*Library of Congress Cataloging-in-Publication Data*

Shakespeare, William, 1564–1616.
King Lear / William Shakespeare.
p. cm. — (Dover thrift study edition)
Includes bibliographical references.
ISBN-13: 978-0-486-47581-3
ISBN-10: 0-486-47581-6
1. Shakespeare, William, 1564–1616. King Lear—Examinations—Study guides. 2. Lear, King (Legendary character)—Drama. 3. Inheritance and succession—Drama. 4. Fathers and daughters—Drama. 5. Kings and rulers—Drama. 6. Aging parents—Drama. 7. Britons—Drama. I. Title.

PR2819.A1 2011
822.3'3—dc22

2010029455

Manufactured in the United States by Courier Corporation
47581601
www.doverpublications.com

## Publisher's Note

Combining the complete text of a classic novel or drama with a comprehensive study guide, Dover Thrift Study Editions are the most effective way to gain a thorough understanding of the major works of world literature.

The study guide features up-to-date and expert analysis of every chapter or section from the source work. Questions and fully explained answers follow, allowing readers to analyze the material critically. Character lists, author bios, and discussions of the work's historical context are also provided.

Each Dover Thrift Study Edition includes everything a student needs to prepare for homework, discussions, reports, and exams.

## Contents

# King Lear

WILLIAM SHAKESPEARE

# Contents

## Dramatis Personæ

LEAR, King of Britain.
KING OF FRANCE.
DUKE OF BURGUNDY.
DUKE OF CORNWALL.
DUKE OF ALBANY.
EARL OF KENT.
EARL OF GLOUCESTER.
EDGAR, *son to Gloucester.*
EDMUND, *bastard son to Gloucester.*
CURAN, *a courtier.*
Old Man, *tenant to Gloucester.*
Doctor.
Fool.
OSWALD, *steward to Goneril.*
A Captain employed by Edmund.
Gentleman attendant on Cordelia.
A Herald.
Servants to Cornwall.

GONERIL, } *daughters to Lear.*
REGAN, }
CORDELIA, }

Knights of Lear's train, Captains,
Messengers, Soldiers, *and* Attendants.

# ACT I

## SCENE I—*King Lear's Palace*

*Enter* KENT, GLOUCESTER, *and* EDMUND

KENT. I thought the king had more affected[1] the Duke of Albany than Cornwall.

GLOU. It did always seem so to us: but now, in the division of the kingdom, it appears not which of the dukes he values most; for equalities are so weighed that curiosity in neither can make choice of either's moiety.[2]

KENT. Is not this your son, my lord?

GLOU. His breeding, sir, hath been at my charge: I have so often blushed to acknowledge him that now I am brazed[3] to it.

KENT. I cannot conceive[4] you.

GLOU. Sir, this young fellow's mother could: whereupon she grew round-wombed, and had indeed, sir, a son for her cradle ere she had a husband for her bed. Do you smell a fault?

KENT. I cannot wish the fault undone, the issue of it being so proper.[5]

GLOU. But I have, sir, a son by order of law, some year elder than this, who yet is no dearer in my account: though this knave came something saucily into the world before he was sent for, yet was his mother fair; there was good sport at his making, and the whoreson must be acknowledged. Do you know this noble gentleman, Edmund?

---

1. *more affected*] showed greater affection for.
2. *moiety*] portion, part.
3. *brazed*] brazened, hardened.
4. *conceive*] understand.
5. *proper*] goodly, handsome.

EDM. No, my lord.

GLOU. My lord of Kent: remember him hereafter as my honourable friend.

EDM. My services to your lordship.

KENT. I must love you, and sue[6] to know you better.

EDM. Sir, I shall study deserving.[7]

GLOU. He hath been out nine years, and away he shall again. The king is coming.

*Sennet.*[8] *Enter one bearing a coronet,* KING LEAR, CORNWALL, ALBANY, GONERIL, REGAN, CORDELIA, *and* Attendants

LEAR. Attend the lords of France and Burgundy, Gloucester.

GLOU. I shall, my liege. [*Exeunt Gloucester and Edmund.*]

LEAR. Meantime we shall express our darker purpose.
Give me the map there. Know we have divided
In three our kingdom: and 't is our fast[9] intent
To shake all cares and business from our age,
Conferring them on younger strengths, while we
Unburthen'd crawl toward death. Our son of Cornwall,
And you, our no less loving son of Albany,
We have this hour a constant will to publish
Our daughters' several dowers, that future strife
May be prevented now. The princes, France and Burgundy,
Great rivals in our youngest daughter's love,
Long in our court have made their amorous sojourn,
And here are to be answer'd. Tell me, my daughters,
Since now we will divest us both of rule,
Interest of territory,[10] cares of state,
Which of you shall we say doth love us most?
That we our largest bounty may extend
Where nature doth with merit challenge.[11] Goneril,
Our eldest-born, speak first.

---

6. *sue*] beg, entreat.
7. *study deserving*] study to be worthy (of your acquaintance).
8. *Sennet*] a note of music commonly indicating the entrance or exit of important characters.
9. *fast*] firmly fixed.
10. *Interest of territory*] profit derived from possession of territory.
11. *Where nature . . . challenge*] Where natural affection prefers a claim equally with merit, where the due of natural affection coincides with the due of merit.

GON. Sir, I love you more than words can wield the matter,
Dearer than eye-sight, space and liberty,
Beyond what can be valued, rich or rare,
No less than life, with grace, health, beauty, honour,
As much as child e'er loved or father found;
A love that makes breath poor and speech unable;
Beyond all manner of so much I love you.

COR. [*Aside*] What shall Cordelia do? Love, and be silent.

LEAR. Of all these bounds, even from this line to this,
With shadowy forests and with champains[12] rich'd,
With plenteous rivers and wide-skirted meads,
We make thee lady. To thine and Albany's issue
Be this perpetual. What says our second daughter,
Our dearest Regan, wife to Cornwall? Speak.

REG. I am made of that self[13] metal as my sister,
And prize me at her worth. In my true heart
I find she names my very deed of love;
Only she comes too short: that I profess
Myself an enemy to all other joys
Which the most precious square of sense possesses,[14]
And find I am alone felicitate[15]
In your dear highness' love.

COR. [*Aside*] Then poor Cordelia!
And yet not so, since I am sure my love's
More ponderous than my tongue.

LEAR. To thee and thine hereditary ever
Remain this ample third of our fair kingdom,
No less in space, validity and pleasure,
Than that conferr'd on Goneril. Now, our joy,
Although the last, not least, to whose young love
The vines of France and milk of Burgundy
Strive to be interess'd,[16] what can you say to draw
A third more opulent than your sisters? Speak.

---

12. *champains*] open country.
13. *self*] self-same.
14. *most . . . possesses*] i.e., which the soundest sense acknowledges as joy.
15. *felicitate*] made happy.
16. *to be interess'd*] to establish a claim, right.

COR. Nothing, my lord.
LEAR. Nothing!
COR. Nothing.
LEAR. Nothing will come of nothing: speak again.
COR. Unhappy that I am, I cannot heave
My heart into my mouth: I love your majesty
According to my bond;[17] nor more nor less.
LEAR. How, how, Cordelia! mend your speech a little,
Lest it mar your fortunes.
COR. Good my lord,
You have begot me, bred me, loved me: I
Return those duties back as are right fit,
Obey you, love you, and most honour you.
Why have my sisters husbands, if they say
They love you all? Haply, when I shall wed,
That lord whose hand must take my plight shall carry
Half my love with him, half my care and duty:
Sure, I shall never marry like my sisters,
To love my father all.
LEAR. But goes thy heart with this?
COR. Ay, good my lord.
LEAR. So young, and so untender?
COR. So young, my lord, and true.
LEAR. Let it be so; thy truth then be thy dower:
For, by the sacred radiance of the sun,
The mysteries of Hecate, and the night;
By all the operation of the orbs
From whom we do exist and cease to be;
Here I disclaim all my paternal care,
Propinquity and property of blood,
And as a stranger to my heart and me
Hold thee from this for ever. The barbarous Scythian,[18]
Or he that makes his generation messes[19]
To gorge his appetite, shall to my bosom

17. *According to my bond*] According to my duty as your daughter.
18. *Scythian*] the inhabitants of Scythia, part of what was Russia, were considered the extreme types of barbarity.
19. *he that . . . messes*] he that makes meals of his children.

Be as well neighbour'd, pitied and relieved,
As thou my sometime daughter.

KENT. Good my liege, —

LEAR. Peace, Kent!
Come not between the dragon and his wrath.
I loved her most, and thought to set my rest
On her kind nursery. Hence, and avoid my sight!
So be my grave my peace, as here I give
Her father's heart from her! Call France. Who stirs?
Call Burgundy. Cornwall and Albany.
With my two daughters' dowers digest[20] this third:
Let pride, which she calls plainness, marry her.
I do invest you jointly with my power,
Pre-eminence and all the large effects[21]
That troop with majesty. Ourself, by monthly course,
With reservation of an hundred knights
By you to be sustain'd, shall our abode
Make with you by due turns. Only we still retain
The name and all the additions to a king;[22]
The sway, revenue, execution of the rest,
Beloved sons, be yours: which to confirm,
This coronet part betwixt you.

KENT. Royal Lear,
Whom I have ever honour'd as my king,
Loved as my father, as my master follow'd,
As my great patron thought on in my prayers, —

LEAR. The bow is bent and drawn; make from the shaft.[23]

KENT. Let it fall rather, though the fork[24] invade
The region of my heart: be Kent unmannerly,
When Lear is mad. What wouldst thou do, old man?
Think'st thou that duty shall have dread to speak,
When power to flattery bows? To plainness honour's bound,
When majesty stoops to folly. Reverse thy doom,

20. *digest*] absorb.
21. *the large effects*] the spacious attributes or dignities.
22. *additions to a king*] titles of a king.
23. *make from the shaft*] take the risk, come what may (Lear is telling Kent, now that he's gone so far, to finish his speech).
24. *fork*] arrowhead.

And in thy best consideration check
This hideous rashness: answer my life my judgement,
Thy youngest daughter does not love thee least;
Nor are those empty-hearted whose low sound
Reverbs no hollowness.[25]

LEAR. Kent, on thy life, no more.

KENT. My life I never held but as a pawn
To wage against thy enemies, nor fear to lose it,
Thy safety being the motive.

LEAR. Out of my sight!

KENT. See better, Lear, and let me still remain
The true blank[26] of thine eye.

LEAR. Now, by Apollo,—

KENT. Now, by Apollo, king,
Thou swear'st thy gods in vain.

LEAR. O, vassal! miscreant!
[*Laying his hand on his sword.*]

ALB.
CORN. } Dear sir, forbear.

KENT. Do;
Kill thy physician, and the fee bestow
Upon the foul disease. Revoke thy doom;
Or, whilst I can vent clamour from my throat,
I'll tell thee thou dost evil.

LEAR. Hear me, recreant!
On thy allegiance, hear me!
Since thou hast sought to make us break our vow,
Which we durst never yet, and with strain'd pride
To come between our sentence and our power,
Which nor our nature nor our place can bear,
Our potency made good, take thy reward.
Five days we do allot thee, for provision
To shield thee from diseases[27] of the world,
And on the sixth to turn thy hated back

25. *Reverbs no hollowness*] reverberates no insincerity or emptiness.
26. *blank*] The white mark forming the bull's eye of the target. Kent appeals to Lear to let him remain by him as the mark by which to guide the aim of his vision.
27. *diseases*] troubles, distresses.

Upon our kingdom: if on the tenth day following
Thy banish'd trunk be found in our dominions,
The moment is thy death. Away! By Jupiter,
This shall not be revoked.

KENT. Fare thee well, king: sith[28] thus thou wilt appear,
Freedom lives hence,[29] and banishment is here.
[*To Cordelia*] The gods to their dear shelter take thee, maid,
That justly think'st and hast most rightly said!
[*To Regan and Goneril*] And your large speeches may your deeds approve,
That good effects may spring from words of love.
Thus Kent, O princes, bids you all adieu;
He'll shape his old course in a country new. [*Exit.*]

*Flourish. Re-enter* GLOUCESTER, *with* FRANCE, BURGUNDY, *and* Attendants

GLOU. Here's France and Burgundy, my noble lord.

LEAR. My lord of Burgundy,
We first address towards you, who with this king
Hath rivall'd for our daughter: what, in the least,
Will you require in present dower with her,
Or cease your quest of love?

BUR. Most royal majesty,
I crave no more than what your highness offer'd,
Nor will you tender less.

LEAR. Right noble Burgundy,
When she was dear to us, we did hold her so;
But now her price is fall'n. Sir, there she stands:
If aught within that little seeming substance,
Or all of it, with our displeasure pieced,[30]
And nothing more, may fitly like your grace,
She's there, and she is yours.

BUR. I know no answer.

LEAR. Will you, with those infirmities she owes,[31]

---

28. *sith*] since, seeing that.
29. *hence*] not here, at a distance.
30. *pieced*] supplemented.
31. *owes*] has, possesses.

Unfriended, new adopted to our hate,
Dower'd with our curse and stranger'd with our oath,[32]
Take her, or leave her?

BUR. Pardon me, royal sir;
Election makes not up on[33] such conditions.

LEAR. Then leave her, sir; for, by the power that made me,
I tell you all her wealth. [*To France*] For you, great king,
I would not from your love make such a stray,
To match[34] you where I hate; therefore beseech you
To avert your liking a more worthier way
Than on a wretch whom nature is ashamed
Almost to acknowledge hers.

FRANCE. This is most strange,
That she, that even but now was your best object,
The argument of your praise, balm of your age,
Most best, most dearest, should in this trice of time
Commit a thing so monstrous, to dismantle
So many folds of favour. Sure, her offence
Must be of such unnatural degree
That monsters it, or your fore-vouch'd affection
Fall'n into taint:[35] which to believe of her,
Must be a faith that reason without miracle
Could never plant in me.

COR. I yet beseech your majesty,—
If for I want that glib and oily art,
To speak and purpose not, since what I well intend,
I'll do't before I speak,—that you make known
It is no vicious blot, murder, or foulness,
No unchaste action, or dishonour'd step,
That hath deprived me of your grace and favour;
But even for want of that for which I am richer,
A still-soliciting eye,[36] and such a tongue

---

32. *stranger'd . . . oath*] made a stranger to us, alienated from us by oath.
33. *Election makes not up*] No choice is possible.
34. *I would not. . . . To match*] I would not neglect or ignore your love to such an extent as to match. . . .
35. *her offence . . . taint*] Cordelia's offence must have been extremely monstrous to have caused Lear's previous affection to become tainted.
36. *still-soliciting*] constantly importuning.

As I am glad I have not, though not to have it
Hath lost me in your liking.

LEAR. Better thou
Hadst not been born than not to have pleased me better.

FRANCE. Is it but this? a tardiness in nature
Which often leaves the history unspoke
That it intends to do? My lord of Burgundy,
What say you to the lady? Love's not love
When it is mingled with regards that stand
Aloof from the entire point.[37] Will you have her?
She is herself a dowry.

BUR. Royal Lear,
Give but that portion which yourself proposed,
And here I take Cordelia by the hand,
Duchess of Burgundy.

LEAR. Nothing: I have sworn; I am firm.

BUR. I am sorry then you have so lost a father
That you must lose a husband.

COR. Peace be with Burgundy!
Since that respects[38] of fortune are his love,
I shall not be his wife.

FRANCE. Fairest Cordelia, that art most rich being poor,
Most choice forsaken, and most loved despised,
Thee and thy virtues here I seize upon:
Be it lawful I take up what's cast away.
Gods, gods! 't is strange that from their cold'st neglect
My love should kindle to inflamed respect.
Thy dowerless daughter, king, thrown to my chance,
Is queen of us, of ours, and our fair France:
Not all the dukes of waterish[39] Burgundy
Can buy this unprized[40] precious maid of me.
Bid them farewell, Cordelia, though unkind:
Thou losest here, a better where to find.

---

37. *with regards . . . the entire point*] with scruples that are irrelevant to the essential or main point.
38. *respects*] considerations.
39. *waterish*] well-watered.
40. *unprized*] priceless.

LEAR. Thou hast her, France: let her be thine, for we
Have no such daughter, nor shall ever see
That face of hers again. Therefore be gone
Without our grace, our love, our benison.[41]
Come, noble Burgundy.
[*Flourish. Exeunt all but France, Goneril, Regan, and Cordelia.*]

FRANCE. Bid farewell to your sisters.

COR. The jewels of our father, with wash'd eyes
Cordelia leaves you: I know you what you are;
And, like a sister, am most loath to call
Your faults as they are named. Use well our father:
To your professed bosoms I commit him:
But yet, alas, stood I within his grace,
I would prefer him to a better place.
So farewell to you both.

REG. Prescribe not us our duties.

GON. Let your study
Be to content your lord, who hath received you
At fortune's alms. You have obedience scanted,
And well are worth the want that you have wanted.[42]

COR. Time shall unfold what plaited cunning hides:
Who cover faults, at last shame them derides.[43]
Well may you prosper!

FRANCE. Come, my fair Cordelia.
[*Exeunt France and Cordelia.*]

GON. Sister, it is not a little I have to say of what most nearly appertains to us both. I think our father will hence to-night.

REG. That's most certain, and with you; next month with us.

GON. You see how full of changes his age is; the observation we have made of it hath not been little: he always loved our sister most; and with what poor judgement he hath now cast her off appears too grossly.

REG. 'T is the infirmity of his age: yet he hath ever but slenderly known himself.

---

41. *benison*] blessing.
42. *well . . . wanted*] well deserve to suffer the want of that affection (from your husband) which you have shown yourself to be without (for your father).
43. *Who . . . derides*] Shame will eventually deride those who try to hide their faults.

GON. The best and soundest of his time hath been but rash; then must we look to receive from his age, not alone the imperfections of long ingrafted condition, but therewithal the unruly waywardness that infirm and choleric years bring with them.

REG. Such unconstant starts are we like to have from him as this of Kent's banishment.

GON. There is further compliment of leave-taking between France and him. Pray you, let's hit together: if our father carry authority with such dispositions as he bears, this last surrender of his will but offend us.[44]

REG. We shall further think on 't.

GON. We must do something, and i' the heat.[45] [*Exeunt.*]

## SCENE II—*The Earl of Gloucester's Castle*

*Enter* EDMUND, *with a letter*

EDM. Thou, nature, art my goddess; to thy law
My services are bound. Wherefore should I
Stand in the plague of custom, and permit
The curiosity of nations to deprive me,
For that I am some twelve or fourteen moonshines
Lag of a brother? Why bastard? wherefore base?[1]
When my dimensions are as well compact,[2]
My mind as generous and my shape as true,

---

44. *let's hit together . . . offend us*] let's join together in our course of action; if our father asserts his authority in such headstrong temper as he now shows, this final surrender to us of his kingdom will merely breed trouble for us.
45. *i' the heat*] now; as in the proverb, "Strike while the iron's hot."

---

1. *Lag of a brother*] Lagging behind a brother, i.e., older than my brother.
*base*] "A *base* son" was a synonym for "a bastard." The words have no etymological connection.
2. *my dimensions . . . compact*] my proportions are put together as well.

As honest madam's issue? Why brand they us
With base? with baseness? bastardy? base, base?
Who in the lusty stealth of nature take
More composition[3] and fierce quality
Than doth, within a dull, stale, tired bed,
Go to the creating a whole tribe of fops,
Got 'tween asleep and wake? Well then,
Legitimate Edgar, I must have your land:
Our father's love is to the bastard Edmund
As to the legitimate: fine word, "legitimate"!
Well, my legitimate, if this letter speed
And my invention thrive, Edmund the base
Shall top the legitimate. I grow; I prosper:
Now, gods, stand up for bastards!

*Enter* GLOUCESTER

GLOU. Kent banish'd thus! and France in choler parted!
And the king gone to-night! subscribed[4] his power!
Confined to exhibition![5] All this done
Upon the gad! Edmund, how now! what news?

EDM. So please your lordship, none. [*Putting up the letter.*]

GLOU. Why so earnestly seek you to put up that letter?

EDM. I know no news, my lord.

GLOU. What paper were you reading?

EDM. Nothing, my lord.

GLOU. No? What needed then that terrible dispatch of it into your pocket? the quality of nothing hath not such need to hide itself. Let's see: come, if it be nothing, I shall not need spectacles.

EDM. I beseech you, sir, pardon me: it is a letter from my brother, that I have not all o'er-read; and for so much as I have perused, I find it not fit for your o'er-looking.

GLOU. Give me the letter, sir.

EDM. I shall offend, either to detain or give it. The contents, as in part I understand them, are to blame.

---

3. *More composition*] More effective blending.
4. *subscribed*] yielded (by a written surrender).
5. *Confined to exhibition*] Restricted to an allowance.

GLOU. Let's see, let's see.

EDM. I hope, for my brother's justification, he wrote this but as an essay or taste[6] of my virtue.

GLOU. [*Reads*]:

"This policy and reverence of age makes the world bitter to the best of our times; keeps our fortunes from us till our oldness cannot relish them. I begin to find an idle and fond[7] bondage in the oppression of aged tyranny; who sways, not as it hath power, but as it is suffered. Come to me, that of this I may speak more. If our father would sleep till I waked him, you should enjoy half his revenue for ever, and live the beloved of your brother,

EDGAR.

Hum! Conspiracy! — "Sleep till I waked him, you should enjoy half his revenue!" — My son Edgar! Had he a hand to write this? a heart and brain to breed it in? When came this to you? who brought it?

EDM. It was not brought me, my lord; there's the cunning of it; I found it thrown in at the casement of my closet.

GLOU. You know the character[8] to be your brother's?

EDM. If the matter were good, my lord, I durst swear it were his; but, in respect of that, I would fain think it were not.

GLOU. It is his.

EDM. It is his hand, my lord; but I hope his heart is not in the contents.

GLOU. Hath he never heretofore sounded you in this business?

EDM. Never, my lord: but I have heard him oft maintain it to be fit, that, sons at perfect age, and fathers declining, the father should be as ward to the son, and the son manage his revenue.

GLOU. O villain, villain! His very opinion in the letter! Abhorred villain! Unnatural, detested, brutish villain! worse than brutish! Go, sirrah, seek him; ay, apprehend him: abominable villain! Where is he?

EDM. I do not well know, my lord. If it shall please you to suspend your indignation against my brother till you can derive from him

---

6. *essay or taste*] trial or test.
7. *fond*] foolish.
8. *character*] handwriting.

better testimony of his intent, you should run a certain course; where, if you violently proceed against him, mistaking his purpose, it would make a great gap in your own honour and shake in pieces the heart of his obedience. I dare pawn down my life for him that he hath wrote this to feel my affection to your honour and to no further pretence of danger.

GLOU. Think you so?

EDM. If your honour judge it meet, I will place you where you shall hear us confer of this, and by an auricular assurance have your satisfaction, and that without any further delay than this very evening.

GLOU. He cannot be such a monster—

EDM. Nor is not, sure.

GLOU. To his father, that so tenderly and entirely loves him. Heaven and earth! Edmund, seek him out; wind me into him, I pray you: frame the business after your own wisdom. I would unstate myself, to be in a due resolution.[9]

EDM. I will seek him, sir, presently, convey[10] the business as I shall find means, and acquaint you withal.

GLOU. These late eclipses in the sun and moon portend no good to us: though the wisdom of nature can reason it thus and thus, yet nature finds itself scourged by the sequent effects: love cools, friendship falls off, brothers divide: in cities, mutinies; in countries, discord; in palaces, treason; and the bond cracked 'twixt son and father. This villain of mine comes under the prediction; there's son against father: the king falls from bias of nature; there's father against child. We have seen the best of our time: machinations, hollowness, treachery and all ruinous disorders follow us disquietly to our graves. Find out this villain, Edmund; it shall lose thee nothing; do it carefully. And the noble and true-hearted Kent banished! his offence, honesty! 'T is strange. [*Exit.*]

EDM. This is the excellent foppery of the world, that when we are

---

9. *I would unstate . . . resolution*] I would give up my rank and estate in order to assure myself (of the facts).

10. *convey*] tactfully manage.

sick in fortune — often the surfeit[11] of our own behaviour — we make guilty of our disasters the sun, the moon and the stars: as if we were villains by necessity, fools by heavenly compulsion; knaves, thieves and treachers, by spherical predominance; drunkards, liars and adulterers, by an enforced obedience of planetary influence; and all that we are evil in, by a divine thrusting on: an admirable evasion of whoremaster man, to lay his goatish disposition to the charge of a star! My father compounded with my mother under the dragon's tail, and my nativity was under Ursa major; so that it follows I am rough and lecherous. Tut, I should have been that I am, had the maidenliest star in the firmament twinkled on my bastardizing. Edgar —

*Enter* EDGAR

And pat he comes like the catastrophe of the old comedy:[12] my cue is villanous melancholy, with a sigh like Tom o' Bedlam.[13] O, these eclipses do portend these divisions! fa, sol, la, mi.

EDG. How now, brother Edmund! what serious contemplation are you in?

EDM. I am thinking, brother, of a prediction I read this other day, what should follow these eclipses.

EDG. Do you busy yourself about that?

EDM. I promise you, the effects he writ of succeed unhappily; as of unnaturalness between the child and the parent; death, dearth, dissolutions of ancient amities; divisions in state, menaces and maledictions against king and nobles; needless diffidences, banishment of friends, dissipation of cohorts, nuptial breaches, and I know not what.

EDG. How long have you been a sectary astronomical?[14]

---

11. *the surfeit*] the morbid excesses.
12. *pat he comes . . . old comedy*] In ancient comedies, the catastrophe was brought about in defiance of the natural order of things by the entry of a dominant character in quite unjustifiable circumstances.
13. *Tom o' Bedlam*] a generic name for mad beggars who often roamed the countryside; Bedlam refers to the London insane asylum at the Hospital of St. Mary of Bethlehem.
14. *a sectary astronomical*] a devotee of astronomy.

EDM. Come, come; when saw you my father last?
EDG. Why, the night gone by.
EDM. Spake you with him?
EDG. Ay, two hours together.
EDM. Parted you in good terms? Found you no displeasure in him by word or countenance?
EDG. None at all.
EDM. Bethink yourself wherein you may have offended him: and at my entreaty forbear his presence till some little time hath qualified the heat of his displeasure, which at this instant so rageth in him that with the mischief of your person it would scarcely allay.
EDG. Some villain hath done me wrong.
EDM. That's my fear. I pray you, have a continent forbearance[15] till the speed of his rage goes slower, and, as I say, retire with me to my lodging, from whence I will fitly bring you to hear my lord speak: pray ye, go; there's my key: if you do stir abroad, go armed.
EDG. Armed, brother!
EDM. Brother, I advise you to the best: go armed: I am no honest man if there be any good meaning towards you: I have told you what I have seen and heard; but faintly, nothing like the image and horror of it: pray you, away.
EDG. Shall I hear from you anon?
EDM. I do serve you in this business. [*Exit Edgar.*]
A credulous father, and a brother noble,
Whose nature is so far from doing harms
That he suspects none; on whose foolish honesty
My practices ride easy. I see the business.
Let me, if not by birth, have lands by wit:
All with me's meet that I can fashion fit.[16] [*Exit.*]

---

15. *have a continent forbearance*] keep a well-controlled distance, a restrained aloofness, deliberately keep away (from him).
16. *All with me's meet . . . fit*] With me every device that I can adapt to my purpose is fair game.

## SCENE III — *The Duke of Albany's Palace*

*Enter* GONERIL *and* OSWALD, *her steward*

GON. Did my father strike my gentleman for chiding of his fool?
OSW. Yes, madam.
GON. By day and night he wrongs me; every hour
He flashes into one gross crime or other,
That sets us all at odds: I'll not endure it:
His knights grow riotous, and himself upbraids us
On every trifle. When he returns from hunting,
I will not speak with him; say I am sick:
If you come slack of[1] former services,
You shall do well; the fault of it I'll answer.
OSW. He's coming, madam; I hear him. [*Horns within.*]
GON. Put on what weary negligence you please,
You and your fellows; I'ld have it come to question:
If he distaste it, let him to our sister,
Whose mind and mine, I know, in that are one,
Not to be over-ruled. Idle old man,
That still would manage those authorities
That he hath given away! Now, by my life,
Old fools are babes again, and must be used
With checks as flatteries, when they are seen abused.
Remember what I tell you.
OSW. Very well, madam.
GON. And let his knights have colder looks among you;
What grows of it, no matter; advise your fellows so:
I would breed from hence occasions, and I shall,
That I may speak: I'll write straight to my sister,
To hold my very course. Prepare for dinner. [*Exeunt.*]

1. *come slack of*] be remiss in.

## SCENE IV—*A Hall in the Same*

*Enter* KENT, *disguised*

KENT. If but as well I other accents borrow,
That can my speech defuse,[1] my good intent
May carry through itself to that full issue
For which I razed my likeness. Now, banish'd Kent,
If thou canst serve where thou dost stand condemn'd,
So may it come, thy master whom thou lovest
Shall find thee full of labours.[2]

*Horns within. Enter* LEAR, Knights, *and* Attendants

LEAR. Let me not stay a jot for dinner; go get it ready. [*Exit an Attendant.*] How now! what art thou?

KENT. A man, sir.

LEAR. What dost thou profess? What wouldst thou with us?

KENT. I do profess to be no less than I seem; to serve him truly that will put me in trust; to love him that is honest; to converse with him that is wise and says little; to fear judgement; to fight when I cannot choose, and to eat no fish.[3]

LEAR. What art thou?

KENT. A very honest-hearted fellow, and as poor as the king.

LEAR. If thou be as poor for a subject as he is for a king, thou art poor enough. What wouldst thou?

KENT. Service.

LEAR. Who wouldst thou serve?

KENT. You.

LEAR. Dost thou know me, fellow?

---

1. *defuse*] disorder, confuse. Kent is anxious to complete his disguise by adopting an accent which shall make his speech indistinct.
2. *full of labours*] ready for any service.
3. *to eat no fish*] Eating fish was held to be the sign of a Roman Catholic, of one disaffected to the government. Hence "to eat no fish" is equivalent to a profession of loyalty and orthodoxy.

KENT. No, sir; but you have that in your countenance which I would fain call master.

LEAR. What's that?

KENT. Authority.

LEAR. What services canst thou do?

KENT. I can keep honest counsel, ride, run, mar a curious tale in telling it, and deliver a plain message bluntly: that which ordinary men are fit for, I am qualified in, and the best of me is diligence.

LEAR. How old art thou?

KENT. Not so young, sir, to love a woman for singing, nor so old to dote on her for any thing: I have years on my back forty eight.

LEAR. Follow me; thou shalt serve me: if I like thee no worse after dinner, I will not part from thee yet. Dinner, ho, dinner! Where's my knave? my fool? Go you, and call my fool hither.

[*Exit an Attendant.*]

*Enter* OSWALD

You, you, sirrah, where's my daughter?

OSW. So please you,— [*Exit.*]

LEAR. What says the fellow there? Call the clotpoll[4] back. [*Exit a Knight.*] Where's my fool, ho? I think the world's asleep.

*Re-enter* Knight

How now! where's that mongrel?

KNIGHT. He says, my lord, your daughter is not well.

LEAR. Why came not the slave back to me when I called him?

KNIGHT. Sir, he answered me in the roundest[5] manner, he would not.

LEAR. He would not!

KNIGHT. My lord, I know not what the matter is; but, to my judgement, your highness is not entertained with that ceremonious affection as you were wont; there's a great abatement of kindness appears as well in the general dependants as in the duke himself also and your daughter.

LEAR. Ha! sayest thou so?

---

4. *clotpoll*] clodpate, blockhead.
5. *roundest*] bluntest.

KNIGHT. I beseech you, pardon me, my lord, if I be mistaken; for my duty cannot be silent when I think your highness wronged.

LEAR. Thou but rememberest me of mine own conception: I have perceived a most faint[6] neglect of late; which I have rather blamed as mine own jealous curiosity than as a very pretence and purpose of unkindness: I will look further into't. But where's my fool? I have not seen him this two days.

KNIGHT. Since my young lady's going into France, sir, the fool hath much pined away.

LEAR. No more of that; I have noted it well. Go you, and tell my daughter I would speak with her. [*Exit an Attendant.*] Go you, call hither my fool. [*Exit an Attendant.*]

*Re-enter* OSWALD

O, you sir, you, come you hither, sir: who am I, sir?

OSW. My lady's father.

LEAR. My lady's father! my lord's knave: you whoreson dog! you slave! you cur!

OSW. I am none of these, my lord; I beseech your pardon.

LEAR. Do you bandy looks with me, you rascal? [*Striking him.*]

OSW. I'll not be struck, my lord.

KENT. Nor tripped neither, you base foot-ball player. [*Tripping up his heels.*]

LEAR. I thank thee, fellow; thou servest me, and I'll love thee.

KENT. Come, sir, arise, away! I'll teach you differences:[7] away, away! If you will measure your lubber's length again, tarry: but away! go to; have you wisdom? so. [*Pushes Oswald out.*]

LEAR. Now, my friendly knave, I thank thee: there's earnest[8] of thy service. [*Giving Kent money.*]

*Enter* Fool

FOOL. Let me hire him too: here's my coxcomb.[9] [*Offering Kent his cap.*]

LEAR. How now, my pretty knave! how dost thou?

6. *faint*] listless, languid.
7. *differences*] differences of rank.
8. *earnest*] earnest money, payment in advance.
9. *coxcomb*] the fool's cap.

FOOL. Sirrah, you were best take my coxcomb.
KENT. Why, fool?
FOOL. Why, for taking one's part that's out of favour: nay, an thou canst not smile as the wind sits, thou'lt catch cold shortly: there, take my coxcomb: why, this fellow hath banished two on's daughters, and done the third a blessing against his will; if thou follow him, thou must needs wear my coxcomb. How now, nuncle![10] Would I had two coxcombs and two daughters!
LEAR. Why, my boy?
FOOL. If I gave them all my living, I'ld keep my coxcombs myself. There's mine; beg another of thy daughters.
LEAR. Take heed, sirrah; the whip.
FOOL. Truth 's a dog must to kennel; he must be whipped out, when Lady the brach may stand by the fire and stink.
LEAR. A pestilent gall to me!
FOOL. Sirrah, I'll teach thee a speech.
LEAR. Do.
FOOL. Mark it, nuncle:

Have more than thou showest,
Speak less than thou knowest,
Lend less than thou owest,[11]
Ride more than thou goest,[12]
Learn more than thou trowest,
Set less than thou throwest;
Leave thy drink and thy whore,
And keep in-a-door,
And thou shalt have more
Than two tens to a score.

KENT. This is nothing, fool.
FOOL. Then 't is like the breath of an unfee'd lawyer, you gave me nothing for't. Can you make no use of nothing, nuncle?
LEAR. Why, no, boy; nothing can be made out of nothing.
FOOL. [*To Kent*] Prithee, tell him, so much the rent of his land comes to: he will not believe a fool.

---

10. *nuncle*] a contraction of "mine uncle." Fools usually addressed their superiors this way.
11. *owest*] ownest, possessest.
12. *goest*] walkest on foot.

LEAR. A bitter fool!

FOOL. Dost thou know the difference, my boy, between a bitter fool and a sweet fool?

LEAR. No, lad; teach me.

FOOL.

That lord that counsell'd thee
To give away thy land,
Come place him here by me;
Do thou for him stand:
The sweet and bitter fool
Will presently appear;
The one in motley[13] here,
The other found out there.

LEAR. Dost thou call me fool, boy?

FOOL. All thy other titles thou hast given away; that thou wast born with.

KENT. This is not altogether fool, my lord.

FOOL. No, faith, lords and great men will not let me; if I had a monopoly out,[14] they would have part on't: and ladies too, they will not let me have all the fool to myself; they'll be snatching. Give me an egg, nuncle, and I'll give thee two crowns.

LEAR. What two crowns shall they be?

FOOL. Why, after I have cut the egg in the middle and eat up the meat, the two crowns of the egg. When thou clovest thy crown i' the middle and gavest away both parts, thou borest thine ass on thy back[15] o'er the dirt: thou hadst little wit in thy bald crown when thou gavest thy golden one away. If I speak like myself[16] in this, let him be whipped that first finds it so.

[*Singing*] Fools had ne'er less wit in a year;
For wise men are grown foppish,
And know not how their wits to wear,
Their manners are so apish.

---

13. *motley*] the ordinary parti-coloured dress of the domestic fool.
14. *if I had a monopoly out*] in folly.
15. *borest thine ass . . . back*] An allusion to Æsop's fable of the old man who tried to please everybody.
16. *like myself*] like a fool.

LEAR. When were you wont to be so full of songs, sirrah?

FOOL. I have used it, nuncle, ever since thou madest thy daughters thy mother: for when thou gavest them the rod and puttest down thine own breeches,

> [*Singing*] Then they for sudden joy did weep,
> And I for sorrow sung,
> That such a king should play bo-peep,
> And go the fools among.

Prithee, nuncle, keep a schoolmaster that can teach thy fool to lie: I would fain learn to lie.

LEAR. An you lie, sirrah, we'll have you whipped.

FOOL. I marvel what kin thou and thy daughters are: they'll have me whipped for speaking true, thou'lt have me whipped for lying, and sometimes I am whipped for holding my peace. I had rather be any kind o' thing than a fool: and yet I would not be thee, nuncle; thou hast pared thy wit o' both sides and left nothing i' the middle. Here comes one o' the parings.

*Enter* GONERIL

LEAR. How now, daughter! what makes that frontlet[17] on? Methinks you are too much of late i' the frown.

FOOL. Thou wast a pretty fellow when thou hadst no need to care for her frowning; now thou art an O without a figure:[18] I am better than thou art now; I am a fool, thou art nothing. [*To Gon.*] Yes, forsooth, I will hold my tongue; so your face bids me, though you say nothing.

> Mum, mum:
> He that keeps nor crust nor crumb,
> Weary of all, shall want some.

[*Pointing to Lear*] That's a shealed peascod.[19]

GON. Not only, sir, this your all-licensed fool,
But other of your insolent retinue
Do hourly carp and quarrel, breaking forth

17. *frontlet*] a tight band worn on women's foreheads, but here a frown.
18. *an O without a figure*] a cipher.
19. *a shealed peascod*] an empty husk, or pod without the peas; "shealed" is the old spelling of "shelled."

In rank and not to be endured riots. Sir,
I had thought, by making this well known unto you,
To have found a safe redress; but now grow fearful,
By what yourself too late have spoke and done,
That you protect this course and put it on
By your allowance; which if you should, the fault
Would not 'scape censure, nor the redresses sleep,
Which, in the tender of a wholesome weal,
Might in their working do you that offence
Which else were shame, that then necessity
Will call discreet proceeding.

FOOL. For, you know, nuncle,

> The hedge-sparrow fed the cuckoo so long,
> That it had it head bit off by it young.[20]

So out went the candle, and we were left darkling.[21]

LEAR. Are you our daughter?

GON. Come, sir,
I would you would make use of that good wisdom
Whereof I know you are fraught, and put away
These dispositions that of late transform you
From what you rightly are.

FOOL. May not an ass know when the cart draws the horse? Whoop, Jug! I love thee.[22]

LEAR. Doth any here know me? This is not Lear:
Doth Lear walk thus? speak thus? Where are his eyes?
Either his notion weakens, his discernings
Are lethargied — Ha! waking? 't is not so.
Who is it that can tell me who I am?

FOOL. Lear's shadow.

LEAR. I would learn that; for, by the marks of sovereignty, knowledge and reason, I should be false persuaded I had daughters.

---

20. *it head . . . it young*] in both cases "it" is the old form of "its." The lines refer to the cuckoo's habit of laying her eggs in the sparrow's nest. The sparrow is wont to hatch and nurture the cuckoo's chicks, though when they grow up they often kill the bird which has cherished them.
21. *darkling*] in the dark.
22. *Whoop, Jug! I love thee*] Possibly the burden of an old song. "Jug" was the pet name for Joan.

**FOOL.** Which they will make an obedient father.
**LEAR.** Your name, fair gentlewoman?
**GON.** This admiration, sir, is much o' the savour
Of other your new pranks. I do beseech you
To understand my purposes aright:
As you are old and reverend, you should be wise.
Here do you keep a hundred knights and squires;
Men so disorder'd, so debosh'd[23] and bold,
That this our court, infected with their manners,
Shows like a riotous inn: epicurism and lust
Make it more like a tavern or a brothel
Than a graced palace. The shame itself doth speak
For instant remedy: be then desired
By her that else will take the thing she begs
A little to disquantity[24] your train,
And the remainder that shall still depend,
To be such men as may besort your age,
Which know themselves and you.
**LEAR.** Darkness and devils!
Saddle my horses; call my train together.
Degenerate bastard! I'll not trouble thee:
Yet have I left a daughter.
**GON.** You strike my people, and your disorder'd rabble
Make servants of their betters.

*Enter* ALBANY

**LEAR.** Woe, that too late repents,— [*To Alb.*] O, sir, are you come?
Is it your will? Speak, sir. Prepare my horses.
Ingratitude, thou marble-hearted fiend,
More hideous when thou show'st thee in a child
Than the sea-monster![25]
**ALB.** Pray, sir, be patient.
**LEAR.** [*To Gon.*] Detested kite! thou liest.
My train are men of choice and rarest parts,
That all particulars of duty know,

23. *debosh'd*] an old spelling of "debauched."
24. *disquantity*] diminish the quantity of.
25. *the sea-monster*] a vague reference to a sea-monster described in Ovid's *Metamorphoses*.

And in the most exact regard support
The worships[26] of their name. O most small fault,
How ugly didst thou in Cordelia show!
That, like an engine,[27] wrench'd my frame of nature
From the fix'd place, drew from my heart all love
And added to the gall. O Lear, Lear, Lear!
Beat at this gate, that let thy folly in [*Striking his head.*]
And thy dear judgement out! Go, go, my people.

ALB. My lord, I am guiltless, as I am ignorant
Of what hath moved you.

LEAR. It may be so, my lord.
Hear, nature, hear; dear goddess, hear!
Suspend thy purpose, if thou didst intend
To make this creature fruitful:
Into her womb convey sterility:
Dry up in her the organs of increase,
And from her derogate[28] body never spring
A babe to honour her! If she must teem,
Create her child of spleen, that it may live
And be a thwart disnatured torment to her.
Let it stamp wrinkles in her brow of youth;
With cadent[29] tears fret channels in her cheeks;
Turn all her mother's pains and benefits
To laughter and contempt; that she may feel
How sharper than a serpent's tooth it is
To have a thankless child! Away, away! [*Exit.*]

ALB. Now, gods that we adore, whereof comes this?

GON. Never afflict yourself to know the cause,
But let his disposition have that scope
That dotage gives it.

*Re-enter* LEAR

LEAR. What, fifty of my followers at a clap!
Within a fortnight!

ALB. What's the matter, sir?

---

26. *The worships*] The honourable repute.
27. *like an engine*] like the rack.
28. *derogate*] degenerate or degraded.
29. *cadent*] falling.

LEAR. I'll tell thee. [*To Gon.*] Life and death! I am ashamed
That thou hast power to shake my manhood thus;
That these hot tears, which break from me perforce,
Should make thee worth them. Blasts and fogs upon thee!
The untented[30] woundings of a father's curse
Pierce every sense about thee! Old fond eyes,
Beweep this cause again, I'll pluck ye out
And cast you with the waters that you lose
To temper clay. Yea, is it come to this?
Let it be so: yet have I left a daughter,
Who, I am sure, is kind and comfortable:
When she shall hear this of thee, with her nails
She'll flay thy wolvish visage. Thou shalt find
That I'll resume the shape which thou dost think
I have cast off for ever: thou shalt, I warrant thee.
[*Exeunt Lear, Kent, and Attendants.*]

GON. Do you mark that, my lord?

ALB. I cannot be so partial, Goneril,
To the great love I bear you, —

GON. Pray you, content. What, Oswald, ho!
[*To the Fool*] You, sir, more knave than fool, after your master.

FOOL. Nuncle Lear, nuncle Lear, tarry; take the fool with thee.

A fox, when one has caught her,
And such a daughter,
Should sure to the slaughter,
If my cap would buy a halter:
So the fool follows after. [*Exit.*]

GON. This man hath had good counsel: a hundred knights!
'T is politic and safe to let him keep
At point[31] a hundred knights: yes, that on every dream,
Each buzz, each fancy, each complaint, dislike,
He may enguard his dotage with their powers
And hold our lives in mercy. Oswald, I say!

ALB. Well, you may fear too far.

GON. Safer than trust too far:

30. *untented*] not to be healed, incapable of yielding to the surgeon's healing "tent" or probe.

31. *At point*] Equipped.

Let me still take away the harms I fear,
Not fear still to be taken: I know his heart.
What he hath utter'd I have writ my sister:
If she sustain him and his hundred knights,
When I have show'd the unfitness,—

*Re-enter* OSWALD

How now, Oswald!
What, have you writ that letter to my sister?

OSW. Yes, madam.

GON. Take you some company, and away to horse
Inform her full of my particular fear,
And thereto add such reasons of your own
As may compact it more.[32] Get you gone;
And hasten your return. [*Exit Oswald.*] No, no, my lord,
This milky gentleness and course of yours
Though I condemn not, yet, under pardon,
You are much more attask'd[33] for want of wisdom
Than praised for harmful mildness.

ALB. How far your eyes may pierce I cannot tell:
Striving to better, oft we mar what's well.

GON. Nay, then—

ALB. Well, well; the event.[34] [*Exeunt.*]

---

32. *compact it more*] strengthen it.
33. *attask'd*] (to be) taken to task, reproved.
34. *the event*] (we'll wait to see) how it turns out.

## SCENE V—*Court Before the Same*

*Enter* LEAR, KENT, *and* Fool

LEAR. Go you before to Gloucester with these letters. Acquaint my daughter no further with any thing you know than comes from her demand out of the letter. If your diligence be not speedy, I shall be there afore you.

KENT. I will not sleep, my lord, till I have delivered your letter. [*Exit.*]

FOOL. If a man's brains were in 's heels, were't not in danger of kibes?[1]

LEAR. Ay, boy.

FOOL. Then, I prithee, be merry; thy wit shall ne'er go slip-shod.[2]

LEAR. Ha, ha, ha!

FOOL. Shalt see thy other daughter will use thee kindly; for though she's as like this as a crab 's like an apple, yet I can tell what I can tell.

LEAR. Why, what canst thou tell, my boy?

FOOL. She will taste as like this as a crab[3] does to a crab. Thou canst tell why one's nose stands i' the middle on 's face?

LEAR. No.

FOOL. Why, to keep one's eyes of either side's nose, that what a man cannot smell out he may spy into.

LEAR. I did her[4] wrong—

FOOL. Canst tell how an oyster makes his shell?

LEAR. No.

FOOL. Nor I neither; but I can tell why a snail has a house.

LEAR. Why?

FOOL. Why, to put's head in; not to give it away to his daughters, and leave his horns without a case.

---

1. *kibes*] chilblains.
2. *thy wit . . . slip-shod*] "slipshod" means "in slippers," the natural footgear for sore heels. The Fool means that Lear has no brains, and thus will never need slippers.
3. *crab*] crabapple.
4. *her*] Cordelia.

LEAR. I will forget my nature.—So kind a father!—Be my horses ready?

FOOL. Thy asses are gone about 'em. The reason why the seven stars are no more than seven is a pretty reason.

LEAR. Because they are not eight?

FOOL. Yes, indeed: thou wouldst make a good fool.

LEAR. To take 't again perforce![5] Monster ingratitude!

FOOL. If thou wert my fool, nuncle, I'ld have thee beaten for being old before thy time.

LEAR. How's that?

FOOL. Thou shouldst not have been old till thou hadst been wise.

LEAR. O, let me not be mad, not mad, sweet heaven!
Keep me in temper: I would not be mad!

*Enter* Gentleman

How now! are the horses ready?

GENT. Ready, my lord.

LEAR. Come, boy.

FOOL. She that's a maid now and laughs at my departure
Shall not be a maid long, unless things be cut shorter.

[*Exeunt.*]

---

5. *To take 't again perforce*] No doubt Lear is meditating a forcible resumption of his royal power.

# ACT II

## SCENE I—*The Earl of Gloucester's Castle*

*Enter* EDMUND *and* CURAN, *meeting*

EDM. Save thee, Curan.

CUR. And you, sir. I have been with your father, and given him notice that the Duke of Cornwall and Regan his duchess will be here with him this night.

EDM. How comes that?

CUR. Nay, I know not. You have heard of the news abroad, I mean the whispered ones, for they are yet but ear-kissing arguments?[1]

EDM. Not I: pray you, what are they?

CUR. Have you heard of no likely wars toward, 'twixt the Dukes of Cornwall and Albany?

EDM. Not a word.

CUR. You may do then in time. Fare you well, sir.

[*Exit.*]

EDM. The duke be here to-night? The better! best!
This weaves itself perforce into my business.
My father hath set guard to take my brother;
And I have one thing, of a queasy question,[2]
Which I must act: briefness and fortune, work!
Brother, a word; descend: brother, I say!

*Enter* EDGAR

---

1. *ear-kissing arguments*] expressions that lightly touch the ear, topics merely spoken of in an undertone.
2. *of a queasy question*] of a delicate or ticklish character.

My father watches: O sir, fly this place;
Intelligence is given where you are hid;
You have now the good advantage of the night:
Have you not spoken 'gainst the Duke of Cornwall?
He's coming hither, now, i' the night, i' the haste,
And Regan with him: have you nothing said
Upon his party 'gainst the Duke of Albany?
Advise yourself.

EDG. I am sure on't, not a word.

EDM. I hear my father coming: pardon me:
In cunning I must draw my sword upon you:[3]
Draw: seem to defend yourself: now quit you well.
Yield: come before my father. Light, ho, here!
Fly, brother. Torches, torches! So farewell.
[*Exit Edgar.*]
Some blood drawn on me would beget opinion[4]
[*Wounds his arm.*]
Of my more fierce endeavour: I have seen drunkards
Do more than this in sport. Father, father!
Stop, stop! No help?

Enter GLOUCESTER, *and* Servants *with torches*

GLOU. Now, Edmund, where's the villain?

EDM. Here stood he in the dark, his sharp sword out,
Mumbling of wicked charms, conjuring the moon
To stand's auspicious mistress.

GLOU. But where is he?

EDM. Look, sir, I bleed.

GLOU. Where is the villain, Edmund?

EDM. Fled this way, sir. When by no means he could—

GLOU. Pursue him, ho!—Go after. [*Exeunt some Servants.*] "By no means" what?

EDM. Persuade me to the murder of your lordship;
But that I told him the revenging gods
'Gainst parricides did all their thunders bend,
Spoke with how manifold and strong a bond

3. *In cunning . . . you*] I must pretend to draw my sword on you.
4. *beget opinion*] create the illusion.

The child was bound to the father; sir, in fine,
Seeing how loathly opposite I stood
To his unnatural purpose, in fell motion
With his prepared sword he charges home
My unprovided body, lanced mine arm:
But when he saw my best alarum'd spirits[5]
Bold in the quarrel's right, roused to the encounter,
Or whether gasted by[6] the noise I made,
Full suddenly he fled.

GLOU. Let him fly far:
Not in this land shall he remain uncaught;
And found—dispatch.[7] The noble duke my master,
My worthy arch and patron, comes to-night:
By his authority I will proclaim it,
That he which finds him shall deserve our thanks,
Bringing the murderous caitiff[8] to the stake;
He that conceals him, death.

EDM. When I dissuaded him from his intent
And found him pight[9] to do it, with curst speech
I threaten'd to discover him: he replied,
"Thou unpossessing bastard! dost thou think,
If I would stand against thee, could the reposure[10]
Of any trust, virtue, or worth, in thee
Make thy words faith'd? No: what I should deny—
As this I would; ay, though thou didst produce
My very character—I'ld turn it all
To thy suggestion, plot, and damned practice:
And thou must make a dullard of the world,
If they not thought the profits of my death
Were very pregnant and potential spurs
To make thee seek it."

GLOU. Strong and fasten'd villain!

---

5. *my best alarum'd spirits*] my finest courage roused to action.
6. *gasted by*] frightened by, aghast at.
7. *And found—dispatch*] An elliptical expression for "and when he is *found* there shall be no delay; he shall be killed outright."
8. *caitiff*] wretch.
9. *pight*] settled or pledged.
10. *reposure*] the act of ascribing, attributing.

Would he deny his letter? I never got[11] him.

[*Tucket within.*]

Hark, the duke's trumpets! I know not why he comes.
All ports I'll bar; the villain shall not 'scape;
The duke must grant me that: besides, his picture
I will send far and near, that all the kingdom
May have due note of him; and of my land,
Loyal and natural boy, I'll work the means
To make thee capable.[12]

*Enter* CORNWALL, REGAN, *and* Attendants

CORN. How now, my noble friend! since I came hither,
Which I can call but now, I have heard strange news.

REG. If it be true, all vengeance comes too short
Which can pursue the offender. How dost, my lord?

GLOU. O, madam, my old heart is crack'd, is crack'd!

REG. What, did my father's godson seek your life?
He whom my father named? your Edgar?

GLOU. O, lady, lady, shame would have it hid!

REG. Was he not companion with the riotous knights
That tend upon my father?

GLOU. I know not, madam: 't is too bad, too bad.

EDM. Yes, madam, he was of that consort.

REG. No marvel then, though he were ill affected:
'T is they have put him on the old man's death,
To have the waste and spoil of his revenues.
I have this present evening from my sister
Been well inform'd of them, and with such cautions
That if they come to sojourn at my house,
I'll not be there.

CORN. Nor I, assure thee, Regan.
Edmund, I hear that you have shown your father
A child-like office.

EDM. 'T was my duty, sir.

GLOU. He did bewray his practice,[13] and received
This hurt you see, striving to apprehend him.

---

11. *got*] begot.
12. *I'll work . . . capable*] I'll make sure you fall heir to (my land).
13. *bewray his practice*] betray his (Edgar's) plot.

CORN. Is he pursued?
GLOU. Ay, my good lord.
CORN. If he be taken, he shall never more
Be fear'd of doing harm: make your own purpose,
How in my strength you please. For you, Edmund,
Whose virtue and obedience doth this instant
So much commend itself, you shall be ours:
Natures of such deep trust we shall much need:
You we first seize on.
EDM. I shall serve you, sir,
Truly, however else.
GLOU. For him I thank your grace.
CORN. You know not why we came to visit you,—
REG. Thus out of season, threading dark-eyed night:
Occasions, noble Gloucester, of some poise,[14]
Wherein we must have use of your advice:
Our father he hath writ, so hath our sister,
Of differences, which I least thought it fit
To answer from our home; the several messengers
From hence attend dispatch.[15] Our good old friend,
Lay comforts to your bosom, and bestow
Your needful counsel to our business,
Which craves the instant use.
GLOU. I serve you, madam:
Your graces are right welcome. [*Flourish. Exeunt.*]

---

14. *poise*] weight, importance.
15. *attend dispatch*] wait to be dispatched.

## SCENE II — *Before Gloucester's Castle*

*Enter* KENT *and* OSWALD, *severally*

OSW. Good dawning[1] to thee, friend: art of this house?
KENT. Ay.
OSW. Where may we set our horses?
KENT. I' the mire.
OSW. Prithee, if thou lovest me, tell me.
KENT. I love thee not.
OSW. Why then I care not for thee.
KENT. If I had thee in Lipsbury pinfold,[2] I would make thee care for me.
OSW. Why dost thou use me thus? I know thee not.
KENT. Fellow, I know thee.
OSW. What dost thou know me for?
KENT. A knave; a rascal; an eater of broken meats; a base, proud, shallow, beggarly, three-suited, hundred-pound, filthy, worsted-stocking[3] knave; a lily-livered action-taking knave; a whoreson, glass-gazing, superserviceable,[4] finical rogue; one-trunk-inheriting[5] slave; one that wouldst be a bawd in way of good service, and art nothing but the composition of a knave, beggar, coward, pandar, and the son and heir of a mongrel bitch: one whom I will beat into clamorous whining, if thou deniest the least syllable of thy addition.[6]

---

1. *dawning*] the time about daybreak.
2. *Lipsbury pinfold*] "Pinfold" is a synonym for "pound," a public enclosure for the confinement of stray cattle. Lipsbury is unexplained. It is perhaps a coined word sarcastically meaning "the lips." Kent might be threatening to get Oswald between his teeth.
3. *worsted-stocking*] Poor people wore worsted stockings, while the stockings of rich people were invariably of silk.
4. *action-taking knave*] one who resorts to legal action when assaulted instead of challenging an assailant to fight.
   *glass-gazing*] surveying his person in a looking-glass.
   *superserviceable*] one above his duties.
5. *one-trunk-inheriting*] possessing a stock of clothes which would all go into a single trunk.
6. *addition*] title.

OSW. Why, what a monstrous fellow art thou, thus to rail on one that is neither known of thee nor knows thee!

KENT. What a brazen-faced varlet art thou, to deny thou knowest me! Is it two days ago since I tripped up thy heels and beat thee before the king? Draw, you rogue: for, though it be night, yet the moon shines; I'll make a sop o' the moonshine of you: draw, you whoreson cullionly barber-monger,[7] draw. [*Drawing his sword.*]

OSW. Away! I have nothing to do with thee.

KENT. Draw, you rascal: you come with letters against the king, and take vanity the puppet's part against the royalty of her father: draw, you rogue, or I'll so carbonado[8] your shanks: draw, you rascal; come your ways.

OSW. Help, ho! murder! help!

KENT. Strike, you slave; stand, rogue; stand, you neat slave, strike. [*Beating him.*]

OSW. Help, ho! murder! murder!

*Enter* EDMUND, *with his rapier drawn*, CORNWALL, REGAN, GLOUCESTER, *and* Servants

EDM. How now! What's the matter? [*Parting them.*]

KENT. With you, goodman boy, an you please: come, I'll flesh you; come on, young master.

GLOU. Weapons! arms! What's the matter here?

CORN. Keep peace, upon your lives;
He dies that strikes again. What is the matter?

REG. The messengers from our sister and the king.

CORN. What is your difference? speak.

OSW. I am scarce in breath, my lord.

KENT. No marvel, you have so bestirred your valour. You cowardly rascal, nature disclaims in thee: a tailor made thee.

CORN. Thou art a strange fellow: a tailor make a man?

KENT. Ay, a tailor, sir: a stone-cutter or a painter could not have made him so ill, though he had been but two hours at the trade.

CORN. Speak yet, how grew your quarrel?

---

7. *cullionly barber-monger*] rascally frequenter of barbers' shops, who was forever getting his hair and beard trimmed.

8. *carbonado*] slash; a culinary term.

OSW. This ancient ruffian, sir, whose life I have spared at suit of his gray beard, —

KENT. Thou whoreson zed! thou unnecessary letter![9] My lord, if you will give me leave, I will tread this unbolted villain into mortar, and daub the walls of a jakes[10] with him. Spare my gray beard, you wagtail?

CORN. Peace, sirrah!
You beastly knave, know you no reverence?

KENT. Yes, sir; but anger hath a privilege.

CORN. Why art thou angry?

KENT. That such a slave as this should wear a sword,
Who wears no honesty. Such smiling rogues as these,
Like rats, oft bite the holy cords[11] a-twain
Which are too intrinse[12] to unloose; smooth every passion
That in the natures of their lords rebel;
Bring oil to fire, snow to their colder moods;
Renege, affirm, and turn their halcyon[13] beaks
With every gale and vary of their masters,
Knowing nought, like dogs, but following.
A plague upon your epileptic visage!
Smile you my speeches, as I were a fool?
Goose, if I had you upon Sarum[14] plain,
I'ld drive ye cackling home to Camelot.

CORN. What, art thou mad, old fellow?

GLOU. How fell you out? say that.

KENT. No contraries hold more antipathy
Than I and such a knave.

CORN. Why dost thou call him knave? What is his fault?

KENT. His countenance likes me not.

---

9. *zed . . . letter*] According to Ben Jonson's *English Grammar*, "Zed is a letter often heard among us, but seldom seen."
10. *a jakes*] an outhouse or privy.
11. *holy cords*] bonds of filial affection.
12. *intrinse*] tightly knotted.
13. *halcyon*] the kingfisher. There was a popular belief that if the bird was suspended in the air by a cord round its neck, its bill would always point to the quarter from which the wind blew.
14. *Sarum*] Salisbury.

CORN. No more perchance does mine, nor his, nor hers.
KENT. Sir, 't is my occupation to be plain:
I have seen better faces in my time
Than stands on any shoulder that I see
Before me at this instant.
CORN. This is some fellow,
Who, having been praised for bluntness, doth affect
A saucy roughness, and constrains the garb
Quite from his nature:[15] he cannot flatter, he, —
An honest mind and plain, — he must speak truth
An they will take it, so; if not, he's plain.
These kind of knaves I know, which in this plainness
Harbour more craft and more corrupter ends
Than twenty silly ducking observants
That stretch their duties nicely.
KENT. Sir, in good faith, in sincere verity,
Under the allowance of your great aspect,
Whose influence, like the wreath of radiant fire
On flickering Phoebus' front, —
CORN. What mean'st by this?
KENT. To go out of my dialect, which you discommend so much. I know, sir, I am no flatterer: he that beguiled you in a plain accent was a plain knave; which, for my part, I will not be, though I should win your displeasure to entreat me to 't.
CORN. What was the offence you gave him?
OSW. I never gave him any:
It pleased the king his master very late
To strike at me, upon his misconstruction;[16]
When he, conjunct,[17] and flattering his displeasure,
Tripp'd me behind; being down, insulted, rail'd,
And put upon him such a deal of man,
That worthied him, got praises of the king
For him attempting who was self-subdued,

15. *constrains . . . nature*] his frankness conceals a deceitful nature.
16. *misconstruction*] misapprehension.
17. *conjunct*] in concert or alliance (with Lear).

And in the fleshment[18] of this dread exploit
Drew on me here again.

KENT. None of these rogues and cowards
But Ajax[19] is their fool.

CORN. Fetch forth the stocks!
You stubborn ancient knave, you reverend braggart,
We'll teach you—

KENT. Sir, I am too old to learn:
Call not your stocks for me: I serve the king,
On whose employment I was sent to you:
You shall do small respect, show too bold malice
Against the grace and person of my master,
Stocking his messenger.

CORN. Fetch forth the stocks! As I have life and honour,
There shall he sit till noon.

REG. Till noon! till night, my lord, and all night too.

KENT. Why, madam, if I were your father's dog,
You should not use me so.

REG. Sir, being his knave, I will.

CORN. This is a fellow of the self-same colour
Our sister speaks of. Come, bring away the stocks!
[*Stocks brought out.*]

GLOU. Let me beseech your grace not to do so:
His fault is much, and the good king his master
Will check him for 't: your purposed low correction
Is such as basest and contemned'st wretches
For pilferings and most common trespasses
Are punish'd with: the king must take it ill,
That he, so slightly valued in his messenger,
Should have him thus restrain'd.

CORN. I'll answer that.

REG. My sister may receive it much more worse,
To have her gentleman abused, assaulted,
For following her affairs. Put in his legs.
[*Kent is put in the stocks.*]

---

18. *fleshment*] insolence, fierceness.
19. *Ajax*] a synonym for a brave, blunt man, whom designing villains always make their butt or get the better of.

Come, my good lord, away.
[*Exeunt all but Gloucester and Kent.*]

GLOU. I am sorry for thee, friend; 't is the duke's pleasure,
Whose disposition, all the world well knows,
Will not be rubb'd[20] nor stopp'd: I'll entreat for thee.

KENT. Pray, do not, sir: I have watch'd and travell'd hard;
Some time I shall sleep out, the rest I'll whistle.
A good man's fortune may grow out at heels:
Give you good morrow!

GLOU. The duke's to blame in this; 't will be ill taken. [*Exit.*]

KENT. Good king, that must approve the common saw,
Thou out of heaven's benediction comest
To the warm sun![21]
Approach, thou beacon to this under globe,
That by thy comfortable beams I may
Peruse this letter! Nothing almost sees miracles
But misery.[22] I know 't is from Cordelia,
Who hath most fortunately been inform'd
Of my obscured course; and shall find time
From this enormous state, seeking to give
Losses their remedies. All weary and o'er-watch'd,
Take vantage, heavy eyes, not to behold
This shameful lodging.
Fortune, good night: smile once more; turn thy wheel!
[*Sleeps.*]

20. *rubb'd*] impeded, hindered.
21. *must approve . . . sun*] must make good the common proverb ("saw"), which says "out of God's blessing into the warm sun," meaning from a better to a worse place.
22. *Nothing . . . misery*] It is almost only by the unfortunate that miracles are looked for or seen; prosperous people stand in no need of them.

## Scene III—A Wood

*Enter* Edgar

Edg. I heard myself proclaim'd;
And by the happy hollow of a tree
Escaped the hunt. No port is free; no place,
That guard and most unusual vigilance
Does not attend my taking. Whiles I may 'scape
I will preserve myself: and am bethought
To take the basest and most poorest shape
That ever penury in contempt of man
Brought near to beast: my face I'll grime with filth,
Blanket my loins, elf all my hair in knots,
And with presented nakedness out-face
The winds and persecutions of the sky.
The country gives me proof and precedent
Of Bedlam beggars,[1] who with roaring voices
Strike in their numb'd and mortified bare arms
Pins, wooden pricks,[2] nails, sprigs of rosemary;
And with this horrible object,[3] from low farms,
Poor pelting[4] villages, sheep-cotes and mills,
Sometime with lunatic bans,[5] sometime with prayers,
Enforce their charity. Poor Turlygod![6] poor Tom!
That's something yet: Edgar I nothing am.[7] [*Exit.*]

---

1. *Bedlam beggars*] half-crazy beggars, strictly applied to mendicant patients discharged from Bethlehem or Bedlam hospital, but often generally applied to pauper idiots.
2. *wooden pricks*] skewers of wood.
3. *object*] appearance.
4. *pelting*] paltry, contemptible.
5. *lunatic bans*] mad imprecations.
6. *Turlygod*] Perhaps a reference to a strange fraternity of naked beggars, which infested the continent of Europe in the fourteenth century, known as Turlupins; Turlygod has been doubtfully interpreted as a corrupted form of Turlupins.
7. *Edgar I nothing am*] I am no longer likely to be mistaken for Edgar. I have rid myself of his likeness.

## SCENE IV — *Before Gloucester's Castle*

*Kent in the Stocks*

*Enter* LEAR, FOOL, *and* Gentleman

LEAR. 'T is strange that they should so depart from home,
And not send back my messenger.

GENT. As I learn'd,
The night before there was no purpose in them
Of this remove.

KENT. Hail to thee, noble master!

LEAR. Ha!
Makest thou this shame thy pastime?

KENT. No, my lord.

FOOL. Ha, ha! he wears cruel garters. Horses are tied by the heads, dogs and bears by the neck, monkeys by the loins, and men by the legs: when a man's over-lusty at legs, then he wears wooden nether-stocks.[1]

LEAR. What's he that hath so much thy place mistook
To set thee here?

KENT. It is both he and she;
Your son and daughter.

LEAR. No.

KENT. Yes.

LEAR. No, I say.

KENT. I say, yea.

LEAR. No, no, they would not.

KENT. Yes, they have.

LEAR. By Jupiter, I swear, no.

KENT. By Juno, I swear, ay.

LEAR. They durst not do't;
They could not, would not do't; 't is worse than murder,

1. *nether-stocks*] stockings or socks, as opposed to knee breeches, the upper-stocks.

To do upon respect[2] such violent outrage:
Resolve me with all modest haste[3] which way
Thou mightst deserve, or they impose, this usage,
Coming from us.

KENT. My lord, when at their home
I did commend your highness' letters to them,
Ere I was risen from the place that show'd
My duty kneeling, came there a reeking post,
Stew'd in his haste, half breathless, panting forth
From Goneril his mistress salutations;
Deliver'd letters, spite of intermission,[4]
Which presently they read: on whose contents
They summon'd up their meiny,[5] straight took horse;
Commanded me to follow and attend
The leisure of their answer; gave me cold looks:
And meeting here the other messenger,
Whose welcome, I perceived, had poison'd mine—
Being the very fellow that of late
Display'd so saucily against your highness—
Having more man than wit about me, drew:
He raised the house with loud and coward cries.
Your son and daughter found this trespass worth
The shame which here it suffers.

FOOL. Winter's not gone yet, if the wild geese fly that way.

Fathers that wear rags
Do make their children blind;
But fathers that bear bags
Shall see their children kind.
Fortune, that arrant whore,
Ne'er turns the key[6] to the poor.

But, for all this, thou shalt have as many dolours[7] for thy daughters as thou canst tell in a year.

---

2. *upon respect*] with deliberation.
3. *Resolve me . . . haste*] Inform me with all the speed that becomes a truthful statement.
4. *spite of intermission*] without any delay, at the cost of postponing my audience with them.
5. *meiny*] retinue, household.
6. *turns the key*] offers the key of her favours.
7. *dolours*] a pun on the word in the sense of the coin, and of grief.

LEAR. O, how this mother[8] swells up toward my heart!
Hysterica passio, down, thou climbing sorrow,
Thy element's below! Where is this daughter?

KENT. With the earl, sir, here within.

LEAR. Follow me not; stay here. [*Exit.*]

GENT. Made you no more offence but what you speak of?

KENT. None.
How chance the king comes with so small a train?

FOOL. An thou hadst been set i' the stocks for that question, thou hadst well deserved it.

KENT. Why, fool?

FOOL. We'll set thee to school to an ant, to teach thee there's no labouring i' the winter.[9] All that follow their noses are led by their eyes but blind men; and there's not a nose among twenty but can smell him that's stinking. Let go thy hold when a great wheel runs down a hill, lest it break thy neck with following it; but the great one that goes up the hill, let him draw thee after. When a wise man gives thee better counsel, give me mine again: I would have none but knaves follow it, since a fool gives it.

That sir which serves and seeks for gain,
And follows but for form,
Will pack when it begins to rain,
And leave thee in the storm.
But I will tarry; the fool will stay,
And let the wise man fly:
The knave turns fool that runs away;
The fool no knave, perdy.

KENT. Where learned you this, fool?

FOOL. Not i' the stocks, fool.

*Re-enter* LEAR, *with* GLOUCESTER

LEAR. Deny to speak with me? They are sick? they are weary?
They have travell'd all the night? Mere fetches;

---

8. *this mother*] the popular name of an hysterical malady, the chief symptom of which was a choking sensation in the throat. The disease was technically known as "hysterica passio."
9. *We'll set thee . . . winter*] A reference to Proverbs 6:6–8: "Go to the ant, thou sluggard; consider her ways, and be wise: which having no guide, overseer, or ruler, provideth her meat in the summer, and gathereth her food in the harvest."

The images of revolt and flying off.[10]
Fetch me a better answer.

GLOU. My dear lord,
You know the fiery quality of the duke;
How unremoveable and fix'd he is
In his own course.

LEAR. Vengeance! plague! death! confusion!
Fiery? what quality? Why, Gloucester, Gloucester,
I'ld speak with the Duke of Cornwall and his wife.

GLOU. Well, my good lord, I have inform'd them so.

LEAR. Inform'd them! Dost thou understand me, man?

GLOU. Ay, my good lord.

LEAR. The king would speak with Cornwall; the dear father
Would with his daughter speak, commands her service:
Are they inform'd of this? My breath and blood!
"Fiery"? "the fiery duke"? Tell the hot duke that—
No, but not yet: may be he is not well:
Infirmity doth still neglect all office
Whereto our health is bound; we are not ourselves
When nature being oppress'd commands the mind
To suffer with the body: I'll forbear;
And am fall'n out with my more headier will,
To take the indisposed and sickly fit
For the sound man. [*Looking on Kent*] Death on my state! wherefore
Should he sit here? This act persuades me
That this remotion[11] of the duke and her
Is practice only. Give me my servant forth.
Go tell the duke and's wife I'ld speak with them,
Now, presently: bid them come forth and hear me,
Or at their chamber-door I'll beat the drum
Till it cry sleep to death.

GLOU. I would have all well betwixt you. [*Exit.*]

LEAR. O me, my heart, my rising heart! But down!

---

10. *fetches . . . flying off*] tricks or subterfuges; the tokens of rebellion and disaffection.
11. *remotion*] removal.

FOOL. Cry to it, nuncle, as the cockney[12] did to the eels when she put 'em i' the paste alive; she knapped[13] 'em o' the coxcombs with a stick, and cried "Down, wantons, down!" 'T was her brother that, in pure kindness to his horse, buttered his hay.[14]

*Re-enter* GLOUCESTER, *with* CORNWALL, REGAN, *and* Servants

LEAR. Good morrow to you both.
CORN. Hail to your grace!
[*Kent is set at liberty.*]
REG. I am glad to see your highness.
LEAR. Regan, I think you are; I know what reason
I have to think so: if thou shouldst not be glad,
I would divorce me from thy mother's tomb,
Sepulchring an adultress. [*To Kent*] O, are you free?
Some other time for that. Beloved Regan,
Thy sister's naught: O Regan, she hath tied
Sharp-tooth'd unkindness, like a vulture, here:
[*Points to his heart.*]
I can scarce speak to thee; thou'lt not believe
With how depraved a quality — O Regan!
REG. I pray you, sir, take patience: I have hope
You less know how to value her desert
Than she to scant her duty.
LEAR. Say, how is that?
REG. I cannot think my sister in the least
Would fail her obligation: if, sir, perchance
She have restrain'd the riots of your followers,
'T is on such ground and to such wholesome end
As clears her from all blame.
LEAR. My curses on her!
REG. O, sir, you are old;
Nature in you stands on the very verge

12. *cockney*] here used in the rare sense of a female "cook" or "scullion." It is more often applied to an effeminate man or woman.
13. *knapped*] cracked.
14. *buttered his hay*] a reference to the practice of dishonest ostlers, who sold for their own profit greased hay which the horses refused.

Of her confine: you should be ruled and led
By some discretion that discerns your state
Better than you yourself. Therefore I pray you
That to our sister you do make return;
Say you have wrong'd her, sir.

LEAR. Ask her forgiveness?
Do you but mark how this becomes the house:[15]
[*Kneeling*] "Dear daughter, I confess that I am old;
Age is unnecessary: on my knees I beg
That you'll vouchsafe me raiment, bed and food."

REG. Good sir, no more; these are unsightly tricks:
Return you to my sister.

LEAR. [*Rising*] Never, Regan:
She hath abated me of half my train;
Look'd black upon me; struck me with her tongue,
Most serpent-like, upon the very heart:
All the stored vengeances of heaven fall
On her ingrateful top! Strike her young bones,[16]
You taking airs,[17] with lameness.

CORN. Fie, sir, fie!

LEAR. You nimble lightnings, dart your blinding flames
Into her scornful eyes. Infect her beauty,
You fen-suck'd fogs, drawn by the powerful sun
To fall and blast her pride.

REG. O the blest gods! so will you wish on me,
When the rash mood is on.

LEAR. No, Regan, thou shalt never have my curse:
Thy tender-hefted[18] nature shall not give
Thee o'er to harshness: her eyes are fierce, but thine
Do comfort and not burn. 'T is not in thee
To grudge my pleasures, to cut off my train,
To bandy hasty words, to scant my sizes,[19]

15. *becomes the house*] fits family relations, suits the domestic ties between father and daughter.
16. *young bones*] unborn infants.
17. *taking airs*] airs that bewitch, strike with disease.
18. *tender-hefted*] Perhaps *tender-hefted* here means "of tender disposition."
19. *scant my sizes*] contract my allowances.

And in conclusion to oppose the bolt
Against my coming in: thou better know'st
The offices of nature, bond of childhood,
Effects of courtesy, dues of gratitude;
Thy half o' the kingdom hast thou not forgot,
Wherein I thee endow'd.

REG. Good sir, to the purpose.

LEAR. Who put my man i' the stocks? [*Tucket within.*]

CORN. What trumpet's that?

REG. I know't; my sister's: this approves[20] her letter,
That she would soon be here.

*Enter* OSWALD

Is your lady come?

LEAR. This is a slave whose easy-borrow'd pride
Dwells in the fickle grace of her he follows.
Out, varlet, from my sight!

CORN. What means your grace?

LEAR. Who stock'd my servant? Regan, I have good hope
Thou didst not know on't. Who comes here?

*Enter* GONERIL

O heavens,
If you do love old men, if your sweet sway
Allow[21] obedience, if yourselves are old,
Make it your cause; send down, and take my part!
[*To Gon.*] Art not ashamed to look upon this beard?
O Regan, wilt thou take her by the hand?

GON. Why not by the hand, sir? How have I offended?
All's not offence that indiscretion finds[22]
And dotage terms so.

LEAR. O sides, you are too tough;
Will you yet hold? How came my man i' the stocks?

CORN. I set him there, sir: but his own disorders
Deserved much less advancement.

LEAR. You! did you?

20. *approves*] corroborates, confirms.
21. *Allow*] Approve of.
22. *finds*] judges, esteems.

REG. I pray you, father, being weak, seem so.
If, till the expiration of your month,
You will return and sojourn with my sister,
Dismissing half your train, come then to me:
I am now from home and out of that provision
Which shall be needful for your entertainment.

LEAR. Return to her, and fifty men dismiss'd?
No, rather I abjure all roofs, and choose
To wage against the enmity o' the air,
To be a comrade with the wolf and owl,—
Necessity's sharp pinch! Return with her?
Why, the hot-blooded France, that dowerless took
Our youngest born, I could as well be brought
To knee his throne, and, squire-like, pension beg
To keep base life afoot. Return with her?
Persuade me rather to be slave and sumpter[23]
To this detested groom. [*Pointing at Oswald.*]

GON. At your choice, sir.

LEAR. I prithee, daughter, do not make me mad:
I will not trouble thee, my child; farewell:
We'll no more meet, no more see one another:
But yet thou art my flesh, my blood, my daughter;
Or rather a disease that 's in my flesh,
Which I must needs call mine: thou art a boil,
A plague-sore, an embossed[24] carbuncle,
In my corrupted blood. But I'll not chide thee;
Let shame come when it will, I do not call it:
I do not bid the thunder-bearer shoot,
Nor tell tales of thee to high-judging Jove:
Mend when thou canst; be better at thy leisure:
I can be patient; I can stay with Regan,
I and my hundred knights.

REG. Not altogether so:
I look'd not for you yet, nor am provided
For your fit welcome. Give ear, sir, to my sister;

---

23. *sumpter*] literally a pack-horse, but often found in the sense of "drudge."
24. *embossed*] swollen.

For those that mingle reason with your passion
Must be content to think you old, and so —
But she knows what she does.

LEAR. Is this well spoken?

REG. I dare avouch it, sir: what, fifty followers?
Is it not well? What should you need of more?
Yea, or so many, sith that both charge[25] and danger
Speak 'gainst so great a number? How in one house
Should many people under two commands
Hold amity? 'T is hard, almost impossible.

GON. Why might not you, my lord, receive attendance
From those that she calls servants or from mine?

REG. Why not, my lord? If then they chanced to slack you,
We could control them. If you will come to me,
For now I spy a danger, I entreat you
To bring but five and twenty: to no more
Will I give place or notice.

LEAR. I gave you all —

REG. And in good time you gave it.

LEAR. Made you my guardians, my depositaries,[26]
But kept a reservation[27] to be follow'd
With such a number. What, must I come to you
With five and twenty, Regan? said you so?

REG. And speak 't again, my lord; no more with me.

LEAR. Those wicked creatures yet do look well-favour'd,
When others are more wicked; not being the worst
Stands in some rank of praise. [*To Gon.*] I'll go with thee:
Thy fifty yet doth double five and twenty,
And thou art twice her love.

GON. Hear me, my lord:
What need you five and twenty, ten, or five,
To follow in a house where twice so many
Have a command to tend you?

REG. What need one?

---

25. *charge*] expense.
26. *depositaries*] trustees.
27. *reservation*] used in the legal sense of saving clause.

LEAR. O, reason not the need: our basest beggars
Are in the poorest thing superfluous:[28]
Allow not nature more than nature needs,
Man's life 's as cheap as beast's: thou art a lady;
If only to go warm were gorgeous,
Why, nature needs not what thou gorgeous wear'st,
Which scarcely keeps thee warm. But for true need,—
You heavens, give me that patience, patience I need!
You see me here, you gods, a poor old man,
As full of grief as age; wretched in both:
If it be you that stirs these daughters' hearts
Against their father, fool me not so much
To bear it tamely; touch me with noble anger,
And let not women's weapons, water-drops,
Stain my man's cheeks! No, you unnatural hags,
I will have such revenges on you both
That all the world shall—I will do such things,—
What they are, yet I know not, but they shall be
The terrors of the earth. You think I'll weep;
No, I'll not weep:
I have full cause of weeping; but this heart
Shall break into a hundred thousand flaws,
Or ere I'll weep. O fool, I shall go mad!
[*Exeunt Lear, Gloucester, Kent, and Fool.*]

CORN. Let us withdraw; 't will be a storm.
[*Storm and tempest.*]

REG. This house is little: the old man and his people
Cannot be well bestow'd.

GON. 'T is his own blame; hath put himself from rest,
And must needs taste his folly.

REG. For his particular, I'll receive him gladly,
But not one follower.

GON. So am I purposed.
Where is my lord of Gloucester?

CORN. Follow'd the old man forth: he is return'd.

---

28. *Are . . . superfluous*] Have in the very depths of poverty something above their actual need.

*Re-enter* GLOUCESTER

GLOU. The king is in high rage.
CORN. Whither is he going?
GLOU. He calls to horse; but will I know not whither.
CORN. 'T is best to give him way; he leads himself.
GON. My lord, entreat him by no means to stay.
GLOU. Alack, the night comes on, and the bleak winds
Do sorely ruffle; for many miles about
There's scarce a bush.
REG. O, sir, to wilful men
The injuries that they themselves procure
Must be their schoolmasters. Shut up your doors:
He is attended with a desperate train;[29]
And what they may incense him to, being apt
To have his ear abused, wisdom bids fear.
CORN. Shut up your doors, my lord; 't is a wild night:
My Regan counsels well: come out o' the storm.

[*Exeunt.*]

---

29. *He is attended . . . train*] Regan appears to falsify the present facts. Lear departs unattended by any train of followers. The fool is now the king's only companion.

# ACT III

## SCENE I — *A Heath*

*Storm still. Enter* KENT *and a* Gentleman, *meeting*

KENT. Who's there, besides foul weather?
GENT. One minded like the weather, most unquietly.
KENT. I know you. Where's the king?
GENT. Contending with the fretful elements;
Bids the wind blow the earth into the sea,
Or swell the curled waters 'bove the main,[1]
That things might change or cease; tears his white hair,
Which the impetuous blasts, with eyeless rage,
Catch in their fury, and make nothing of;
Strives in his little world of man to out-scorn
The to-and-fro-conflicting wind and rain.
This night, wherein the cub-drawn[2] bear would couch,
The lion and the belly-pinched wolf
Keep their fur dry, unbonneted he runs,
And bids what will take all.
KENT. But who is with him?
GENT. None but the fool; who labours to out-jest
His heart-struck injuries.
KENT. Sir, I do know you;
And dare, upon the warrant of my note,[3]
Commend a dear thing[4] to you. There is division,

1. *main*] mainland.
2. *cub-drawn*] sucked dry by the cubs, and thereby rendered hungry and ferocious.
3. *upon the warrant of my note*] on the strength of my knowledge of you.
4. *a dear thing*] an urgent, desperate matter.

Although as yet the face of it be cover'd
With mutual cunning, 'twixt Albany and Cornwall;
Who have—as who have not, that their great stars
Throned and set high?—servants, who seem no less,
Which are to France the spies and speculations
Intelligent of our state; what hath been seen,
Either in snuffs and packings[5] of the dukes,
Or the hard rein which both of them have borne
Against the old kind king, or something deeper,
Whereof perchance these are but furnishings,[6]—
But true it is, from France there comes a power[7]
Into this scatter'd kingdom; who already,
Wise in our negligence, have secret feet[8]
In some of our best ports, and are at point
To show their open banner. Now to you:
If on my credit you dare build so far
To make your speed to Dover, you shall find
Some that will thank you, making just report
Of how unnatural and bemadding sorrow
The king hath cause to plain.[9]
I am a gentleman of blood and breeding,
And from some knowledge and assurance offer
This office to you.

GENT. I will talk further with you.

KENT. No, do not.
For confirmation that I am much more
Than my out-wall,[10] open this purse and take
What it contains. If you shall see Cordelia,—
As fear not but you shall,—show her this ring,
And she will tell you who your fellow is
That yet you do not know. Fie on this storm!

---

5. *snuffs and packings*] jealous quarrels and underhand intrigues.
6. *furnishings*] trimmings, appendages.
7. *a power*] a military force.
8. *have secret feet*] have secretly set foot.
9. *plain*] complain.
10. *out-wall*] exterior.

I will go seek the king.

GENT. Give me your hand:

Have you no more to say?

KENT. Few words, but, to effect, more than all yet;

That when we have found the king, — in which your pain

That way, I'll this,[11] — he that first lights on him

Holla the other. [*Exeunt severally.*]

## SCENE II — *Another Part of the Heath*

### *Storm Still*

*Enter* LEAR *and* Fool

LEAR. Blow, winds, and crack your cheeks! rage! blow!

You cataracts and hurricanoes, spout

Till you have drench'd our steeples, drown'd the cocks![1]

You sulphurous and thought-executing[2] fires,

Vaunt-couriers[3] to oak-cleaving thunderbolts,

Singe my white head! And thou, all-shaking thunder,

Smite flat the thick rotundity o' the world!

Crack nature's moulds, all germins[4] spill at once

That make ingrateful man!

FOOL. O nuncle, court holy-water[5] in a dry house is better than this rain-water out o' door. Good nuncle, in, and ask thy daughters' blessing: here's a night pities neither wise man nor fool.

LEAR. Rumble thy bellyful! Spit, fire! spout, rain!

Nor rain, wind, thunder, fire, are my daughters:

---

11. *in which your pain . . . I'll this*] in which your endeavors shall take that way, while I'll take this direction.

---

1. *cocks*] the cocks on the tops of steeples.
2. *thought-executing*] working with the rapidity of thought.
3. *Vaunt-couriers*] Heralds, forerunners.
4. *germins*] seeds.
5. *court holy-water*] flattering speeches.

I tax not you, you elements, with unkindness;
I never gave you kingdom, call'd you children,
You owe me no subscription:[6] then let fall
Your horrible pleasure; here I stand, your slave,
A poor, infirm, weak and despised old man:
But yet I call you servile ministers,
That have with two pernicious daughters join'd
Your high-engender'd battles[7] 'gainst a head
So old and white as this. O! O! 't is foul!

FOOL. He that has a house to put's head in has a good head-piece.

The cod-piece that will house
Before the head has any,
The head and he shall louse
So beggars marry many.
The man that makes his toe
What he his heart should make
Shall of a corn cry woe,
And turn his sleep to wake.[8]

For there was never yet fair woman but she made mouths in a glass.

LEAR. No, I will be the pattern of all patience;
I will say nothing.

*Enter* KENT

KENT. Who's there?

FOOL. Marry, here's grace and a cod-piece; that's a wise man and a fool.

KENT. Alas, sir, are you here? things that love night
Love not such nights as these; the wrathful skies
Gallow[9] the very wanderers of the dark,
And make them keep their caves: since I was man,
Such sheets of fire, such bursts of horrid thunder,

---

6. *subscription*] allegiance.
7. *high-engender'd battles*] armies bred on high (i.e., in the sky); battalions recruited in the heavens.
8. *The man . . . wake*] The general meaning is that the man who cherishes a mean part of his being, instead of a really vital part, is likely to suffer pain from the very part to which he shows the unwise preference.
9. *Gallow*] Frighten.

Such groans of roaring wind and rain, I never
Remember to have heard: man's nature cannot carry
The affliction nor the fear.

LEAR. Let the great gods,
That keep this dreadful pother o'er our heads,
Find out their enemies now. Tremble, thou wretch,
That hast within thee undivulged crimes,
Unwhipp'd of justice: hide thee, thou bloody hand;
Thou perjured, and thou simular[10] man of virtue
That art incestuous: caitiff, to pieces shake,
That under covert and convenient seeming[11]
Hast practised on man's life: close pent-up guilts,
Rive your concealing continents and cry
These dreadful summoners grace. I am a man
More sinn'd against than sinning.

KENT. Alack, bare-headed!
Gracious my lord, hard by here is a hovel;
Some friendship will it lend you 'gainst the tempest:
Repose you there; while I to this hard house —
More harder than the stones whereof 't is raised;
Which even but now, demanding after you,
Denied me to come in — return, and force
Their scanted courtesy.

LEAR. My wits begin to turn.
Come on, my boy: how dost, my boy? art cold?
I am cold myself. Where is this straw, my fellow?
The art[12] of our necessities is strange,
That can make vile things precious. Come, your hovel.
Poor fool and knave, I have one part in my heart
That's sorry yet for thee.

FOOL. [*Singing*]

He that has and a little tiny wit, —
With hey, ho, the wind and the rain, —
Must make content with his fortunes fit,
For the rain it raineth every day.

---

10. *simular*] simulating.
11. *seeming*] hypocrisy.
12. *art*] alchemy.

LEAR. True, my good boy. Come, bring us to this hovel.

[*Exeunt Lear and Kent.*]

FOOL. This is a brave night to cool a courtezan. I'll speak a prophecy ere I go:

When priests are more in word than matter;
When brewers mar their malt with water;
When nobles are their tailors' tutors;
No heretics burn'd, but wenches' suitors;
When every case in law is right;
No squire in debt, nor no poor knight;
When slanders do not live in tongues,
Nor cutpurses come not to throngs;
When usurers tell their gold i' the field,
And bawds and whores do churches build;
Then shall the realm of Albion
Come to great confusion:
Then comes the time, who lives to see 't,
That going shall be used with feet.

This prophecy Merlin shall make; for I live before his time. [*Exit.*]

## SCENE III — *Gloucester's Castle*

*Enter* GLOUCESTER *and* EDMUND

GLOU. Alack, alack, Edmund, I like not this unnatural dealing. When I desired their leave that I might pity him, they took from me the use of mine own house; charged me, on pain of their perpetual displeasure, neither to speak of him, entreat for him, nor any way sustain him.

EDM. Most savage and unnatural!

GLOU. Go to; say you nothing. There's a division betwixt the dukes, and a worse matter than that: I have received a letter this night; 't is dangerous to be spoken; I have locked the letter in my closet: these injuries the king now bears will be revenged home; there is part of a power already footed:[1] we must incline to the king. I will seek him

---

1. *a power already footed*] a military force has already landed.

and privily relieve him: go you, and maintain talk with the duke, that my charity be not of him perceived: if he ask for me, I am ill and gone to bed. Though I die for it, as no less is threatened me, the king my old master must be relieved. There is some strange thing toward, Edmund; pray you, be careful.

[*Exit.*]

EDM. This courtesy, forbid thee, shall the duke
Instantly know, and of that letter too:
This seems a fair deserving,[2] and must draw me
That which my father loses; no less than all:
The younger rises when the old doth fall. [*Exit.*]

## SCENE IV — *The Heath*
### *Before a Hovel*

*Enter* LEAR, KENT, *and* Fool

KENT. Here is the place, my lord: good my lord, enter:
The tyranny of the open night 's too rough
For nature to endure. [*Storm still.*]

LEAR. Let me alone.

KENT. Good my lord, enter here.

LEAR. Wilt break my heart?

KENT. I had rather break mine own. Good my lord, enter.

LEAR. Thou think'st 't is much that this contentious storm
Invades us to the skin: so 't is to thee;
But where the greater malady is fix'd
The lesser is scarce felt. Thou'ldst shun a bear,
But if thy flight lay toward the raging sea
Thou'ldst meet the bear i' the mouth. When the mind's free
The body's delicate: the tempest in my mind
Doth from my senses take all feeling else

---

2. *a fair deserving*] an action deserving fair recognition.

Save what beats there. Filial ingratitude!
Is it not as this mouth should tear this hand
For lifting food to 't? But I will punish home.
No, I will weep no more. In such a night
To shut me out! Pour on; I will endure.
In such a night as this! O Regan, Goneril!
Your old kind father, whose frank heart gave you all, —
O, that way madness lies; let me shun that;
No more of that.

KENT. Good my lord, enter here.

LEAR. Prithee, go in thyself; seek thine own ease:
This tempest will not give me leave to ponder
On things would hurt me more. But I'll go in.
[*To the Fool*] In, boy; go first. You houseless poverty,[1] —
Nay, get thee in. I'll pray, and then I'll sleep.

[*Fool goes in.*]

Poor naked wretches, wheresoe'er you are,
That bide the pelting of this pitiless storm,
How shall your houseless heads and unfed sides,
Your loop'd and window'd[2] raggedness, defend you
From seasons such as these? O, I have ta'en
Too little care of this! Take physic, pomp;
Expose thyself to feel what wretches feel,
That thou mayst shake the superflux to them
And show the heavens more just.

EDG. [*Within*] Fathom and half, fathom and half![3]
Poor Tom! [*The Fool runs out from the hovel.*]

FOOL. Come not in here, nuncle, here's a spirit. Help me, help me!

KENT. Give me thy hand. Who's there?

FOOL. A spirit, a spirit: he says his name's poor Tom.

KENT. What art thou that dost grumble there i' the straw?
Come forth.

*Enter* EDGAR *disguised as a madman*

1. *poverty*] poor creature, pauper, beggar.
2. *loop'd and window'd*] full of holes and apertures.
3. *Fathom and half*] Perhaps Edgar refers to the depth of the flood of rain from which he is taking refuge in the hovel.

EDG. Away! the foul fiend follows me!

Through the sharp hawthorn blows the cold wind.

Hum! go to thy cold bed and warm thee.

LEAR. Hast thou given all to thy two daughters? and art thou come to this?

EDG. Who gives any thing to poor Tom? whom the foul fiend hath led through fire and through flame, through ford and whirlpool, o'er bog and quagmire; that hath laid knives under his pillow and halters in his pew; set ratsbane by his porridge;[4] made him proud of heart, to ride on a bay trotting-horse over four-inched bridges, to course his own shadow for a traitor. Bless thy five wits! Tom's a-cold. O, do de, do de, do de. Bless thee from whirlwinds, star-blasting, and taking![5] Do poor Tom some charity, whom the foul fiend vexes. There could I have him now, and there, and there again, and there. [*Storm still.*]

LEAR. What, have his daughters brought him to this pass?
Couldst thou save nothing? Didst thou give them all?

FOOL. Nay, he reserved a blanket, else we had been all shamed.

LEAR. Now, all the plagues that in the pendulous air
Hang fated o'er men's faults light on thy daughters!

KENT. He hath no daughters, sir.

LEAR. Death, traitor! nothing could have subdued nature
To such a lowness but his unkind daughters.
Is it the fashion that discarded fathers
Should have thus little mercy on their flesh?
Judicious punishment! 't was this flesh begot
Those pelican daughters.[6]

EDG. Pillicock sat on Pillicock-hill:[7]
Halloo, halloo, loo, loo!

FOOL. This cold night will turn us all to fools and madmen.

EDG. Take heed o' the foul fiend: obey thy parents; keep thy word

4. *laid knives . . . by his porridge*] The devil was popularly credited with placing such temptations to suicide in the way of the possessed or the insane.

5. *taking*] bewitchment, infection by witches.

6. *pelican daughters*] The young of the pelican was commonly credited with drinking its parent's blood.

7. *Pillicock . . . Pillicock-hill*] A nursery rhyme. "Pillicock," which had a double meaning, was often used as a term of endearment for children.

justly; swear not; commit not with man's sworn spouse; set not thy sweet heart on proud array. Tom's a-cold.

LEAR. What hast thou been?

EDG. A serving-man, proud in heart and mind; that curled my hair; wore gloves in my cap; served the lust of my mistress' heart and did the act of darkness with her; swore as many oaths as I spake words and broke them in the sweet face of heaven: one that slept in the contriving of lust and waked to do it: wine loved I deeply, dice dearly, and in woman out-paramoured the Turk: false of heart, light of ear,[8] bloody of hand; hog in sloth, fox in stealth, wolf in greediness, dog in madness, lion in prey. Let not the creaking of shoes nor the rustling of silks betray thy poor heart to woman: keep thy foot out of brothels, thy hand out of plackets,[9] thy pen from lenders' books, and defy the foul fiend.

"Still through the hawthorn blows the cold wind."
Says suum, mun, ha, no, nonny.
Dolphin my boy, my boy, sessa! let him trot by.

[*Storm still.*]

LEAR. Why, thou wert better in thy grave than to answer with thy uncovered body this extremity of the skies. Is man no more than this? Consider him well. Thou owest the worm no silk, the beast no hide, the sheep no wool, the cat no perfume. Ha! here's three on 's are sophisticated.[10] Thou art the thing itself: unaccommodated man is no more but such a poor, bare, forked[11] animal as thou art. Off, off, you lendings![12] come, unbutton here.

[*Tearing off his clothes.*]

FOOL. Prithee, nuncle, be contented; 't is a naughty night to swim in. Now a little fire in a wild field were like an old lecher's heart, a small spark, all the rest on's body cold. Look, here comes a walking fire.

*Enter* GLOUCESTER, *with a torch*

EDG. This is the foul fiend Flibbertigibbet:[13] he begins at curfew

8. *light of ear*] credulous of slanderous gossip or of obscenity.
9. *plackets*] the openings in petticoats.
10. *sophisticated*] artificially made up (by wearing clothes).
11. *forked*] two-pronged, two-legged.
12. *lendings*] borrowed clothes.
13. *Flibbertigibbet*] a traditional name of an imp or demon.

and walks till the first cock; he gives the web and the pin,[14] squints the eye and makes the hare-lip; mildews the white wheat[15] and hurts the poor creature of earth.

Saint Withold footed thrice the 'old;[16]
He met the night-mare and her nine-fold;[17]
Bid her alight,
And her troth plight,
And aroint thee,[18] witch, aroint thee!

KENT. How fares your grace?
LEAR. What's he?
KENT. Who's there? What is't you seek?
GLOU. What are you there? Your names?
EDG. Poor Tom, that eats the swimming frog, the toad, the tadpole, the wall-newt and the water;[19] that in the fury of his heart, when the foul fiend rages, eats cow-dung for sallets;[20] swallows the old rat and the ditch-dog; drinks the green mantle of the standing pool; who is whipped from tithing to tithing,[21] and stock-punished, and imprisoned; who hath had three suits to his back, six shirts to his body, horse to ride and weapon to wear;

But mice and rats and such small deer
Have been Tom's food for seven long year.

Beware my follower. Peace, Smulkin;[22] peace, thou fiend!
GLOU. What, hath your grace no better company?
EDG. The prince of darkness is a gentleman: Modo he's call'd, and Mahu.[23]
GLOU. Our flesh and blood is grown so vile, my lord,
That it doth hate what gets it.

---

14. *the web and the pin*] cataract of the eye.
15. *the white wheat*] the ripening wheat.
16. *Saint Withold . . . 'old*] No such saint apparently is noticed elsewhere, but he has been doubtfully identified with Saint Vitalis, who was invoked against nightmares. "The 'old" clearly stands for "the wold," low-lying country.
17. *nine-fold*] nine foals.
18. *aroint thee*] begone.
19. *the water*] the water-newt.
20. *sallets*] salads.
21. *tithing*] district or parish.
22. *Smulkin*] the name of one of the fiends.
23. *Modo . . . Mahu*] names for devils.

EDG. Poor Tom's a-cold.

GLOU. Go in with me: my duty cannot suffer
To obey in all your daughters' hard commands:
Though their injunction be to bar my doors
And let this tyrannous night take hold upon you,
Yet have I ventured to come seek you out
And bring you where both fire and food is ready.

LEAR. First let me talk with this philosopher.
What is the cause of thunder?

KENT. Good my lord, take his offer; go into the house.

LEAR. I'll talk a word with this same learned Theban.[24]
What is your study?

EDG. How to prevent the fiend and to kill vermin.

LEAR. Let me ask you one word in private.

KENT. Importune him once more to go, my lord;
His wits begin to unsettle.

GLOU. Canst thou blame him?

[*Storm still.*]

His daughters seek his death: ah, that good Kent!
He said it would be thus, poor banish'd man!
Thou say'st the king grows mad; I'll tell thee, friend,
I am almost mad myself: I had a son,
Now outlaw'd from my blood;[25] he sought my life,
But lately, very late: I loved him, friend,
No father his son dearer: truth to tell thee,
The grief hath crazed my wits. What a night's this!
I do beseech your grace, —

LEAR. O, cry you mercy, sir.
Noble philosopher, your company.

EDG. Tom's a-cold.

GLOU. In, fellow, there, into the hovel: keep thee warm.

LEAR. Come, let's in all.

KENT. This way, my lord.

LEAR. With him;
I will keep still with my philosopher.

---

24. *learned Theban*] an ironical incoherence. A Theban or Boeotian — Thebes was the chief city of Boeotia — commonly connotes stupidity.
25. *outlaw'd from my blood*] disowned and disinherited.

KENT. Good my lord, soothe him; let him take the fellow.
GLOU. Take him you on.
KENT. Sirrah, come on; go along with us.
LEAR. Come, good Athenian.
GLOU. No words, no words: hush.
EDG.
Child Rowland to the dark tower came:
His word was still "Fie, foh, and fum,
I smell the blood of a British man." [*Exeunt.*]

## SCENE V — *Gloucester's Castle*

*Enter* CORNWALL *and* EDMUND

CORN. I will have my revenge ere I depart his house.
EDM. How, my lord, I may be censured, that nature thus gives way to loyalty, something fears me to think of.
CORN. I now perceive, it was not altogether your brother's evil disposition made him seek his death, but a provoking merit, set a-work by a reproveable badness in himself.
EDM. How malicious is my fortune, that I must repent to be just! This is the letter he spoke of, which approves him an intelligent party to the advantages of France. O heavens! that this treason were not, or not I the detector!
CORN. Go with me to the duchess.
EDM. If the matter of this paper be certain, you have mighty business in hand.
CORN. True or false, it hath made thee earl of Gloucester. Seek out where thy father is, that he may be ready for our apprehension.
EDM. [*Aside*] If I find him comforting[1] the king, it will stuff his suspicion more fully.—I will persever in my course of loyalty, though the conflict be sore between that and my blood.[2]
CORN. I will lay trust upon thee, and thou shalt find a dearer father in my love. [*Exeunt.*]

1. *comforting*] supporting (as a legal accessory); the word is used in its legal sense.
2. *my blood*] my natural feeling.

## SCENE VI—*A Chamber in a Farmhouse Adjoining the Castle*

*Enter* GLOUCESTER, LEAR, KENT, Fool, *and* EDGAR

GLOU. Here is better than the open air; take it thankfully. I will piece out the comfort with what addition I can: I will not be long from you.

KENT. All the power of his wits have given way to his impatience: the gods reward your kindness!

[*Exit Gloucester.*]

EDG. Frateretto[1] calls me, and tells me Nero is an angler in the lake of darkness. Pray, innocent, and beware the foul fiend.

FOOL. Prithee, nuncle, tell me whether a madman be a gentleman or a yeoman.

LEAR. A king, a king!

FOOL. No, he's a yeoman that has a gentleman to his son, for he's a mad yeoman that sees his son a gentleman before him.

LEAR. To have a thousand with red burning spits
Come hissing in upon 'em,—

EDG. The foul fiend bites my back.

FOOL. He's mad that trusts in the tameness of a wolf, a horse's health, a boy's love, or a whore's oath.

LEAR. It shall be done; I will arraign them straight.
[*To Edgar*] Come, sit thou here, most learned justicer;[2]
[*To the Fool*] Thou, sapient sir, sit here. Now, you she foxes![3]

EDG. Look, where he stands and glares! Wantest thou eyes at trial, madam?

FOOL.
Come o'er the bourn,[4] Bessy, to me.
Her boat hath a leak,
And she must not speak
Why she dares not come over to thee.

---

1. *Frateretto*] the name of a fiend.
2. *justicer*] justiciar, judge of a high court.
3. *she foxes*] addressed to Goneril or her sister.
4. *bourn*] brook, stream.

EDG. The foul fiend haunts poor Tom in the voice of a nightingale. Hopdance[5] cries in Tom's belly for two white herring. Croak not, black angel; I have no food for thee.

KENT. How do you, sir? Stand you not so amazed:
Will you lie down and rest upon the cushions?

LEAR. I'll see their trial first. Bring in the evidence.
[*To Edgar*] Thou robed man of justice, take thy place;
[*To the Fool*] And thou, his yoke-fellow of equity,
Bench by his side. [*To Kent*] You are o' the commission;[6]
Sit you too.

EDG. Let us deal justly.

Sleepest or wakest thou, jolly shepherd?
Thy sheep be in the corn;
And for one blast of thy minikin[7] mouth,
Thy sheep shall take no harm.

Pur! the cat is gray.

LEAR. Arraign her first; 't is Goneril. I here take my oath before this honourable assembly, she kicked the poor king her father.

FOOL. Come hither, mistress. Is your name Goneril?

LEAR. She cannot deny it.

FOOL. Cry you mercy, I took you for a joint-stool.

LEAR. And here's another, whose warp'd looks proclaim
What store her heart is made on. Stop her there!
Arms, arms, sword, fire! Corruption in the place!
False justicer, why hast thou let her 'scape?

EDG. Bless thy five wits!

KENT. O pity! Sir, where is the patience now,
That you so oft have boasted to retain?

EDG. [*Aside*] My tears begin to take his part so much,
They'll mar my counterfeiting.

LEAR. The little dogs and all,
Tray, Blanch, and Sweet-heart, see, they bark at me.

EDG. Tom will throw his head at them. Avaunt, you curs!

---

5. *Hopdance*] the name of another fiend; possibly derived from the fiend Hobberdidaunce.
6. *the commission*] the commission of justices of the peace.
7. *minikin*] pretty, dainty.

Be thy mouth or black or white,
Tooth that poisons if it bite;
Mastiff, greyhound, mongrel grim,
Hound or spaniel, brach or lym,[8]
Or bobtail tike or trundle-tail,[9]
Tom will make them weep and wail:
"For, with throwing thus my head,"
Dogs leap the hatch,[10] and all are fled.

Do de, de, de. Sessa! Come, march to wakes and fairs and market-towns. Poor Tom, thy horn is dry.

LEAR. Then let them anatomize Regan; see what breeds about her heart. Is there any cause in nature that makes these hard hearts? [*To Edgar*] You, sir, I entertain for one of my hundred; only I do not like the fashion of your garments. You will say they are Persian attire; but let them be changed.

KENT. Now, good my lord, lie here and rest awhile.

LEAR. Make no noise, make no noise; draw the curtains: so, so, so. We'll go to supper i' the morning. So, so, so.

FOOL. And I'll go to bed at noon.

*Re-enter* GLOUCESTER

GLOU. Come hither, friend: where is the king my master?

KENT. Here, sir; but trouble him not: his wits are gone.

GLOU. Good friend, I prithee, take him in thy arms;
I have o'erheard a plot of death upon him:
There is a litter ready; lay him in 't,
And drive toward Dover, friend, where thou shalt meet
Both welcome and protection. Take up thy master:
If thou shouldst dally half an hour, his life,
With thine and all that offer to defend him,
Stand in assured loss. Take up, take up,
And follow me, that will to some provision
Give thee quick conduct.

KENT. Oppressed nature sleeps.
This rest might yet have balm'd thy broken sinews,[11]

---

8. *brach or lym*] bitch hound or bloodhound.
9. *trundle-tail*] a dog with a curled tail.
10. *the hatch*] the half-door.
11. *broken sinews*] shattered nerves.

Which, if convenience will not allow,
Stand in hard cure.[12] [*To the Fool*] Come, help to bear thy master;
Thou must not stay behind.

GLOU. Come, come, away.

[*Exeunt all but Edgar.*]

EDG. When we our betters see bearing our woes,
We scarcely think our miseries our foes.
Who alone suffers suffers most i' the mind,
Leaving free things[13] and happy shows behind:
But then the mind much sufferance doth o'erskip,
When grief hath mates, and bearing[14] fellowship.
How light and portable my pain seems now,
When that which makes me bend makes the king bow,
He childed as I father'd! Tom, away!
Mark the high noises, and thyself bewray[15]
When false opinion, whose wrong thought defiles thee,
In thy just proof repeals and reconciles thee.
What will hap more to-night, safe 'scape the king!
Lurk, lurk. [*Exit.*]

---

12. *Stand in hard cure*] Must prove difficult to cure.
13. *free things*] things free of trouble.
14. *bearing*] suffering.
15. *bewray*] discover, reveal.

## SCENE VII — *Gloucester's Castle*

*Enter* CORNWALL, REGAN, GONERIL, EDMUND, *and* Servants

CORN. Post speedily to my lord your husband; show him this letter:[1] the army of France is landed. Seek out the traitor Gloucester.

[*Exeunt some of the Servants.*]

REG. Hang him instantly.

GON. Pluck out his eyes.

CORN. Leave him to my displeasure. Edmund, keep you our sister company: the revenges we are bound to take upon your traitorous father are not fit for your beholding. Advise the duke, where you are going, to a most festinate[2] preparation: we are bound to the like. Our posts shall be swift and intelligent betwixt us. Farewell, dear sister: farewell, my lord of Gloucester.

*Enter* OSWALD

How now! where's the king?

OSW. My lord of Gloucester hath convey'd him hence:
Some five or six and thirty of his knights,
Hot questrists[3] after him, met him at gate;
Who, with some other of the lords dependants,
Are gone with him toward Dover; where they boast
To have well-armed friends.

CORN. Get horses for your mistress.

GON. Farewell, sweet lord, and sister.

CORN. Edmund, farewell.

[*Exeunt Goneril, Edmund, and Oswald.*]

Go seek the traitor Gloucester.
Pinion him like a thief, bring him before us.

[*Exeunt other Servants.*]

Though well we may not pass upon his life

1. *this letter*] the letter which Edmund has already given to Cornwall.
2. *festinate*] hurried.
3. *questrists*] searchers or pursuers (engaged in the quest); a very rare word.

Without the form of justice, yet our power
Shall do a courtesy to our wrath, which men
May blame but not control. Who's there? the traitor?

*Enter* GLOUCESTER, *brought in by two or three*

REG. Ingrateful fox! 't is he.
CORN. Bind fast his corky[4] arms.
GLOU. What mean your graces? Good my friends, consider
You are my guests: do me no foul play, friends.
CORN. Bind him, I say. [*Servants bind him.*]
REG. Hard, hard. O filthy traitor!
GLOU. Unmerciful lady as you are, I'm none.
CORN. To this chair bind him. Villain, thou shalt find—
[*Regan plucks his beard.*]
GLOU. By the kind gods, 't is most ignobly done
To pluck me by the beard.
REG. So white, and such a traitor!
GLOU. Naughty lady,
These hairs which thou dost ravish from my chin
Will quicken[5] and accuse thee: I am your host:
With robbers' hands my hospitable favours[6]
You should not ruffle thus. What will you do?
CORN. Come, sir, what letters had you late from France?
REG. Be simple answerer, for we know the truth.
CORN. And what confederacy have you with the traitors
Late footed in the kingdom?
REG. To whose hands have you sent the lunatic king?
Speak.
GLOU. I have a letter guessingly set down,[7]
Which came from one that's of a neutral heart,
And not from one opposed.
CORN. Cunning.
REG. And false.
CORN. Where hast thou sent the king?
GLOU. To Dover.

4. *corky*] sapless, shrivelled with age.
5. *quicken*] assume life.
6. *my hospitable favours*] the face or features of me your host.
7. *guessingly set down*] written from conjecture.

REG. Wherefore to Dover? Wast thou not charged at peril —
CORN. Wherefore to Dover? Let him first answer that.
GLOU. I am tied to the stake, and I must stand the course.[8]
REG. Wherefore to Dover, sir?
GLOU. Because I would not see thy cruel nails
Pluck out his poor old eyes, nor thy fierce sister
In his anointed flesh stick boarish fangs.
The sea, with such a storm as his bare head
In hell-black night endured, would have buoy'd up,
And quench'd the stelled[9] fires:
Yet, poor old heart, he holp[10] the heavens to rain.
If wolves had at thy gate howl'd that stern time,
Thou shouldst have said, "Good porter, turn the key,"
All cruels else subscribed:[11] but I shall see
The winged vengeance overtake such children.
CORN. See 't shalt thou never. Fellows, hold the chair.
Upon these eyes of thine I'll set my foot.
GLOU. He that will think to live till he be old,
Give me some help! O cruel! O you gods!
REG. One side will mock another; the other too.
CORN. If you see vengeance —
FIRST SERV. Hold your hand, my lord:
I have served you ever since I was a child;
But better service have I never done you
Than now to bid you hold.
REG. How now, you dog!
FIRST SERV. If you did wear a beard upon your chin,
I'ld shake it on this quarrel. What do you mean?
CORN. My villain![12] [*They draw and fight.*]
FIRST SERV. Nay, then, come on, and take the chance of anger.
REG. Give me thy sword. A peasant stand up thus!
[*Takes a sword and runs at him behind.*]

---

8. *the course*] the attack; the bout; the onset of dogs baiting the bear, according to the custom of the sport.
9. *stelled*] probably "fixed," "everlasting."
10. *holp*] helped.
11. *All cruels else subscribed*] All their cruelty and fierceness in other circumstances being forgiven or condoned.
12. *My villain*] My serf; one legally bound to me in ties of servitude.

FIRST SERV. O, I am slain! My lord, you have one eye left
To see some mischief on him. O! [*Dies.*]

CORN. Lest it see more, prevent it. Out, vile jelly!
Where is thy lustre now?

GLOU. All dark and comfortless. Where's my son Edmund?
Edmund, enkindle all the sparks of nature,
To quit[13] this horrid act.

REG. Out, treacherous villain!
Thou call'st on him that hates thee: it was he
That made the overture[14] of thy treasons to us;
Who is too good to pity thee.

GLOU. O my follies! Then Edgar was abused.
Kind gods, forgive me that, and prosper him!

REG. Go thrust him out at gates, and let him smell
His way to Dover. [*Exit one with Gloucester.*] How is't, my lord? how look you?

CORN. I have received a hurt: follow me, lady.
Turn out that eyeless villain: throw this slave
Upon the dunghill. Regan, I bleed apace:
Untimely comes this hurt: give me your arm.
[*Exit Cornwall, led by Regan.*]

SEC. SERV. I'll never care what wickedness I do,
If this man come to good.

THIRD SERV. If she live long,
And in the end meet the old course of death,
Women will all turn monsters.

SEC. SERV. Let 's follow the old earl, and get the Bedlam[15]
To lead him where he would: his roguish madness
Allows itself[16] to any thing.

THIRD SERV. Go thou: I'll fetch some flax and whites of eggs
To apply to his bleeding face. Now, heaven help him!
[*Exeunt severally.*]

---

13. *quit*] requite, repay.
14. *overture*] disclosure.
15. *the Bedlam*] the crazy beggar, Edgar.
16. *Allows itself*] Adapts itself, is amenable.

## ACT IV

### SCENE I — *The Heath*

*Enter* EDGAR

EDG. Yet better thus, and known to be contemn'd,
Than still contemn'd and flatter'd.[1] To be worst,
The lowest and most dejected thing of fortune,
Stands still in esperance,[2] lives not in fear:
The lamentable change is from the best;
The worst returns to laughter. Welcome then,
Thou unsubstantial air that I embrace!
The wretch that thou hast blown unto the worst
Owes nothing to thy blasts. But who comes here?

*Enter* GLOUCESTER, *led by an* Old Man

My father, poorly led? World, world, O world!
But that thy strange mutations make us hate thee,
Life would not yield to age.[3]

OLD MAN. O, my good lord, I have been your tenant, and your father's tenant, these fourscore years.

GLOU. Away, get thee away; good friend, be gone:
Thy comforts can do me no good at all;
Thee they may hurt.

---

1. *Yet better . . . flatter'd*] The general meaning is, "It is better to know that one is despised than for one to be really despised and at the same time to be treated with false flattery which conceals the truth."
2. *esperance*] hope.
3. *But that . . . age*] If reverses of fortune did not make us despise existence altogether, we should never resign ourselves to the hateful incidents of infirm age. In other words, the world with all its uncertainties of fortune is such a repellent object to us that it doesn't really matter whether we are young or old, strong or weak.

OLD MAN. Alack, sir, you cannot see your way.

GLOU. I have no way and therefore want no eyes;
I stumbled when I saw: full oft 't is seen,
Our means secure[4] us, and our mere defects
Prove our commodities. Ah, dear son Edgar,
The food of thy abused father's wrath!
Might I but live to see thee in my touch,
I'ld say I had eyes again!

OLD MAN. How now! Who's there?

EDG. [*Aside*] O gods! Who is 't can say "I am at the worst"?
I am worse than e'er I was.

OLD MAN. 'T is poor mad Tom.

EDG. [*Aside*] And worse I may be yet: the worst is not
So long as we can say "This is the worst."

OLD MAN. Fellow, where goest?

GLOU. Is it a beggar-man?

OLD MAN. Madman and beggar too.

GLOU. He has some reason, else he could not beg.
I' the last night's storm I such a fellow saw,
Which made me think a man a worm: my son
Came then into my mind, and yet my mind
Was then scarce friends with him: I have heard more since.
As flies to wanton boys, are we to the gods;
They kill us for their sport.

EDG. [*Aside*] How should this be?
Bad is the trade that must play fool to sorrow,[5]
Angering itself and others. Bless thee, master!

GLOU. Is that the naked fellow?

OLD MAN. Ay, my lord.

GLOU. Then, prithee, get thee gone: if for my sake
Thou wilt o'ertake us hence a mile or twain
I' the way toward Dover, do it for ancient love;
And bring some covering for this naked soul,
Who I'll entreat to lead me.

OLD MAN. Alack, sir, he is mad.

---

4. *secure*] to render careless.
5. *play fool to sorrow*] divert sorrow by making merriment.

GLOU. 'T is the times' plague, when madmen lead the blind.
Do as I bid thee, or rather do thy pleasure;
Above the rest, be gone.

OLD MAN. I'll bring him the best 'parel that I have,
Come on 't what will. [*Exit.*]

GLOU. Sirrah, naked fellow,—

EDG. Poor Tom's a-cold. [*Aside*] I cannot daub[6] it further.

GLOU. Come hither, fellow.

EDG. [*Aside*] And yet I must.—Bless thy sweet eyes, they bleed.

GLOU. Know'st thou the way to Dover?

EDG. Both stile and gate, horse-way and foot-path. Poor Tom hath been scared out of his good wits. Bless thee, good man's son, from the foul fiend! Five fiends have been in poor Tom at once; of lust, as Obidicut; Hobbididence, prince of dumbness; Mahu, of stealing; Modo, of murder; Flibbertigibbet,[7] of mopping and mowing;[8] who since possesses chambermaids and waiting-women. So, bless thee, master!

GLOU. Here, take this purse, thou whom the heavens' plagues
Have humbled to all strokes: that I am wretched
Makes thee the happier. Heavens, deal so still!
Let the superfluous and lust-dieted man,
That slaves your ordinance, that will not see
Because he doth not feel, feel your power quickly;
So distribution should undo excess
And each man have enough. Dost thou know Dover?

EDG. Ay, master.

GLOU. There is a cliff whose high and bending head
Looks fearfully in the confined deep:
Bring me but to the very brim of it,
And I'll repair the misery thou dost bear
With something rich about me: from that place
I shall no leading need.

EDG. Give me thy arm:
Poor Tom shall lead thee. [*Exeunt.*]

---

6. *daub*] disguise.
7. *Obidicut . . . Flibbertigibbet*] the names of five fiends.
8. *mopping and mowing*] grinning and grimacing (like an ape).

## SCENE II — *Before the Duke of Albany's Palace*

*Enter* GONERIL *and* EDMUND

GON. Welcome, my lord: I marvel our mild husband
Not met us on the way.

*Enter* Oswald

Now, where's your master?
OSW. Madam, within; but never man so changed.
I told him of the army that was landed;
He smiled at it: I told him you were coming;
His answer was, "The worse:" of Gloucester's treachery
And of the loyal service of his son
When I inform'd him, then he call'd me sot[1]
And told me I had turn'd the wrong side out:[2]
What most he should dislike seems pleasant to him;
What like, offensive.
GON. [*To Edm.*] Then shall you go no further.
It is the cowish terror of his spirit,
That dares not undertake: he'll not feel wrongs,
Which tie him to an answer. Our wishes on the way
May prove effects. Back, Edmund, to my brother;
Hasten his musters and conduct his powers:
I must change arms[3] at home and give the distaff
Into my husband's hands. This trusty servant
Shall pass between us: ere long you are like to hear,
If you dare venture in your own behalf,
A mistress's command. Wear this; spare speech;
[*Giving a favour.*]
Decline your head: this kiss, if it durst speak,
Would stretch thy spirits up into the air:
Conceive, and fare thee well.

---

1. *sot*] fool.
2. *turn'd the wrong side out*] completely misinterpreted the facts.
3. *change arms*] exchange implements (*i.e.*, spears for spindles).

EDM. Yours in the ranks of death.

GON. My most dear Gloucester!

[*Exit Edmund.*]

O, the difference of man and man!
To thee a woman's services are due:
My fool usurps my body.

OSW. Madam, here comes my lord.

[*Exit.*]

*Enter* Albany

GON. I have been worth the whistle.[4]

ALB. O Goneril!
You are not worth the dust which the rude wind
Blows in your face. I fear your disposition:
That nature which contemns it origin
Cannot be border'd certain in itself;
She that herself will sliver and disbranch
From her material sap,[5] perforce must wither
And come to deadly use.

GON. No more; the text is foolish.

ALB. Wisdom and goodness to the vile seem vile:
Filths savour but themselves. What have you done?
Tigers, not daughters, what have you perform'd?
A father, and a gracious aged man,
Whose reverence even the head-lugg'd bear[6] would lick,
Most barbarous, most degenerate! have you madded.
Could my good brother suffer you to do it?
A man, a prince, by him so benefited!
If that the heavens do not their visible spirits
Send quickly down to tame these vile offences,
It will come,
Humanity must perforce prey on itself,
Like monsters of the deep.

GON. Milk-liver'd man!

---

4. *I have been worth the whistle*] an adaptation of the common proverb, "A poor dog is not worth the whistling." Goneril usually received an elaborate welcome on her return home.
5. *material sap*] sap giving essential nourishment.
6. *the head-lugg'd bear*] the bear dragged about by a cord round its head, and thereby infuriated.

That bear'st a cheek for blows, a head for wrongs;
Who hast not in thy brows an eye discerning
Thine honour from thy suffering; that not know'st
Fools do those villains pity who are punish'd
Ere they have done their mischief.[7] Where's thy drum?
France spreads his banners in our noiseless land,
With plumed helm thy state begins to threat,
Whiles thou, a moral[8] fool, sit'st still and criest
"Alack, why does he so?"

ALB. See thyself, devil!
Proper deformity seems not in the fiend
So horrid as in woman.

GON. O vain fool!

ALB. Thou changed and self-cover'd thing, for shame,
Be-monster not thy feature. Were 't my fitness
To let these hands obey my blood,[9]
They are apt enough to dislocate and tear
Thy flesh and bones: howe'er thou art a fiend,
A woman's shape doth shield thee.

GON. Marry, your manhood! mew![10]

*Enter a* Messenger

ALB. What news?

MESS. O, my good lord, the Duke of Cornwall's dead,
Slain by his servant, going to put out
The other eye of Gloucester.

ALB. Gloucester's eyes!

MESS. A servant that he bred, thrill'd with remorse,[11]
Opposed against the act, bending his sword
To his great master; who thereat enraged
Flew on him and amongst them fell'd him dead,
But not without that harmful stroke which since

---

7. *Who hast not . . . mischief*] Whose eyes are not able to distinguish the injury to honour in tamely suffering wrong; who does not know that only fools show pity for those wretches who are punished before they have wrought the mischief they have designed.
8. *moral*] moralising.
9. *blood*] disposition or impulse.
10. *mew!*] a derisive interjection.
11. *remorse*] compassion.

Hath pluck'd him after.

ALB. This shows you are above,
You justicers, that these our nether crimes
So speedily can venge. But, O poor Gloucester!
Lost he his other eye?

MESS. Both, both, my lord.
This letter, madam, craves a speedy answer;
'T is from your sister.

GON. [*Aside*] One way I like this well;
But being widow, and my Gloucester with her,
May all the building in my fancy pluck
Upon my hateful life:[12] another way,
The news is not so tart.—I'll read, and answer. [*Exit.*]

ALB. Where was his son when they did take his eyes?

MESS. Come with my lady hither.

ALB. He is not here.

MESS. No, my good lord; I met him back again.[13]

ALB. Knows he the wickedness?

MESS. Ay, my good lord; 't was he inform'd against him,
And quit the house on purpose, that their punishment
Might have the freer course.

ALB. Gloucester, I live
To thank thee for the love thou show'dst the king,
And to revenge thine eyes. Come hither, friend:
Tell me what more thou know'st. [*Exeunt.*]

---

12. *One way . . . hateful life*] Goneril's cruelty approves the death of Cornwall and the blinding of Gloucester. But seeing that her sister is now a widow and Edmund, whom she calls by his father's title, "my Gloucester," is in her sister's company, she fears that the design of killing her own husband and marrying Edmund herself may be foiled, and that the castle of her imagination may fall and crush her own life, which in its present condition is loathsome to her.
13. *back again*] on his way back.

## SCENE III—*The French Camp Near Dover*

*Enter* Kent *and a* Gentleman

KENT. Why the King of France is so suddenly gone back know you the reason?

GENT. Something he left imperfect in the state which since his coming forth is thought of, which imports to the kingdom so much fear and danger that his personal return was most required and necessary.

KENT. Who hath he left behind him general?

GENT. The Marshal of France, Monsieur La Far.

KENT. Did your letters pierce the queen to any demonstration of grief?

GENT. Ay, sir; she took them, read them in my presence,
And now and then an ample tear trill'd[1] down
Her delicate cheek: it seem'd she was a queen
Over her passion, who most rebel-like
Sought to be king o'er her.

KENT. O, then it moved her.

GENT. Not to a rage: patience and sorrow strove
Who should express her goodliest. You have seen
Sunshine and rain at once: her smiles and tears
Were like a better way: those happy smilets
That play'd on her ripe lip seem'd not to know
What guests were in her eyes; which parted thence
As pearls from diamonds dropp'd. In brief,
Sorrow would be a rarity most beloved,
If all could so become it.

KENT. Made she no verbal question?

GENT. Faith, once or twice she heaved the name of "father"
Pantingly forth, as if it press'd her heart;
Cried "Sisters! sisters! Shame of ladies! sisters!
Kent! father! sisters! What, i' the storm? i' the night?

---

1. *trill'd*] trickled.

Let pity not be believed!" There she shook
The holy water from her heavenly eyes,
And clamour moisten'd: then away she started
To deal with grief alone.

KENT. It is the stars,
The stars above us, govern our conditions;
Else one self mate and mate[2] could not beget
Such different issues. You spoke not with her since?

GENT. No.

KENT. Was this before the king return'd?

GENT. No, since.

KENT. Well, sir, the poor distressed Lear 's i' the town;
Who sometime in his better tune remembers
What we are come about, and by no means
Will yield to see his daughter.

GENT. Why, good sir?

KENT. A sovereign shame so elbows him: his own unkindness
That stripp'd her from his benediction, turn'd her
To foreign casualties, gave her dear rights
To his dog-hearted daughters: these things sting
His mind so venomously that burning shame
Detains him from Cordelia.

GENT. Alack, poor gentleman!

KENT. Of Albany's and Cornwall's powers you heard not?

GENT. 'T is so; they are afoot.

KENT. Well, sir, I'll bring you to our master Lear,
And leave you to attend him: some dear cause[3]
Will in concealment wrap me up awhile;
When I am known aright, you shall not grieve
Lending me this acquaintance. I pray you, go
Along with me. [*Exeunt.*]

---

2. *self mate and mate*] the same husband and wife.
3. *some dear cause*] some very good reason.

## SCENE IV — *The Same*

A *Tent*

*Enter, with drum and colours,* CORDELIA, Doctor, *and* Soldiers

COR. Alack, 't is he: why, he was met even now
As mad as the vex'd sea; singing aloud;
Crown'd with rank fumiter and furrow-weeds,
With bur-docks, hemlock, nettles, cuckoo-flowers,
Darnel,[1] and all the idle weeds that grow
In our sustaining corn. A century send forth;
Search every acre in the high-grown field,
And bring him to our eye. [*Exit an Officer.*] What can man's wisdom
In the restoring his bereaved sense?
He that helps him take all my outward worth.

DOCT. There is means, madam:
Our foster-nurse of nature is repose,
The which he lacks: that to provoke in him,
Are many simples[2] operative, whose power
Will close the eye of anguish.

COR. All blest secrets,
All you unpublish'd virtues of the earth,
Spring with my tears! be aidant and remediate[3]
In the good man's distress! Seek, seek for him;
Lest his ungovern'd rage dissolve the life
That wants the means to lead it.[4]

*Enter a* Messenger

---

1. *rank fumiter . . . bur-docks . . . cuckoo-flowers, Darnel*] Cf. *Hen.* V, V, ii, 44–46: "her fallow leas The *darnel,* hemlock and *rank fumitory* Doth root upon." "Fumiter" is a common sort of weed, of which there seem to be five species known in England. *Burdocks,* or "burdock," is a coarse flower bearing prickly flowerheads called "burs," and having large dock-leaves. "Cuckoo flowers" is applied to many plants flowering in the spring. "Darnel" is raygrass, a weed often found in open cornfields.
2. *simples*] medicinal herbs.
3. *aidant and remediate*] helpful and remedial.
4. *the means to lead it*] the control of reason to guide it.

MESS. News, madam;
The British powers are marching hitherward.
COR. 'T is known before; our preparation stands
In expectation of them. O dear father,
It is thy business that I go about;
Therefore great France
My mourning and important tears[5] hath pitied.
No blown ambition doth our arms incite,
But love, dear love, and our aged father's right:
Soon may I hear and see him!
[*Exeunt.*]

## SCENE V—*Gloucester's Castle*

*Enter* REGAN *and* OSWALD

REG. But are my brother's powers set forth?
OSW. Ay, madam.
REG. Himself in person there?
OSW. Madam, with much ado:
Your sister is the better soldier.
REG. Lord Edmund spake not with your lord at home?
OSW. No, madam.
REG. What might import my sister's letter to him?
OSW. I know not, lady.
REG. Faith, he is posted hence on serious matter.
It was great ignorance, Gloucester's eyes being out,
To let him live: where he arrives he moves
All hearts against us: Edmund, I think, is gone,
In pity of his misery, to dispatch
His nighted life; moreover, to descry
The strength o' the enemy.

5. *important tears*] importunate tears.

OSW. I must needs after him, madam, with my letter.
REG. Our troops set forth to-morrow: stay with us;
The ways are dangerous.
OSW. I may not, madam:
My lady charged my duty in this business.
REG. Why should she write to Edmund? Might not you
Transport her purposes by word? Belike,
Something—I know not what: I'll love thee much,
Let me unseal the letter.
OSW. Madam, I had rather—
REG. I know your lady does not love her husband;
I am sure of that: and at her late being here
She gave strange œillades[1] and most speaking looks
To noble Edmund. I know you are of her bosom.[2]
OSW. I, madam?
REG. I speak in understanding: you are; I know't:
Therefore I do advise you, take this note:
My lord is dead; Edmund and I have talk'd;
And more convenient is he for my hand
Than for your lady's: you may gather more.
If you do find him, pray you, give him this;
And when your mistress hears thus much from you,
I pray, desire her call her wisdom to her.
So, fare you well.
If you do chance to hear of that blind traitor,
Preferment falls on him that cuts him off.
OSW. Would I could meet him, madam! I should show
What party I do follow.
REG. Fare thee well. [*Exeunt.*]

1. *œillades*] amorous glances.
2. *of her bosom*] in her confidence.

## SCENE VI—*Fields Near Dover*

*Enter* GLOUCESTER, *and* EDGAR *dressed like a peasant*

GLOU. When shall we come to the top of that same hill?
EDG. You do climb up it now: look, how we labour.
GLOU. Methinks the ground is even.
EDG. Horrible steep.
Hark, do you hear the sea?
GLOU. No, truly.
EDG. Why then your other senses grow imperfect
By your eyes' anguish.
GLOU. So may it be indeed:
Methinks thy voice is alter'd, and thou speak'st
In better phrase and matter than thou didst.
EDG. You're much deceived: in nothing am I changed
But in my garments.
GLOU. Methinks you're better spoken.
EDG. Come on, sir; here's the place: stand still. How fearful
And dizzy 't is to cast one's eyes so low!
The crows and choughs[1] that wing the midway air
Show scarce so gross as beetles: half way down
Hangs one that gathers samphire,[2] dreadful trade!
Methinks he seems no bigger than his head:
The fishermen that walk upon the beach
Appear like mice; and yond tall anchoring bark
Diminish'd to her cock;[3] her cock, a buoy
Almost too small for sight: the murmuring surge
That on the unnumber'd idle pebbles chafes
Cannot be heard so high. I'll look no more,

1. *choughs*] jackdaws.
2. *samphire*] a rock herb named after St. Pierre or St. Peter, which is much used for pickling. It is sometimes called "sea-fennel."
3. *cock*] a ship's small boat, often called cock-boat.

Lest my brain turn and the deficient sight
Topple down headlong.

GLOU. Set me where you stand.

EDG. Give me your hand: you are now within a foot
Of the extreme verge: for all beneath the moon
Would I not leap upright.

GLOU. Let go my hand.
Here, friend, 's another purse; in it a jewel
Well worth a poor man's taking: fairies and gods
Prosper it with thee! Go thou further off;
Bid me farewell, and let me hear thee going.

EDG. Now fare you well, good sir.

GLOU. With all my heart.

EDG. Why I do trifle thus with his despair
Is done to cure it.

GLOU. [*Kneeling*] O you mighty gods!
This world I do renounce, and in your sights
Shake patiently my great affliction off:
If I could bear it longer and not fall
To quarrel with your great opposeless wills,
My snuff[4] and loathed part of nature should
Burn itself out. If Edgar live, O bless him!
Now, fellow, fare thee well. [*He falls forward.*]

EDG. Gone, sir: farewell.
And yet I know not how conceit[5] may rob
The treasury of life, when life itself
Yields to the theft: had he been where he thought,
By this had thought been past. Alive or dead?
Ho, you sir! friend! Hear you, sir! speak!
Thus might he pass[6] indeed: yet he revives.
What are you, sir?

GLOU. Away, and let me die.

EDG. Hadst thou been aught but gossamer, feathers, air,
So many fathom down precipitating,
Thou'dst shiver'd like an egg: but thou dost breathe;

---

4. *snuff*] refuse or dregs.
5. *conceit*] imagination, false impression.
6. *pass*] pass away, die.

Hast heavy substance; bleed'st not; speak'st; art sound.
Ten masts at each[7] make not the altitude
Which thou hast perpendicularly fell:
Thy life's a miracle. Speak yet again.

GLOU. But have I fall'n, or no?

EDG. From the dread summit of this chalky bourn.
Look up a-height; the shrill-gorged lark so far
Cannot be seen or heard: do but look up.

GLOU. Alack, I have no eyes.
Is wretchedness deprived that benefit,
To end itself by death? 'T was yet some comfort,
When misery could beguile the tyrant's rage
And frustrate his proud will.

EDG. Give me your arm:
Up: so. How is't? Feel you your legs? You stand.

GLOU. Too well, too well.

EDG. This is above all strangeness.
Upon the crown o' the cliff, what thing was that
Which parted from you?

GLOU. A poor unfortunate beggar.

EDG. As I stood here below, methought his eyes
Were two full moons; he had a thousand noses,
Horns whelk'd and waved like the enridged sea:[8]
It was some fiend; therefore, thou happy father,
Think that the clearest[9] gods, who make them honours
Of men's impossibilities, have preserved thee.

GLOU. I do remember now: henceforth I'll bear
Affliction till it do cry out itself
"Enough, enough," and die. That thing you speak of,
I took it for a man; often 't would say
"The fiend, the fiend:" he led me to that place.

EDG. Bear free and patient thoughts. But who comes here?

*Enter* LEAR, *fantastically dressed with wild flowers*

---

7. *Ten masts at each*] Ten masts fastened end to end.
8. *whelk'd and waved . . . sea*] twisted or convolved (like the shell of the whelk fish) and fluted like the furrowed sea.
9. *clearest*] most pure or righteous.

The safer sense will ne'er accommodate
His master thus.[10]

LEAR. No, they cannot touch me for coining; I am the king himself.

EDG. O thou side-piercing[11] sight!

LEAR. Nature 's above art in that respect. There's your press-money.[12] That fellow handles his bow like a crow-keeper;[13] draw me a clothier's yard.[14] Look, look, a mouse! Peace, peace; this piece of toasted cheese will do 't. There's my gauntlet; I'll prove it on a giant. Bring up the brown bills.[15] O, well flown, bird![16] i' the clout, i' the clout:[17] hewgh! Give the word.[18]

EDG. Sweet marjoram.

LEAR. Pass.

GLOU. I know that voice.

LEAR. Ha! Goneril, with a white beard! They flattered me like a dog, and told me I had white hairs in my beard ere the black ones were there. To say "ay" and "no" to every thing that I said! "Ay" and "no" too was no good divinity. When the rain came to wet me once and the wind to make me chatter; when the thunder would not peace at my bidding; there I found 'em, there I smelt 'em out. Go to, they are not men o' their words: they told me I was every thing; 't is a lie, I am not ague-proof.

GLOU. The trick of that voice I do well remember:
Is 't not the king?

LEAR. Ay, every inch a king:
When I do stare, see how the subject quakes.
I pardon that man's life. What was thy cause?

---

10. *The safer sense . . . thus*] The saner sense or the reason would never allow one in full possession of it to dress himself up thus. "His master" would be in modern grammar "its master."
11. *side-piercing*] piercing the heart.
12. *There's your press-money*] Lear imagines himself a recruiting officer handing bounty money to men forcibly impressed.
13. *crow-keeper*] scarecrow.
14. *draw me a clothier's yard*] shoot an arrow the length of a clothier's yard measure.
15. *the brown bills*] the halberdiers, soldiers bearing halberds, which were painted brown to preserve them from rust.
16. *well flown, bird!*] the falconer's cry to the hawk.
17. *i' the clout*] the cry of the archer who hit the "clout," or the bull's eye or pin fixed in the centre of the butt or target.
18. *Give the word*] The mad king imagines himself a sentinel demanding the watchword of Edgar.

Adultery?
Thou shalt not die: die for adultery! No:
The wren goes to 't, and the small gilded fly
Does lecher in my sight.
Let copulation thrive; for Gloucester's bastard son
Was kinder to his father than my daughters
Got 'tween the lawful sheets.
To 't, luxury,[19] pell-mell! for I lack soldiers.
Behold yond simpering dame,
Whose face between her forks[20] presages snow,
That minces virtue and does shake the head
To hear of pleasure's name;
The fitchew,[21] nor the soiled horse,[22] goes to 't
With a more riotous appetite.
Down from the waist they are Centaurs,
Though women all above:
But to the girdle do the gods inherit,
Beneath is all the fiends';
There's hell, there's darkness, there's the sulphurous pit,
Burning, scalding, stench, consumption; fie, fie, fie! pah, pah!
Give me an ounce of civet,[23] good apothecary, to sweeten my imagination: there's money for thee.

GLOU. O, let me kiss that hand!

LEAR. Let me wipe it first; it smells of mortality.

GLOU. O ruin'd piece of nature! This great world
Shall so wear out to nought. Dost thou know me?

LEAR. I remember thine eyes well enough. Dost thou squiny[24] at me? No, do thy worst, blind Cupid; I'll not love. Read thou this challenge; mark but the penning on 't.

GLOU. Were all the letters suns, I could not see one.

EDG. I would not take this from report: it is,
And my heart breaks at it.

LEAR. Read.

---

19. *luxury*] lust.
20. *forks*] legs.
21. *fitchew*] polecat, often applied to a harlot.
22. *the soiled horse*] the horse turned out to new grass, which rendered him wanton.
23. *civet*] a musky perfume, obtained from the glands of the civet cat.
24. *squiny*] look asquint.

GLOU. What, with the case of eyes?[25]

LEAR. O, ho, are you there with me?[26] No eyes in your head, nor no money in your purse? Your eyes are in a heavy case,[27] your purse in a light: yet you see how this world goes.

GLOU. I see it feelingly.

LEAR. What, art mad? A man may see how this world goes with no eyes. Look with thine ears: see how yond justice rails upon yond simple thief. Hark, in thine ear: change places, and, handy-dandy, which is the justice, which is the thief? Thou hast seen a farmer's dog bark at a beggar?

GLOU. Ay, sir.

LEAR. And the creature run from the cur? There thou mightst behold the great image of authority: a dog's obeyed in office.
Thou rascal beadle, hold thy bloody hand!
Why dost thou lash that whore? Strip thine own back;
Thou hotly lust'st to use her in that kind
For which thou whip'st her. The usurer hangs the cozener.
Through tatter'd clothes small vices do appear;
Robes and furr'd gowns hide all. Plate sin with gold,
And the strong lance of justice hurtless breaks;
Arm it in rags, a pigmy's straw does pierce it.
None does offend, none, I say, none; I'll able 'em:[28]
Take that of me, my friend, who have the power
To seal the accuser's lips. Get thee glass eyes,
And, like a scurvy politician, seem
To see the things thou dost not.
Now, now, now, now: pull off my boots: harder, harder: so.

EDG. O, matter and impertinency mix'd!
Reason in madness!

LEAR. If thou wilt weep my fortunes, take my eyes.
I know thee well enough; thy name is Gloucester:
Thou must be patient; we came crying hither:
Thou know'st, the first time that we smell the air,

---

25. *with the case of eyes*] with the sockets which once held eyes.
26. *are you there with me?*] do you understand me?
27. *a heavy case*] a sad plight.
28. *I'll able 'em*] I'll answer or vouch for them.

We wawl and cry. I will preach to thee: mark.

GLOU. Alack, alack the day!

LEAR. When we are born, we cry that we are come
To this great stage of fools. This's a good block.[29]
It were a delicate stratagem, to shoe
A troop of horse with felt: I'll put 't in proof;
And when I have stol'n upon these sons-in-law,
Then, kill, kill, kill, kill, kill, kill!

*Enter a* Gentleman, *with* Attendants

GENT. O, here he is: lay hand upon him. Sir,
Your most dear daughter —

LEAR. No rescue? What, a prisoner? I am even
The natural fool of fortune. Use me well;
You shall have ransom. Let me have a surgeon;
I am cut to the brains.

GENT. You shall have any thing.

LEAR. No seconds? all myself?
Why, this would make a man a man of salt,[30]
To use his eyes for garden water-pots,
Ay, and laying autumn's dust.

GENT. Good sir, —

LEAR. I will die bravely, like a smug[31] bridegroom. What!
I will be jovial: come, come; I am a king,
My masters, know you that.

GENT. You are a royal one, and we obey you.

LEAR. Then there 's life in 't. Nay, an you get it, you shall get it by running. Sa, sa, sa, sa.

[*Exit running; Attendants follow.*]

GENT. A sight most pitiful in the meanest wretch,
Past speaking of in a king! Thou hast one daughter,
Who redeems nature from the general curse

---

29. *This's a good block*] "Block" is frequently used for the mould on which a hat is fashioned, and thus for the hat itself.

30. *salt*] salt tears.

31. *smug*] spruce, without any depreciatory sense.

Which twain have brought her to.

EDG. Hail, gentle sir.

GENT. Sir, speed you: what's your will?

EDG. Do you hear aught, sir, of a battle toward?

GENT. Most sure and vulgar: every one hears that,
Which can distinguish sound.

EDG. But, by your favour,
How near's the other army?

GENT. Near and on speedy foot; the main descry
Stands on the hourly thought.

EDG. I thank you, sir: that's all.

GENT. Though that the queen on special cause is here,
Her army is moved on.

EDG. I thank you, sir.

[*Exit Gent.*]

GLOU. You ever-gentle gods, take my breath from me;
Let not my worser spirit tempt me again
To die before you please!

EDG. Well pray you, father.

GLOU. Now, good sir, what are you?

EDG. A most poor man, made tame to fortune's blows;
Who, by the art of known and feeling sorrows,
Am pregnant to good pity. Give me your hand,
I'll lead you to some biding.[32]

GLOU. Hearty thanks;
The bounty and the benison of heaven
To boot, and boot!

*Enter* OSWALD

OSW. A proclaim'd prize! Most happy!
That eyeless head of thine was first framed flesh
To raise my fortunes. Thou old unhappy traitor,
Briefly thyself remember: the sword is out
That must destroy thee.

GLOU. Now let thy friendly hand
Put strength enough to 't. [*Edgar interposes.*]

OSW. Wherefore, bold peasant,
Darest thou support a publish'd traitor? Hence!

32. *biding*] lodging.

Lest that the infection of his fortune take
Like hold on thee. Let go his arm.

EDG. Chill[33] not let go, zir, without vurther 'casion.

OSW. Let go, slave, or thou diest!

EDG. Good gentleman, go your gait, and let poor volk pass. An chud ha' been zwaggered out of my life, 't would not ha' been zo long as 't is by a vortnight. Nay, come not near th' old man; keep out, che vor ye,[34] or I'se try whether your costard or my ballow[35] be the harder: chill be plain with you.

OSW. Out, dunghill! [*They fight.*]

EDG. Chill pick your teeth, zir: come; no matter vor your foins.[36]
[*Oswald falls.*]

OSW. Slave, thou hast slain me. Villain, take my purse:
If ever thou wilt thrive, bury my body;
And give the letters which thou find'st about me
To Edmund earl of Gloucester; seek him out
Upon the British party. O, untimely death!
Death! [*Dies.*]

EDG. I know thee well: a serviceable villain,
As duteous[37] to the vices of thy mistress
As badness would desire.

GLOU. What, is he dead?

EDG. Sit you down, father; rest you.
Let 's see these pockets: the letters that he speaks of
May be my friends. He 's dead; I am only sorry
He had no other deathsman.[38] Let us see:
Leave, gentle wax; and, manners, blame us not:
To know our enemies' minds, we 'ld rip their hearts;
Their papers, is more lawful.

[*Reads*] "Let our reciprocal vows be remembered. You have many opportunities to cut him off: if your will want not, time and place will be fruitfully offered. There is nothing done, if he return the conqueror: then am I the prisoner, and his bed my gaol; from the

33. *Chill*] I will.
34. *che vor ye*] I warn you.
35. *your costard or my ballow*] your head or my cudgel.
36. *foins*] thrusts in fencing.
37. *duteous*] obsequious, obedient.
38. *deathsman*] executioner.

loathed warmth whereof deliver me, and supply the place for your labour.

"Your — wife, so I would say — affectionate servant,

"GONERIL."

O undistinguish'd space of woman's will!
A plot upon her virtuous husband's life;
And the exchange my brother! Here, in the sands,
Thee I'll rake up,[39] the post unsanctified
Of murderous lechers; and in the mature time
With this ungracious paper strike the sight
Of the death-practised[40] duke: for him 't is well
That of thy death and business I can tell.

GLOU. The king is mad: how stiff is my vile sense,
That I stand up, and have ingenious feeling[41]
Of my huge sorrows! Better I were distract:
So should my thoughts be sever'd from my griefs,
And woes by wrong imaginations lose
The knowledge of themselves. [*Drum afar off.*]

EDG. Give me your hand:
Far off, methinks, I hear the beaten drum:
Come, father, I'll bestow you with a friend. [*Exeunt.*]

39. *rake up*] cover.
40. *death-practised*] whose death is plotted.
41. *ingenious feeling*] lively consciousness.

## SCENE VII — *A Tent in the French Camp. Lear on a Bed Asleep, Soft Music Playing; Gentleman, and Others Attending*

*Enter* CORDELIA, KENT, *and* Doctor

COR. O thou good Kent, how shall I live and work,
To match thy goodness? My life will be too short,
And every measure fail me.

KENT. To be acknowledged, madam, is o'erpaid.
All my reports go with the modest truth,
Nor more nor clipp'd, but so.

COR. Be better suited:[1]
These weeds are memories of those worser hours:
I prithee, put them off.

KENT. Pardon me, dear madam;
Yet to be known shortens my made intent:
My boon I make it, that you know me not
Till time and I think meet.

COR. Then be 't so, my good lord. [*To the Doctor*] How does the king?

DOCT. Madam, sleeps still.

COR. O you kind gods,
Cure this great breach in his abused nature!
The untuned and jarring senses, O, wind up
Of this child-changed father!

DOCT. So please your majesty
That we may wake the king: he hath slept long.

COR. Be govern'd by your knowledge, and proceed
I' the sway of your own will. Is he array'd?

GENT. Ay, madam; in the heaviness of his sleep
We put fresh garments on him.

DOCT. Be by, good madam, when we do awake him;

1. *suited*] dressed.

I doubt not of his temperance.[2]

COR. Very well.

DOCT. Please you, draw near. Louder the music there!

COR. O my dear father! Restoration hang
Thy medicine on my lips, and let this kiss
Repair those violent harms that my two sisters
Have in thy reverence made!

KENT. Kind and dear princess!

COR. Had you not been their father, these white flakes[3]
Had challenged pity of them. Was this a face
To be opposed against the warring winds?
To stand against the deep dread-bolted thunder?
In the most terrible and nimble stroke
Of quick, cross lightning? to watch — poor perdu![4] —
With this thin helm? Mine enemy's dog,
Though he had bit me, should have stood that night
Against my fire; and wast thou fain, poor father,
To hovel thee with swine and rogues forlorn,
In short[5] and musty straw? Alack, alack!
'T is wonder that thy life and wits at once
Had not concluded all. He wakes; speak to him.

DOCT. Madam, do you; 't is fittest.

COR. How does my royal lord? How fares your majesty?

LEAR. You do me wrong to take me out o' the grave:
Thou art a soul in bliss; but I am bound
Upon a wheel of fire, that mine own tears
Do scald like molten lead.

COR. Sir, do you know me?

LEAR. You are a spirit, I know: when did you die?

COR. Still, still, far wide![6]

DOCT. He's scarce awake: let him alone awhile.

LEAR. Where have I been? Where am I? Fair daylight?
I am mightily abused. I should e'en die with pity,

---

2. *temperance*] sanity, calmness.
3. *white flakes*] snow-white hair.
4. *perdu*] from "enfans perdus" or "perdus," soldiers intrusted with very perilous service.
5. *short*] scanty, insufficient.
6. *wide*] astray.

To see another thus. I know not what to say.
I will not swear these are my hands: let's see;
I feel this pin prick. Would I were assured
Of my condition!

COR. O, look upon me, sir,
And hold your hands in benediction o'er me.
No, sir, you must not kneel.

LEAR. Pray, do not mock me:
I am a very foolish fond old man,
Fourscore and upward, not an hour more nor less;
And, to deal plainly,
I fear I am not in my perfect mind.
Methinks I should know you and know this man;
Yet I am doubtful; for I am mainly ignorant
What place this is, and all the skill I have
Remembers not these garments, nor I know not
Where I did lodge last night. Do not laugh at me;
For, as I am a man, I think this lady
To be my child Cordelia.

COR. And so I am, I am.

LEAR. Be your tears wet? yes, faith. I pray, weep not:
If you have poison for me, I will drink it.
I know you do not love me; for your sisters
Have, as I do remember, done me wrong:
You have some cause, they have not.

COR. No cause, no cause.

LEAR. Am I in France?

KENT. In your own kingdom, sir.

LEAR. Do not abuse me.

DOCT. Be comforted, good madam: the great rage,
You see, is kill'd in him: and yet it is danger
To make him even o'er[7] the time he has lost.
Desire him to go in; trouble him no more
Till further settling.

COR. Will 't please your highness walk?[8]

---

7. *even o'er*] account for, bridge over in his recollection.
8. *walk*] withdraw.

LEAR. You must bear with me. Pray you now, forget and forgive: I am old and foolish.

[*Exeunt all but Kent and Gentleman.*]

GENT. Holds it true, sir, that the Duke of Cornwall was so slain?

KENT. Most certain, sir.

GENT. Who is conductor of his people?

KENT. As 't is said, the bastard son of Gloucester.

GENT. They say Edgar, his banished son, is with the Earl of Kent in Germany.

KENT. Report is changeable. 'T is time to look about; the powers of the kingdom approach apace.

GENT. The arbitrement[9] is like to be bloody. Fare you well, sir.

[*Exit.*]

KENT. My point and period will be thoroughly wrought,
Or well or ill, as this day's battle 's fought.[10] [*Exit.*]

9. *arbitrement*] decision.

10. *My point and period . . . fought*] The aim and end of my life will be fully attained for either good or ill in the course of this day's battle.

# ACT V

## SCENE I — *The British Camp Near Dover*

*Enter, with drum and colours,* EDMUND, REGAN, Gentlemen, *and* Soldiers

EDM. Know of the Duke if his last purpose hold,
Or whether since he is advised by aught
To change the course: he's full of alteration
And self-reproving: bring his constant pleasure.[1]
[*To a Gentleman, who goes out.*]

REG. Our sister's man is certainly miscarried.

EDM. 'T is to be doubted,[2] madam.

REG. Now, sweet lord,
You know the goodness I intend upon you:
Tell me, but truly, but then speak the truth,
Do you not love my sister?

EDM. In honour'd love.

REG. But have you never found my brother's way
To the forfended[3] place?

EDM. That thought abuses you.

REG. I am doubtful that you have been conjunct
And bosom'd with her, as far as we call hers.

EDM. No, by mine honour, madam.

REG. I never shall endure her: dear my lord,

---

1. *constant pleasure*] settled decision.
2. *doubted*] feared.
3. *forfended*] forbidden.

Be not familiar with her.

EDM. Fear me not.—

She and the duke her husband!

*Enter, with drum and colours,* ALBANY, GONERIL, *and* Soldiers

GON. [*Aside*] I had rather lose the battle than that sister
Should loosen him and me.

ALB. Our very loving sister, well be-met.
Sir, this I hear; the king is come to his daughter,
With others whom the rigour of our state
Forced to cry out. Where I could not be honest,
I never yet was valiant: for this business,
It toucheth us, as France invades our land,
Not bolds the king,[4] with others, whom, I fear,
Most just and heavy causes make oppose.

EDM. Sir, you speak nobly.

REG. Why is this reason'd?[5]

GON. Combine together 'gainst the enemy;
For these domestic and particular broils
Are not the question here.

ALB. Let's then determine
With the ancient of war[6] on our proceedings.

EDM. I shall attend you presently at your tent.

REG. Sister, you'll go with us?

GON. No.

REG. 'T is most convenient; pray you, go with us.

GON. [*Aside*] O, ho, I know the riddle.—I will go.

*As they are going out, enter* EDGAR *disguised*

EDG. If e'er your grace had speech with man so poor,
Hear me one word.

ALB. I'll overtake you. Speak.
[*Exeunt all but Albany and Edgar.*]

EDG. Before you fight the battle, ope this letter.

---

4. *It toucheth us . . . king*] It concerns us not because the French support Lear inasmuch as the French are invading our territory.
5. *reason'd*] discussed, talked about.
6. *ancient of war*] military veterans, those of long experience in warfare.

If you have victory, let the trumpet sound
For him that brought it: wretched though I seem,
I can produce a champion that will prove
What is avouched there. If you miscarry,
Your business of the world hath so an end,
And machination ceases. Fortune love you!

ALB. Stay till I have read the letter.

EDG. I was forbid it.
When time shall serve, let but the herald cry,
And I'll appear again.

ALB. Why, fare thee well: I will o'erlook thy paper.

[*Exit Edgar.*]

*Re-enter* Edmund

EDM. The enemy's in view: draw up your powers.
Here is the guess of their true strength and forces
By diligent discovery; but your haste
Is now urged on you.

ALB. We will greet the time. [*Exit.*]

EDM. To both these sisters have I sworn my love;
Each jealous of the other, as the stung
Are of the adder. Which of them shall I take?
Both? one? or neither? Neither can be enjoy'd,
If both remain alive: to take the widow
Exasperates, makes mad her sister Goneril;
And hardly shall I carry out my side,[7]
Her husband being alive. Now then we'll use
His countenance for the battle; which being done,
Let her who would be rid of him devise
His speedy taking off. As for the mercy
Which he intends to Lear and to Cordelia,
The battle done, and they within our power,
Shall never see his pardon; for my state
Stands on me to defend, not to debate. [*Exit.*]

---

7. *carry out my side*] win my game. "Side" is often found as a technical term for a set of partners in a game played by two or more players, and hence was sometimes applied to the game itself or to a bout of play.

## SCENE II—*A Field Between the Two Camps*

*Alarum within. Enter, with drum and colours,* LEAR, CORDELIA, *and* Soldiers, *over the stage; and exeunt*

*Enter* EDGAR *and* GLOUCESTER

EDG. Here, father, take the shadow of this tree
For your good host; pray that the right may thrive:
If ever I return to you again,
I'll bring you comfort.

GLOU. Grace go with you, sir!

[*Exit Edgar.*]

*Alarum and retreat within. Re-enter* EDGAR.

EDG. Away, old man; give me thy hand; away!
King Lear hath lost, he and his daughter ta'en:
Give me thy hand; come on.

GLOU. No further, sir; a man may rot even here.

EDG. What, in ill thoughts again? Men must endure
Their going hence, even as their coming hither:
Ripeness is all: come on.

GLOU. And that's true too. [*Exeunt.*]

## SCENE III — *The British Camp Near Dover*

*Enter, in conquest, with drum and colours,* EDMUND; LEAR *and* CORDELIA, *as prisoners;* Captain, Soldiers, *etc.*

EDM. Some officers take them away: good guard,
Until their greater pleasures first be known
That are to censure them.

COR. We are not the first
Who with best meaning have incurr'd the worst.
For thee, oppressed king, am I cast down;
Myself could else out-frown false fortune's frown.
Shall we not see these daughters and these sisters?

LEAR. No, no, no, no! Come, let's away to prison:
We two alone will sing like birds i' the cage:
When thou dost ask me blessing, I'll kneel down
And ask of thee forgiveness: so we'll live,
And pray, and sing, and tell old tales, and laugh
At gilded butterflies,[1] and hear poor rogues
Talk of court news; and we'll talk with them too,
Who loses and who wins, who's in, who's out;
And take upon 's the mystery of things,
As if we were God's spies: and we'll wear out,
In a wall'd prison, packs and sects[2] of great ones
That ebb and flow by the moon.

EDM. Take them away.

LEAR. Upon such sacrifices, my Cordelia,
The gods themselves throw incense. Have I caught thee?
He that parts us shall bring a brand from heaven,
And fire us hence like foxes.[3] Wipe thine eyes;
The good-years shall devour them, flesh and fell,[4]

1. *gilded butterflies*] fashionable courtiers.
2. *packs and sects*] parties and factions (of politicians).
3. *fire us hence like foxes*] drive us away as foxes are expelled from their holes by burning them out.
4. *flesh and fell*] literally "flesh and skin"; colloquially used for "flesh and bones."

Ere they shall make us weep: we'll see 'em starve first.
Come. [*Exeunt Lear and Cordelia, guarded.*]

EDM. Come hither, captain; hark.
Take thou this note: go follow them to prison:
One step I have advanced thee; if thou dost
As this instructs thee, thou dost make thy way
To noble fortunes: know thou this, that men
Are as the time is: to be tender-minded
Does not become a sword: thy great employment
Will not bear question; either say thou'lt do 't,
Or thrive by other means.

CAPT. I'll do 't, my lord.

EDM. About it; and write happy when thou hast done.
Mark; I say, instantly, and carry it so
As I have set it down.

CAPT. I cannot draw a cart, nor eat dried oats;
If it be man's work, I'll do 't. [*Exit.*]

*Flourish. Enter* ALBANY, GONERIL, REGAN, *another* Captain, *and* Soldiers

ALB. Sir, you have shown to-day your valiant strain,
And fortune led you well: you have the captives
That were the opposites of this day's strife:
We do require them of you, so to use them
As we shall find their merits and our safety
May equally determine.

EDM. Sir, I thought it fit
To send the old and miserable king
To some retention and appointed guard;
Whose age has charms in it, whose title more,
To pluck the common bosom on his side,
And turn our impress'd lances[5] in our eyes
Which do command them. With him I sent the queen:
My reason all the same; and they are ready
To-morrow or at further space to appear
Where you shall hold your session. At this time
We sweat and bleed: the friend hath lost his friend;

5. *our impress'd lances*] weapons of the men we have impressed into our service.

And the best quarrels, in the heat, are cursed
By those that feel their sharpness.[6]
The question of Cordelia and her father
Requires a fitter place.

ALB. Sir, by your patience,
I hold you but a subject of this war,
Not as a brother.

REG. That's as we list to grace him.
Methinks our pleasure might have been demanded,
Ere you had spoke so far. He led our powers,
Bore the commission of my place and person;
The which immediacy may well stand up
And call itself your brother.

GON. Not so hot:
In his own grace he doth exalt himself
More than in your addition.[7]

REG. In my rights,
By me invested, he compeers the best.

GON. That were the most, if he should husband you.

REG. Jesters do oft prove prophets.

GON. Holla, holla!
That eye that told you so look'd but a-squint.

REG. Lady, I am not well; else I should answer
From a full-flowing stomach.[8] General,
Take thou my soldiers, prisoners, patrimony;
Dispose of them, of me; the walls are thine:[9]
Witness the world, that I create thee here
My lord and master.

GON. Mean you to enjoy him?

ALB. The let-alone[10] lies not in your good will.

EDM. Nor in thine, lord.

ALB. Half-blooded fellow, yes.

---

6. *And the best quarrels . . . sharpness*] And those engaged in wars even when waged in the justest of causes curse the quarrel when they suffer the bitter consequences, (either from loss of friends or by reason of their own wounds).
7. *in your addition*] by virtue of the title with which you invest him.
8. *stomach*] anger.
9. *The walls are thine*] Regan surrenders her person as though it were a vanquished citadel.
10. *let-alone*] prohibition.

REG. [*To Edmund*] Let the drum strike, and prove my title thine.
ALB. Stay yet; hear reason. Edmund, I arrest thee
On capital treason; and in thine attaint[11]
This gilded serpent [*pointing to Gon.*]. For your claim, fair sister,
I bar it in the interest of my wife;
'T is she is sub-contracted to this lord,
And I, her husband, contradict your bans.
If you will marry, make your loves to me;
My lady is bespoke.
GON. An interlude![12]
ALB. Thou art arm'd, Gloucester: let the trumpet sound:
If none appear to prove upon thy person
Thy heinous, manifest, and many treasons,
There is my pledge [*throwing down a glove*]: I'll prove it on thy heart,
Ere I taste bread, thou art in nothing less
Than I have here proclaim'd thee.
REG. Sick, O, sick!
GON. [*Aside*] If not, I'll ne'er trust medicine.[13]
EDM. [*Throwing down a glove*] There's my exchange: what in the world he is
That names me traitor, villain-like he lies:
Call by thy trumpet: he that dares approach,
On him, on you,—who not?—I will maintain
My truth and honour firmly.
ALB. A herald, ho!
EDM. A herald, ho, a herald!
ALB. Trust to thy single virtue;[14] for thy soldiers,
All levied in my name, have in my name
Took their discharge.
REG. My sickness grows upon me.
ALB. She is not well; convey her to my tent.
[*Exit Regan, led.*]

*Enter a* Herald

11. *in thine attaint*] in connection with thy impeachment.
12. *An interlude!*] A farce is on foot!
13. *I'll ne'er trust medicine*] Goneril has poisoned Regan.
14. *thy single virtue*] thy personal valour.

Come hither, herald, — Let the trumpet sound, —
And read out this.

CAPT. Sound, trumpet! [*A trumpet sounds.*]

HER. [*Reads*] "If any man of quality or degree within the lists of the army will maintain upon Edmund, supposed Earl of Gloucester, that he is a manifold traitor, let him appear by the third sound of the trumpet: he is bold in his defence."

EDM. Sound! [*First trumpet.*]

HER. Again! [*Second trumpet.*]

HER. Again! [*Third trumpet.*]

[*Trumpet answers within.*]

*Enter* EDGAR, *at the third sound, armed, with a trumpet before him*

ALB. Ask him his purposes, why he appears
Upon this call o' the trumpet.

HER. What are you?
Your name, your quality? and why you answer
This present summons?

EDG. Know, my name is lost;
By treason's tooth bare-gnawn and canker-bit:[15]
Yet am I noble as the adversary
I come to cope.[16]

ALB. Which is that adversary?

EDG. What's he that speaks for Edmund, Earl of Gloucester?

EDM. Himself: what say'st thou to him?

EDG. Draw thy sword,
That if my speech offend a noble heart,
Thy arm may do thee justice: here is mine.
Behold, it is the privilege of mine honours,
My oath, and my profession: I protest,
Maugre[17] thy strength, youth, place and eminence,
Despite thy victor sword and fire-new fortune,
Thy valour and thy heart, thou art a traitor,
False to thy gods, thy brother and thy father,
Conspirant 'gainst this high illustrious prince,

15. *canker-bit*] bitten by the caterpillar, by vermin.
16. *cope*] encounter.
17. *Maugre*] in spite of.

And from the extremest upward of thy head
To the descent and dust below thy foot,
A most toad-spotted traitor. Say thou "No,"
This sword, this arm and my best spirits are bent
To prove upon thy heart, whereto I speak,
Thou liest.

EDM. In wisdom I should ask thy name,
But since thy outside looks so fair and warlike
And that thy tongue some say of breeding breathes,
What safe and nicely I might well delay
By rule of knighthood,[18] I disdain and spurn:
Back do I toss these treasons to thy head;
With the hell-hated[19] lie o'erwhelm thy heart;
Which for they yet glance by and scarcely bruise.
This sword of mine shall give them instant way,
Where they shall rest for ever. Trumpets, speak!
[*Alarums. They fight. Edmund falls.*]

ALB. Save him, save him!

GON. This is practice,[20] Gloucester:
By the law of arms thou wast not bound to answer
An unknown opposite; thou art not vanquish'd,
But cozen'd and beguiled.

ALB. Shut your mouth, dame,
Or with this paper shall I stop it. Hold, sir;
Thou worse than any name, read thine own evil.
No tearing, lady; I perceive you know it.

GON. Say, if I do, the laws are mine, not thine:
Who can arraign me for 't?

ALB. Most monstrous!
Know'st thou this paper?

GON. Ask me not what I know. [*Exit.*]

ALB. Go after her: she's desperate; govern her.

EDM. What you have charged me with, that have I done;
And more, much more; the time will bring it out:

---

18. *What safe . . . knighthood*] That refusal (of your challenge) which I might well and quite accurately make in accordance with the laws of chivalry.
19. *hell-hated*] hated as hell.
20. *practice*] deceitful intrigue.

'T is past, and so am I. But what art thou
That hast this fortune on me? If thou 'rt noble,
I do forgive thee.

EDG. Let's exchange charity.
I am no less in blood than thou art, Edmund;
If more, the more thou hast wrong'd me.
My name is Edgar, and thy father's son.
The gods are just, and of our pleasant vices
Make instruments to plague us:
The dark and vicious place where thee he got
Cost him his eyes.

EDM. Thou hast spoken right, 't is true;
The wheel is come full circle; I am here.

ALB. Methought thy very gait did prophesy
A royal nobleness: I must embrace thee:
Let sorrow split my heart, if ever I
Did hate thee or thy father!

EDG. Worthy prince, I know't.

ALB. Where have you hid yourself?
How have you known the miseries of your father?

EDG. By nursing them, my lord. List a brief tale;
And when 't is told, O, that my heart would burst!
The bloody proclamation to escape
That follow'd me so near,—O, our lives' sweetness!
That we the pain of death would hourly die
Rather than die at once![21]—taught me to shift
Into a madman's rags, to assume a semblance
That very dogs disdain'd: and in this habit
Met I my father with his bleeding rings,[22]
Their precious stones new lost; became his guide,
Led him, begg'd for him, saved him from despair;
Never—O fault!—reveal'd myself unto him,
Until some half-hour past, when I was arm'd;
Not sure, though hoping, of this good success,
I ask'd his blessing, and from first to last

---

21. *we the pain . . . die at once*] we would suffer every hour the pain of death rather than die once for all.
22. *rings*] sockets of the eyes.

Told him my pilgrimage: but his flaw'd heart, —
Alack, too weak the conflict to support! —
'Twixt two extremes of passion, joy and grief,
Burst smilingly.

EDM. This speech of yours hath moved me,
And shall perchance do good: but speak you on;
You look as you had something more to say.

ALB. If there be more, more woful, hold it in;
For I am almost ready to dissolve,
Hearing of this.

EDG. This would have seem'd a period
To such as love not sorrow; but another,
To amplify too much, would make much more,
And top extremity.[23]
Whilst I was big in clamour, came there in a man,
Who, having seen me in my worst estate,
Shunn'd my abhorr'd society; but then, finding
Who 't was that so endured, with his strong arms
He fasten'd on my neck, and bellow'd out
As he'ld burst heaven; threw him on my father;
Told the most piteous tale of Lear and him
That ever ear received: which in recounting
His grief grew puissant, and the strings of life
Began to crack: twice then the trumpets sounded,
And there I left him tranced.

ALB. But who was this?

EDG. Kent, sir, the banish'd Kent; who in disguise
Follow'd his enemy king, and did him service
Improper for a slave.

*Enter a* Gentleman, *with a bloody knife*

GENT. Help, help, O, help!

EDG. What kind of help?

ALB. Speak, man.

EDG. What means this bloody knife?

GENT. 'T is hot, it smokes;

---

23. *but another . . . extremity*] Any further period or conclusion to my story, by adding sorrow to what is already too much, would substantially increase the pathos and exceed the utmost limits of grief.

It came even from the heart of—O, she's dead!

ALB. Who dead? speak, man.

GENT. Your lady, sir, your lady: and her sister
By her is poisoned; she hath confess'd it.

EDM. I was contracted to them both: all three
Now marry in an instant.

EDG. Here comes Kent.

ALB. Produce the bodies, be they alive or dead.

[*Exit Gentleman.*]

This judgement of the heavens, that makes us tremble,
Touches us not with pity.

*Enter* Kent

O, is this he?
The time will not allow the compliment
Which very manners urges.

KENT. I am come
To bid my king and master aye good night:
Is he not here?

ALB. Great thing of us forgot!
Speak, Edmund, where's the king? and where's Cordelia?
See'st thou this object, Kent?

[*The bodies of Goneril and Regan are brought in.*]

KENT. Alack, why thus?

EDM. Yet Edmund was beloved:
The one the other poison'd for my sake,
And after slew herself.

ALB. Even so. Cover their faces.

EDM. I pant for life: some good I mean to do,
Despite of mine own nature. Quickly send,
Be brief in it, to the castle; for my writ
Is on the life of Lear and on Cordelia:
Nay, send in time.

ALB. Run, run, O, run!

EDG. To who, my lord? Who hath the office? send
Thy token of reprieve.

EDM. Well thought on: take my sword,
Give it the captain.

ALB. Haste thee, for thy life. [*Exit Edgar.*]

EDM. He hath commission from thy wife and me
To hang Cordelia in the prison, and
To lay the blame upon her own despair,
That she fordid herself.[24]

ALB. The gods defend her! Bear him hence awhile.
[*Edmund is borne off.*]

*Re-enter* LEAR, *with* CORDELIA *dead in his arms*; EDGAR, Captain, *and others following*

LEAR. Howl, howl, howl, howl! O, you are men of stones:
Had I your tongues and eyes, I'ld use them so
That heaven's vault should crack. She's gone for ever:
I know when one is dead and when one lives;
She's dead as earth. Lend me a looking-glass;
If that her breath will mist or stain the stone,[25]
Why, then she lives.

KENT. Is this the promised end?

EDG. Or image of that horror?

ALB. Fall and cease.

LEAR. This feather stirs; she lives. If it be so,
It is a chance which does redeem all sorrows
That ever I have felt.

KENT. [*Kneeling*] O my good master!

LEAR. Prithee, away.

EDG. 'T is noble Kent, your friend.

LEAR. A plague upon you, murderers, traitors all!
I might have saved her; now she's gone for ever!
Cordelia, Cordelia! stay a little. Ha!
What is't thou say'st? Her voice was ever soft,
Gentle and low, an excellent thing in woman.
I kill'd the slave that was a-hanging thee.

CAPT. 'T is true, my lords, he did.

LEAR. Did I not, fellow?
I have seen the day, with my good biting falchion[26]
I would have made them skip: I am old now,

---

24. *fordid herself*] destroyed herself.
25. *the stone*] the mirror of crystal.
26. *falchion*] scimitar.

And these same crosses[27] spoil me. Who are you?
Mine eyes are not o' the best: I'll tell you straight.

KENT. If fortune brag of two she loved and hated,
One of them we behold.

LEAR. This is a dull sight. Are you not Kent?

KENT. The same,
Your servant Kent. Where is your servant Caius?

LEAR. He's a good fellow, I can tell you that;
He'll strike, and quickly too: he's dead and rotten.

KENT. No, my good lord; I am the very man —

LEAR. I'll see that straight.

KENT. That from your first of difference[28] and decay
Have follow'd your sad steps.

LEAR. You are welcome hither.

KENT. Nor no man else: all's cheerless, dark and deadly.
Your eldest daughters have fordone themselves,
And desperately[29] are dead.

LEAR. Ay, so I think.

ALB. He knows not what he says, and vain is it
That we present us to him.

EDG. Very bootless.

*Enter a* Captain

CAPT. Edmund is dead, my lord.

ALB. That's but a trifle here.
You lords and noble friends, know our intent.
What comfort to this great decay may come
Shall be applied: for us, we will resign,
During the life of this old majesty,
To him our absolute power: [*To Edgar and Kent*] you, to your rights;
With boot, and such addition as your honours
Have more than merited. All friends shall taste

27. *crosses*] misadventures.
28. *from your first of difference*] from the first indication of your change of fortune.
29. *desperately*] in the despair of sin which denies them salvation.

The wages of their virtue, and all foes
The cup of their deservings. O, see, see!

LEAR. And my poor fool[30] is hang'd! No, no, no life!
Why should a dog, a horse, a rat, have life,
And thou no breath at all? Thou'lt come no more,
Never, never, never, never, never!
Pray you, undo this button: thank you, sir.
Do you see this? Look on her, look, her lips,
Look there, look there! [*Dies.*]

EDG. He faints. My lord, my lord!

KENT. Break, heart; I prithee, break!

EDG. Look up, my lord.

KENT. Vex not his ghost: O, let him pass! he hates him
That would upon the rack of this tough world
Stretch him out longer.

EDG. He is gone indeed.

KENT. The wonder is he hath endured so long:
He but usurp'd his life.

ALB. Bear them from hence. Our present business
Is general woe. [*To Kent and Edgar*] Friends of my soul, you twain
Rule in this realm and the gored state sustain.

KENT. I have a journey, sir, shortly to go;
My master calls me, I must not say no.

ALB. The weight of this sad time we must obey,
Speak what we feel, not what we ought to say.
The oldest hath borne most: we that are young
Shall never see so much, nor live so long.
[*Exeunt, with a dead march.*]

---

30. *my poor fool*] a common term of endearment, here applied by Lear to Cordelia.

# Study Guide

*Text by*
**Corinna Siebert Ruth**
*(M.A., California State University-Fresno)*
Department of English
Fresno Pacific College
Fresno, California

# Contents

SECTION ONE

# Introduction

***The Life and Work of William Shakespeare***

Details about William Shakespeare's life are sketchy, mostly mere surmise based upon court or other clerical records. His parents, John and Mary (Arden), were married about 1557; she was of the landed gentry, and he a yeoman—a glover and commodities merchant. By 1568, John had risen through the ranks of town government and held the position of high bailiff, similar to mayor. William, the eldest son and the third of eight children, was born in 1564, probably on April 23, several days before his baptism on April 26 in Stratford-upon-Avon. Shakespeare is also believed to have died on the same date—April 23—in 1616.

It is believed William attended the local grammar school in Stratford where his parents lived, and studied primarily Latin rhetoric, logic, and literature. Shakespeare probably left school at age 15, which was the norm, to take a job, especially since this was the period of his father's financial difficulty. At age 18 (1582), William married Anne Hathaway, a local farmer's daughter who was eight years his senior. Their first daughter (Susanna) was born six months later (1583), and twins Judith and Hamnet were born in 1585.

Shakespeare's life can be divided into three periods: the first 20 years in Stratford, which include his schooling, early marriage, and fatherhood; the next 25 years as an actor and playwright in London; and the last five in retirement back in Stratford where he enjoyed moderate wealth gained from his theatrical successes. The years linking the first two periods are marked by a lack of information about Shakespeare, and are often referred to as the "dark years."

At some point during the "dark years," Shakespeare began his career with a London theatrical company, perhaps in 1589, for he was already an actor and playwright of some note by 1592. Shakespeare apparently wrote and acted for numerous theatrical companies, including Pembroke's Men, and Strange's Men, which later became the Chamberlain's Men, with whom he remained for the rest of his career.

In 1592, the Plague closed the theaters for about two years, and Shakespeare turned to writing book length narrative poetry. Most notable were "Venus and Adonis" and "The Rape of Lucrece," both of which were dedicated to the Earl of Southampton, whom scholars accept as Shakespeare's friend and benefactor despite a lack of documentation. During this same period, Shakespeare was writing his sonnets, which are more likely signs of the time's fashion rather than actual love poems detailing any particular relationship. He returned to playwriting when theaters reopened in 1594, and did not continue to write poetry. His sonnets were published without his consent in 1609, shortly before his retirement.

Amid all of his success, Shakespeare suffered the loss of his only son, Hamnet, who died in 1596 at the age of 11. But Shakespeare's career continued unabated, and in London in 1599, he became one of the partners in the new Globe Theater, which was built by the Chamberlain's Men.

Shakespeare wrote very little after 1612, which was the year he completed *Henry VIII.* It was during a performance of this play in 1613 that the Globe caught fire and burned to the ground. Sometime between 1610 and 1613, Shakespeare returned to Stratford, where he owned a large house and property, to spend his remaining years with his family.

William Shakespeare died on April 23, 1616, and was buried two days later in the chancel of Holy Trinity Church where he had been baptized exactly 52 years earlier. His literary legacy included 37 plays, 154 sonnets and five major poems.

Incredibly, most of Shakespeare's plays had never been published in anything except pamphlet form, and were simply extant as acting scripts stored at the Globe. Theater scripts were not regarded as literary works of art, but only the basis for the performance. Plays were simply a popular form of entertainment for all layers of society in Shakespeare's time. Only the efforts of two of Shakespeare's company, John Heminges and Henry Condell, preserved his 36 plays (minus *Pericles,* the thirty-seventh).



***Historical Background***

Shakespeare's work can be understood more clearly if we follow its development as a reflection of the rapidly-changing world of the sixteenth and early seventeenth centuries in which he lived. After the colorful reign of Henry VIII, which ushered in the Protestant Reformation, England was never the same. The contributions of John Calvin and Michelangelo (who both died the year Shakespeare was born) had a decisive role in the European Reformation and the Renaissance. When Queen Elizabeth I came to the throne in 1558, the time was right to bring in "the golden age" of English history. The arts flourished during the Elizabethan era. Some of Shakespeare's contemporary dramatists were such notables as Christopher Marlowe and Ben Jonson.

King James VI of Scotland succeeded Elizabeth to the throne after her death in 1603 uniting the kingdoms of England and Scotland. The monarch's new title was King James I. Fortunately for Shakespeare, the new king was a patron of the arts and agreed to sponsor the King's Men, Shakespeare's theatrical group, named in the King's honor. According to the *Stationers' Register* recorded on November 26, 1607, *King Lear* was performed for King James I at Whitehall on St. Stephen's night as a Christmas celebration on December 26, 1606.

The legend of King Lear, well-known in Shakespeare's day, was about a mythical British king dating back to the obscurity of ancient times. It was first recorded in 1135 by Geoffrey of Monmouth in *Historia Britonum.* In 1574 it appeared in *A Mirror for Magistrates* and later in Holinshed's *Chronicles* in 1577. The subplot, which concerned Gloucester and his sons, was taken from Philip Sidney's *Arcadia.* An older version of the play called *The True Chronicle History of King Leir* first appeared on the stage in 1590. Comments on public response to the play in Shakespeare's day would necessarily be based on conjecture but in 1681, an adaptation of the original play was published by Nahum Tate, a dramatist of the Restoration period. Tate's sentimental adaptation gives the play a happy ending in which Lear and Gloucester are united with their children. Virtue is rewarded and justice reigns in Tate's version. It was not until 1838 that Macready reinstated Shakespeare's original version on the stage.



### *Major Characters*

**Lear, King of Britain**—*A mythical king of pre-Christian Britain, well-known in the folklore of Shakespeare's day. Lear is a foolish king who intends to divide his kingdom among his three daughters.*

**Cordelia**—*Lear's youngest daughter who speaks the truth.*

**The King of France and the Duke of Burgundy**—*They are both Cordelia's suitors, but the King of France marries her.*

**Regan and Goneril**—*Lear's selfish daughters who flatter him in order to gain his wealth and power.*

**Duke of Albany**—*Goneril's husband whose sympathy for Lear turns him against his wife.*

**Duke of Cornwall**—*Regan's husband who joins his wife in her devious scheme to destroy King Lear and usurp his power.*

**Earl of Gloucester**—*In the subplot, Gloucester's afflictions with his sons parallel those of Lear's with his daughters.*

**Edgar**—*The legitimate son of Gloucester.*

**Edmund**—*The illegitimate son of Gloucester who stops at nothing to gain power.*

**Earl of Kent**—*Kent is banished by King Lear for trying to intervene when Lear disinherits Cordelia.*

**Fool**—*The king's professional court jester whose witty and prophetic remarks are a wise commentary on Lear's shortsightedness.*

**Oswald**—*Goneril's steward who attempts to kill Gloucester.*

### *Summary of the Play*

From the legendary story of King Lear, Shakespeare presents a dramatic version of the relationships between parents and their children. Lear, king of ancient Britain, decides to divide his kingdom among his three daughters: Goneril and Regan, the wives of the Duke of Albany and the Duke of Cornwall, and Cordelia, his youngest and favorite. In an attempt to give the "largest bounty" to the one who loves him most, the king asks for his daughters' expressions of affection. He receives embellished speeches of endearment from the older two, but Cordelia modestly speaks the truth, angering her father who disinherits her and banishes her forever. Trying to intercede on Cordelia's behalf, the Earl of Kent also is banished. The King of France marries Lear's dowerless daughter. Meanwhile, the Earl of Gloucester is deceived by his illegitimate son, Edmund, who leads him to believe that Edgar, the earl's legitimate son, is plotting to murder his father.

Lear's plans to live with his two older daughters are immediately thwarted when Goneril turns on him, reducing his train of followers by half. In shock from her ingratitude, Lear decides to seek refuge with Regan. Instead of admonishing her sister for her actions as Lear expects, Regan is harsh with him, suggesting that he apologize to Goneril. Heartbroken and rejected, Lear totters out into the storm with only his Fool and Kent to keep him company. Kent, who is now in disguise, finds refuge in a hovel for the king, who has been driven mad by his suffering. There they meet Edgar, disguised as Tom o'Bedlam, hiding in fear for his life. Gloucester soon arrives and hurries Lear off to Dover, where Cordelia is waiting with a French army ready to restore her father's kingdom. Cordelia cares for her father in the camp, and their severed relationship is restored.

In the meantime, Cornwall gouges out Gloucester's eyes, calling him a traitor. Still in disguise, Edgar leads his blind father to Dover. Edmund, in command of the English army, defeats the French, taking Cordelia and Lear as prisoners. As Gloucester is dying, Edgar reveals his true identity to his father. Edgar kills Edmund, but cannot save Cordelia whom Edmund has ordered to be hanged. Lear dies, grief-stricken over Cordelia's death. Rivalry over their love for Edmund leads Goneril to poison Regan and then stab herself. Albany, Kent, and Edgar are left to restore some semblance of order to the kingdom.

***Estimated Reading Time***

Shakespeare's poetic drama, written to be viewed by an audience, usually takes approximately three hours to perform on the stage. It would be possible to read it almost as fast the first time around to get the plot of the story. An auditory tape of *King Lear*, available at most university or county libraries, is an excellent device that can be used to follow along with the text, making the drama more interesting by bringing the characters alive. After the initial reading, however, it should be read more carefully, taking special note of the difficult words and phrases that are glossed at the bottom of most Shakespearean an texts. This reading would probably take about six hours for the entire play, allowing a little more than an hour for each of the five acts. Since the acts of *King Lear* vary from three to seven scenes each, the length of reading time for each act will, of course, vary.

# SECTION TWO

## Act I

### Act I, Scene I (pages 1–11)

New Characters:

**King Lear:** *king of pre-Christian Britain; protagonist of the play*

**Goneril:** *King Lear's oldest daughter with whom he lives first*

**Regan:** *King Lear's middle daughter who refuses to take him in*

**Cordelia:** *King Lear's youngest daughter who is banished and disinherited*

**Duke of Cornwall:** *husband of Regan who stops at nothing to gain power*

**Duke of Albany:** *the mild-mannered husband of Goneril*

**Earl of Kent:** *King Lear's devoted courtier who is banished*

**Earl of Gloucester:** *protagonist of the subplot whose family situation is analogous to Lear's*

**Edmund:** *bastard son of Gloucester*

**King of France:** *marries Cordelia without a dowry*

**Duke of Burgundy:** *Cordelia's suitor who rejects Lear's dowerless daughter*

***Summary***

Setting the scene for King Lear's rumored intention of dividing his kingdom, Gloucester and Kent discuss the King's preference between his sons-in-law, the Duke of Albany and Cornwall.

Kent is introduced to Edmund, Gloucester's illegitimate son, whom his father loves no less than his legitimate son, Edgar.

The trumpet sounds and King Lear and his attendants enter with his two sons-in-law and his three daughters, Goneril, Regan, and Cordelia. He immediately orders Gloucester to attend to the King of France and the Duke of Burgundy who are both suitors contending for Cordelia's hand in marriage. Gloucester leaves and without delay Lear clarifies his intended purpose. He plans to divide his kingdom among his three daughters, giving the greatest share to the daughter who publicly professes to love him most.

Goneril, Lear's oldest daughter, is called on first. She flatters her father into believing that she loves him more than "words can wield the matter." Not to be outdone, Regan claims to love the King as much as her sister does, except that Goneril "comes too short." Expecting a grander expression of love from Cordelia, his favorite, the King is surprised and angry when her reply is simply "Nothing, my lord." He implores her to "mend [her] speech a little" or else she "may mar [her] fortunes." She tries to explain to the King that she only speaks the truth, but it is to no avail. Lear banishes her without an inheritance or a dowry.

In a futile attempt to change the King's mind, Kent argues on Cordelia's behalf but is also banished. He bids goodbye to the King, commending Cordelia for speaking truthfully and admonishing Goneril and Regan to live up to their "large speeches" of love for their father.

Gloucester ushers in the King of France and the Duke of Burgundy. They are both made aware of Cordelia's banishment and recent loss of fortune and are given a chance to accept her without a dowry. The King of France is confused, wondering what Cordelia, who had always had been Lear's favorite, could have done to deserve such treatment from her father. Cordelia begs her father to understand that she lacks the "glib and oily art" to speak of her love for him, but he only responds with a wish that she had never been born. Burgundy appeals to Lear to change his mind about the inheritance, but the King is unyielding. When Burgundy rejects Cordelia for lack of a dowry, she responds with a refusal to marry him if he is only interested in her "fortune." The

King of France who has gained a new admiration and respect for Cordelia, happily accepts King Lear's "dow'rless daughter" and offers to make her the new Queen of France.

Without her father's blessing, Cordelia bids farewell to her sisters with tearstained eyes, telling them that she wishes she could leave her father in better hands. Goneril and Regan sneer at her request for them to love Lear well. When they are alone together, the older sisters quickly turn on their father, discussing his "poor judgment" and making plans to usurp his power to prevent any more of his rash behavior.

***Analysis***

The universality of *King Lear* revolves around the theme of appearances versus reality as it relates to the world of filial love and, in Lear's case, ingratitude. In the opening scene we see Lear as a monarch commanding respect and love from his daughters. Lear speaks in the language of the "royal we," which was language given to the nobility in Shakespeare's plays. "Which of you shall we say doth love us most,/ That we our largest bounty may extend." In his illusory world, he mistakes the flattery of Goneril and Regan as the truth and interprets Cordelia's plain speech as a lack of love for her father. Lear completely misses the point of Cordelia's words, which show her love to be "more ponderous" than her tongue. In his selfish attempt to buy his daughters' love with material possessions, however, he is blind to the fact that one cannot manipulate true affection.

Images of Lear's blindness or lack of insight are revealed when Kent coaxes him to "See better, Lear" or when Goneril claims that she loves her father "dearer than eyesight." Unaware of what he is relinquishing to his older daughters, Lear's illusions carry him even further when he hopes to "retain/ The name (king), and all th' addition to the king." He expects to keep his title and all the honors and official privileges and powers inherent in that title. The folly of that illusion will later haunt him as he is driven out to face the reality of the storm with only his Fool to keep him company.

Some critics have censured Cordelia's unbending attitude toward the King in the first scene as evidence of her pride. In allowing Cordelia the "asides" to express her repulsion for her sisters' flowery speeches, however, Shakespeare characterizes her as a completely honest person who acts as a foil to Goneril and Regan. Cordelia's response, "Nothing," and Lear's subsequent repetition of the word, punctuate Aristotle's idea that "Nothing will come of nothing." Ironically, these words, spoken by Lear himself, foreshadow the move from order to chaos throughout the rest of the drama. In the eyes of the King of France, Cordelia is, paradoxically, "most rich being poor." France extols her virtues and acknowledges her loss by promising to make it up to her as his queen.

Lear, in his ill-considered haste, banishes both Cordelia and Kent for speaking the truth. Kent feels duty-bound to stop Lear's rash behavior. "When Lear is mad./ . . . Think'st thou that duty shall have dread to speak/ When power to flattery bows?" Kent alludes to Lear's "madness," which will dominate the action in subsequent scenes of the play.



Writing in the consciousness of his own age, Shakespeare's view of the natural order of things was still heavily influenced by the recent ideas of the Middle Ages. Lear refuses to accept Cordelia's love when it is given only "According to my bond." He fails to abide by her natural allegiance to her king and father and casts her out, thereby, destroying the natural order based on the hierarchy of all beings and things, animate and inanimate. Although this concept of the "chain of being" had its genesis with Plato and Aristotle, it was central to Medieval thought and did, in fact, stretch far beyond. In the seventeenth century, Leibniz writes about it; and as late as the eighteenth century, Alexander Pope explicitly describes the hierarchy and possible destruction of the natural order.

> Vast chain of being! which from God began,
> Natures aethereal, human, angel, man,
> Beast, bird, fish, insect, what no eye can see, . . .
> Where, one step broken, the great scale's destroyed . . .

Shakespeare sets the scene for this disorder in the opening lines of the play. The prose dialogue of Kent and Gloucester discussing the bastardy and illegitimacy of Edmund with a flippant attitude is unnatural for Gloucester's station in life. Kent also joins him with an attitude of acceptance unable to "smell a fault." To make matters worse, Gloucester has a legitimate son whom he loves equally as well. This equality, seeming correct and natural in our modern times, would have been unnatural and shocking in Elizabethan England. It is significant that they both speak in prose rather than verse, since prose is usually set aside for servants and other lowly characters speaking in the colloquial language of the day. Shakespeare often uses prose, however, for humorously coarse or bawdy conversation that does, perhaps, not warrant the use of verse. Later, all three of the characters will speak in blank verse, unrhymed iambic pentameter (10 syllables to a line with the accent on every second syllable), which is befitting their social rank. Gloucester and his sons, Edmund and Edgar are the main characters involving the subplot of the play, which commences in the next scene.

***Study Questions***

1. Explain briefly why King Lear has called his family together in the first scene.
2. Which characters are involved in the subplot of the story?
3. Name one of the major themes of the play.
4. At what period in history does the play take place?
5. Why does Kent defend Cordelia when her father banishes her?
6. Why does the Duke of Burgundy reject the offer of Cordelia's hand in marriage?
7. Who are the Duke of Albany and the Duke of Cornwall?
8. Who eventually marries Lear's dowerless daughter? Where will she live after her marriage?
9. What advice does Cordelia give to her sisters as she leaves with the King of France?
10. What do Goneril and Regan do as soon as everyone is gone and they are alone together?

***Answers***

1. King Lear calls his family together in order to divide his kingdom among his three daughters.
2. Gloucester, his illegitimate son Edmund, and his legitimate son Edgar, are the characters involved in the subplot.
3. A major theme of the play is appearance versus reality. King Lear is more impressed with his older daughters' flowery speeches of love than Cordelia's sincere response.
4. The play supposedly takes place in pre-Christian Britain but exhibits many sixteenth-century values.
5. Kent defends Cordelia because he feels it is his duty to keep the King from making a "rash" decision.
6. The Duke of Burgundy will not accept Cordelia because she has no dowry to bring into the marriage.
7. The Duke of Albany is Goneril's husband, and the Duke of Cornwall is Regan's husband.
8. The King of France marries Cordelia in spite of her banishment and lack of a dowry. He will take her to France.
9. Cordelia asks her sisters to treat their father well.
10. Goneril and Regan immediately begin to plot ways in which to usurp the power of the King, their father.

***Suggested Essay Topics***

1. In the play, King Lear requests his daughters' public profession of love to him. Cordelia is often criticized for being too proud to give her father the response he wants to hear. Analyze the incident where Cordelia responds with "Nothing, my Lord." Discuss her obedience to her father as it relates to the philosophy of the hierarchy of all beings. Support your answer with examples from the play.
2. Goneril and Regan both please King Lear with flowery speeches of love and devotion to him. Compare and contrast

their attitudes before the division of the kingdom with their attitudes at the end of Scene 1. Are they completely evil? Do they show some signs of rational thought regarding the King's future? Cite examples from the play to support your answer.

## Act I, Scene II (pages 11–16)

***Summary***

In Edmund's opening soliloquy, we move from King Lear's palace in the previous scene to the castle of the Earl of Gloucester. The subplot of the play is set in motion when Edmund calls upon his goddess, Nature, to whose law he is bound. As the illegitimate son of Gloucester, Edmund challenges his supposed inferiority to his brother Edgar. He is also aware that Edgar is no dearer to his father than he is and intends to capitalize on the Earl's trust in him. Determined to snatch his half-brother's land and future title as Earl of Gloucester, Edmund forges his brother's name in a letter in which Edgar presumably suggests a plan to murder his father. With the letter in his hand, Edmund confidently invokes the gods to "stand up for bastards" as he prepares to meet his father.

As Gloucester enters, he is preoccupied with the disturbing events of the recent past. Edmund, however, makes sure that his father sees him attempting to hide the letter. Gloucester's curiosity is aroused by Edmund's strange behavior, and he repeatedly questions him about the piece of paper in his hand. Edmund, pretending to spare his father's feelings, cautiously breaks the news. He tells him the letter is from his brother, and "I find it not fit for your o'erlooking." This only increases Gloucester's curiosity, and, after much coaxing, Edmund finally hands it to him. Gloucester, stunned by its contents, questions the handwriting but is easily convinced it is Edgar's. Gloucester's harsh invectives against Edgar, the seeming villain, are promptly checked by Edmund, however. Under the guise of protecting his father's safety, Edmund asks him to leave the matter to him.

In the meantime, Gloucester blames the "late eclipses in the sun and moon" for the recent happenings turning son against father and the king against his child. When his father is out of sight, Edmund ridicules his superstitious beliefs, convinced that people blame the stars as an excuse for their own faults.

When Edgar approaches, Edmund feigns an interest in astrology, much to his brother's surprise. Quickly changing the subject, however, Edmund moves to the matter at hand which is to inform his brother that their father is furiously angry at Edgar for some unknown reason. He advises Edgar to arm himself if he plans to go out in public and gives him a key to his lodgings, where he will be safe until a proper time when Edmund will bring Edgar to his father.

After Edgar leaves, Edmund, realizing he has easily duped his father and brother, revels over their gullibility.

***Analysis***

Edmund's soliloquy, introducing the subplot of the play, reveals an attitude of free will and equality that is easily understood by people in modern society. Our sympathies are certainly with Edmund in his complaint: "Wherefore should I/ Stand in the plague of custom." He pierces our sensibilities with his satirical repetition of the word "legitimate," and the sensation is heightened further with his alliterative "Why brand they us/ With base? with baseness? bastardy? base, base?" Today, in all fairness, we would agree that people are not "base" by virtue of their birth. Reference to legitimate and illegitimate children is seldom seen in today's world. But we must be careful not to mistake Edmund's view as an ideal of modern society. The goddess Nature that Edgar invokes has no righteousness. There is, instead, a devil-may-care attitude where "gods stand up for bastards" regardless of what they do. Edmund's actions are brought about by deception, linking him with the evils of Goneril and Regan as the play progresses. He judges his superiority "by the lusty stealth of nature" in which he has "more composition" than the "dull, stale, tired bed" of marriage. Edmund's idea of Nature is based mostly on matter and animal appetites. Instead of harmony and order in the universe, his law of nature brings chaos and death.

Edmund's response to Gloucester's question concerning the paper he was reading is "Nothing, my lord." It is significant that these same words, spoken by Cordelia, started the action involving Lear's lack of insight, which resulted in her banishment. Gloucester also lacks insight to make good choices concerning Edgar. In his hasty judgment of him, he is immediately gulled into seeing him as a "brutish villain." Shakespeare's use of images pertaining to sight has a symbolic significance in this scene. When Gloucester begs "Let's see, let's see," he does, in fact, lack the insight to see the truth, just as he does when he says, "Come, if it be nothing, I shall not need spectacles." But spectacles do not give him insight, and, consequently, his poor judgment of Edgar parallels Lear's judgment of Cordelia.

Gloucester's view of life in his speech beginning with "These late eclipses in the sun and moon" is seen by Edmund as superstition or an evasive way of blaming the stars or the heavens for his faults. Again, Edmund presents a rebuttal that appeals to our modern sensibilities. At the heart of the matter, however, lies his view of nature as a morally indifferent world that is simply a force with which to be reckoned. In contrast, Gloucester's view of nature reflects the hierarchy of all beings. When son turns against father or father against child, that hierarchy is disturbed and "all ruinous disorders follow us disquietly to our graves." Some critics believe that Edmund's view of nature was a new concept—just beginning to take hold in the sixteenth century—that was radically opposed to the orthodox traditions. Nevertheless, Lear, Gloucester, and Kent will see the relationship between the heavenly bodies and their effect on the lives of people throughout the drama.

***Study Questions***

1. In his soliloquy, what does Edmund want to take from his half-brother Edgar?
2. What is the piece of paper Edmund is supposedly hiding from his father? What does it say?
3. What is Gloucester's reaction to the letter?
4. Give an example of alliteration in Edmund's soliloquy.

5. What does Edmund think of his father's view of nature?
6. What does Edmund tell Edgar about his father?
7. What does Edmund tell Edgar he must do if he intends to walk in public?
8. Where is Edgar instructed to go?
9. How will Edgar be able to talk to his father?
10. Why is Edmund gloating at the end of the scene?

### *Answers*

1. Edmund wants to take land that now rightfully belongs to his half-brother Edgar.
2. The piece of paper is a forged letter supposedly written by Edgar plotting his father's murder.
3. Gloucester's reaction to the letter sends him into a rage against his son Edgar.
4. An example of alliteration in Edmund's soliloquy is "With base? with baseness? bastardy? base, base?"
5. Edmund thinks his father is only blaming the stars for his own failures.
6. Edmund tells Edgar his father is very angry with him and might harm him.
7. Edmund tells Edgar he must arm himself if he intends to "stir abroad."
8. Edgar is instructed to go to Edmund's lodging.
9. Edmund promises to bring Edgar to his father so he can hear him speak.
10. Edmund gloats because he has duped his father and half-brother into believing his story.

### *Suggested Essay Topics*

1. In his soliloquy, Edmund addresses issues of equality and free will. Analyze these issues in the light of our modern-day society. Do you agree with Edmund? Do you disagree? Did

Edmund present a law of nature with harmony and order? Use examples from the play to support your answer.

2. Act I, Scene 2 starts the action of the subplot of *King Lear*. Explain the subplot and tell how it parallels the main plot of the play. Describe the characters in the subplot and tell who they are analogous to in the main plot, giving examples from the play to support your answer.

## Act I, Scene III (page 17)

New Character:

**Oswald:** *Goneril's steward who willingly carries out the evil schemes of his mistress*

***Summary***

This scene is set in the Duke of Albany's palace, the home of Lear's oldest daughter Goneril with whom he has been living since the division of the kingdom. Goneril questions her steward, Oswald, and finds that her father has struck her gentleman for chiding his Fool. She is distraught over the King's behavior, claiming that he "upbraids us/ On every trifle." She says too that his knights "grow riotous." She is, in fact, so angry at her father that she does not want to speak to him and instructs Oswald to tell the King she is sick when he comes back from his hunting trip. In retaliation for her father's behavior, she also gives Oswald a directive to cut back on his usual services to the King. She will answer for it later if he gives Oswald any trouble.

Horns sound as Lear and his entourage return from their hunting trip. Goneril hastily directs Oswald to treat the King with "weary negligence" and instruct the servants under his command to do the same. If her father does not like it, she says, he can go live with her sister Regan. Goneril is well aware that she and Regan are of like mind concerning their father. She calls him foolish for trying to cling to his power and authority after he has officially relinquished it.

Goneril continues to rail bitterly against her father, calling him an old fool who needs to be treated like a baby again. He needs "flatteries" but also "checks" or reprimands. Hastily, she tells Oswald to instruct his knights to greet Lear with cold looks. With that, she hurries off to write to Regan informing her of what has transpired.

***Analysis***

This short scene acts as an interlude between the introduction of the subplot and Lear's dialogue with the disguised Kent. As background for the subsequent action of the play, the scene gives us our first brief glimpse of the signs of deterioration of the father/daughter relationship. It comes as no surprise, however, since we have been forewarned of the intentions of Goneril and Regan at the end of the first act.

Goneril repeatedly insists on blaming Lear's actions on "the infirmity of his age." It should be noted, however, that he has just returned from a strenuous hunting expedition which seems to be quite a feat for an "idle old man." In her eagerness to strip him of his power, Goneril deceives even herself. Her obvious disrespect for her father validates Cordelia's perceptive honesty in Act I when she says, "I know you what you are." Goneril's actions toward her father would have been seen as a clear violation of the natural hierarchy by the Elizabethan audience of Shakespeare's day.

***Study Questions***

1. Where is the scene set?
2. What arrangement have Goneril and Regan made for the care of their father, the king?
3. Where has King Lear gone at the beginning of the scene?
4. What kind of servant is Oswald?
5. What does Goneril instruct Oswald to do in order to anger the king?
6. Why does Goneril pretend to be sick?
7. Where does Goneril plan to tell her father to go if he does not like it at her palace?
8. Why does Goneril decide to write to her sister?

9. What is the significance of the father/daughter relationship in this scene?
10. What would an Elizabethan audience of Shakespeare's day have thought of Goneril's attitude toward her father?

***Answers***

1. It is set in the palace of the Duke of Albany.
2. Goneril will keep her father first. Then she and Regan will alternate each month.
3. The King has gone hunting.
4. Oswald is a steward in charge of other servants.
5. Goneril instructs Oswald and his fellows to treat Lear's knights with cold looks and to put on "weary negligence."
6. Goneril is too angry to speak to her father when he comes home from his hunting trip.
7. Goneril will tell Lear to go live with her sister Regan.
8. Goneril hastily writes to her sister to tell her that Lear is acting badly and might decide to come live with her.
9. This is our first glimpse of the deterioration of the father/daughter relationship.
10. They would have seen Goneril's attitude as a violation of the natural hierarchy.

***Suggested Essay Topics***

1. Act I, Scene 3 is a short scene, but it is essential to the understanding of the play. Explain what purpose it serves. Why are Goneril's speeches important? In what way does the scene help to clarify the deterioration of relationships? Explain your answer.
2. The theme of old age is at the heart of Goneril's attitude toward her father. Discuss Goneril's attitude toward old people in general. How does she view their worth? Cite examples from the play to support your answer.

## Act I, Scene IV (pages 18–28)

New Characters:

**Knight:** *one of Lear's many attendants*

**Fool:** *the king's court jester*

***Summary***

The scene continues in Albany's palace, where Kent is considering the success of his disguise. He is convinced that if he falsifies his accent, the masquerade will be complete. Ironically, he wishes to remain loyal to the King who has banished him. Just as Lear returns from his hunting trip, Kent appears disguised in servant's garb. Lear questions his abilities and his motives for wanting to serve him. Answering each question in a jovial manner, Kent portrays a character unlike his own. Convinced of Kent's qualifications, Lear invites him to join him as his servant and immediately calls for his dinner and his Fool.

Oswald, Goneril's steward, enters and Lear demands to see his daughter. Walking away, Oswald purposely ignores the King's request. Lear calls him back, but when Oswald does not respond, he sends his knight after him. The knight comes back with the news that Oswald rudely refused to obey the King. Shocked at such defiance, Lear discusses the matter with his knight, who has also noticed the recent "abatement of kindness" evident in the servants, Goneril, and the Duke of Albany. Lear again calls for his Fool, whom he has not seen for two weeks and is told that he has been pining away for Cordelia ever since she left for France. Unwilling to discuss it further, Lear quickly dismisses the idea, instructing his knight to bring Goneril and his Fool to him.

In the meantime, Oswald appears and addresses Lear with insolence and disrespect. Lear strikes him and Kent trips his heels and pushes him out. Grateful to Kent, the King hands him money for his service.

Lear's Fool finally appears with humorous and witty remarks about his coxcomb or cap. The Fool's satiric jesting about Lear's loss of his title and the division of his kingdom is a sad but honest commentary on his plight in which his "daughters" have become his "mothers." Goneril enters and the King kindly asks her why she wears a frown on her face. The Fool chastises him for patronizing her. Goneril confronts her father with a long diatribe concerning his quarreling and riotous servants. She blames him for allowing them to exhibit this kind of behavior. Lear cannot believe these words are coming from his own daughter. Goneril is relentless, however, finally demanding that he diminish his "train of servants" so that there will be order in the palace again, and he will be able to act in a manner befitting his age. Lear reacts with rage, calling her a "degenerate bastard" and promising to trouble her no longer.

Unaware of the situation, Albany enters, telling Lear to be patient, but he turns a deaf ear to his son-in-law. Claiming his "train are men of choice," he tells Goneril she is lying about their conduct. Cordelia's faults suddenly seem small compared to Goneril's, and he beats his head, blaming himself for his foolishness and poor judgment in giving up his "fix'd place." Before he leaves, he invokes the goddess Nature to curse Goneril with sterility, or, if she must bear a child, to let it be a spiteful child who will torment her and cause her to grow old before her time. Albany, still puzzled, questions Goneril about her father, but she evades the issue, telling him not to worry.

Having heard that Goneril has just reduced his train of followers by 50, Lear re-enters, cursing his daughter for destroying his manhood. He threatens to leave and stay with Regan, convinced that she would scratch her sister's eyes out if she heard of the way in which Goneril had been treating her father. Goneril, however, quickly sends a letter to her sister, warning her that Lear is coming. Doubting the wisdom of Goneril's actions, Albany censures his wife for her decision, but she criticizes his "milky gentleness" and his "want of wisdom."

***Analysis***

As Kent interviews for a position as a servant in Lear's retinue, he takes on the mannerisms of the Fool. His witty humor, spoken in prose, prompts Lear to respond to him as he would to his Fool. Kent's long list of attributes that he thinks would make him a good servant, includes "to eat no fish," a Protestant virtue easily understood by an Elizabethan audience. At the opening of the scene, Kent speaks in verse but changes to prose when he takes on his disguise as a servant. Later, when he is left alone in the stocks, he will again speak in verse, assuming his true character as the noble Earl of Kent.

Oswald, addressed by Lear as "sirrah," a title for commoners, willingly carries out the wishes of his lady Goneril, linking him with the evil characters in the play. Under Goneril's instructions, he defies the King by ignoring his commands and defending himself against Lear's abusive insults. This behavior, demonstrated by a servant against a king or other noble, would have been unheard of in Shakespeare's day.

When we first meet the Fool, he offers his coxcomb to Kent, demonstrating that anyone aligning himself with the King is a fool and needs to wear the cap of the Fool. The Fool warns Kent that he cannot take "one's (Lear's) part that's out of favor" and at the same time bring himself into the good graces of those now in power, or he will soon "catch cold," or be out in the cold. Lear's Fool is often referred to by critics as a character assuming the role of the "chorus" whose function is to comment on the action of the play. The Fool speaks the bitter truth about King Lear's folly in dividing his kingdom between his two oldest daughters. He is the only character who can speak the truth without the risk of banishment. Lear, in fact, threatens to whip him if he tells a lie. To the implication that he might be calling Lear a fool, he replies, "All thy other titles thou hast given away, that thou wast born with." Kent's response, "This is not altogether fool," shows the wisdom of the Fool, who is not merely there to entertain. The Fool censures Lear for splitting his crown in the middle and giving away both parts to his daughters. "Thou bor'st thine ass on thy back o'er the dirt" alludes to one of Aesop's fables in which the miller and his son foolishly carry a donkey instead of riding on his back. The analogy is clear: both Lear and the miller have foolishly inverted the order of nature. Lear's response when the Fool asks him whether he can make use of "nothing," echoes the words first spoken regarding Cordelia.

Goneril's diatribe concerning Lear's unruly train of followers is, perhaps, not altogether unwarranted, considering the rash behavior her father has exhibited thus far in the play. Lear insists, however, that his "train are men of choice and rarest parts" and curses Goneril with sterility or at least a child who will torment her so that she too will feel the pain of a "thankless child." In spite of his protest, she reduces his train by 50 followers. Lear decides to leave immediately, certain that his daughter Regan will take him in. Confident that her sister will not "sustain him and his hundred knights," Goneril quickly sends word to her sister, informing her of Lear's arrival. Goneril's true motive for reducing Lear's train comes out by the end of the scene. She is afraid that with a hundred armed knights "He may enguard his dotage with their pow'rs,/And hold our lives in mercy." Her husband, Albany, is troubled by her actions, but she accuses him of lacking wisdom which is reminiscent of her treatment of the King.

***Study Questions***

1. Why does Kent speak in verse and then change to prose in the beginning of the scene?
2. Why does the Fool offer his coxcomb to Kent?
3. Why is the Fool often referred to as the chorus?
4. What behavior does Oswald demonstrate to the King?
5. Why is Goneril angry at her father in this scene?
6. In Lear's rage against his daughter Goneril, who does he think he can turn to?
7. How many of Lear's followers does Goneril take from him?
8. What does Goneril do to warn her sister of Lear's departure from Albany's palace?
9. How does the Duke of Albany feel about his wife's actions against the King?
10. What is Goneril's response to Albany's fears?

***Answers***

1. Kent speaks in verse because he is the Earl of Kent. He speaks in prose when he is disguised as a servant.
2. The Fool offers his coxcomb because he thinks Kent is a fool for following Lear.
3. Traditionally the chorus functions as a commentary on the action of the play. The Fool plays the role of the chorus.
4. Oswald is defiant and treats the King with disrespect.
5. Goneril tells her father that his train of followers are unruly and quarrelsome.
6. Lear says Regan will take him in.
7. Goneril reduces Lear's followers by 50.
8. Goneril writes Regan a letter warning her of Lear's arrival.
9. Albany is troubled by his wife's actions.
10. Goneril accuses Albany of a lack of wisdom in his decision-making.

***Suggested Essay Topics***

1. Lear's Fool is often seen as a wise character in the play. Discuss the way in which he acts as a commentator on Lear's folly. Explain why Lear tolerates his truths. Why were Kent and Cordelia banished for telling the truth? Cite examples from the play to support your view.
2. The Duke of Albany has a "milky gentleness" that annoys his wife Goneril. Explain their marriage relationship in light of the hierarchy of nature prevalent in Shakespeare's time. How does this hierarchy apply to Goneril's attitude toward her husband and father. Give examples from the play to support your answer.

## Act I, Scene V (pages 29–30)

New Characters:

**Gentleman:** *one of Lear's train attending to the horses*



### *Summary*

The scene is set in the courtyard in front of Albany's palace. Preparing to leave for Regan's, Lear orders Kent to deliver a letter to her in the city of Gloucester. He urges Kent to make sure he arrives before Lear does. In an attempt to raise his master's spirits, the Fool engages in honest witty metaphors and nonsensical riddles. Lear plays the game for a short time but soon slips back into his preoccupations with his daughter's ingratitude and his fears of madness. His gentleman soon arrives with the horses, and they are on their way to Regan's.

### *Analysis*

This short scene acts as a commentary on Lear's emotional state as he prepares himself for his new living arrangements with his middle daughter, Regan. His Fool, though annoying at times, honestly reflects his master's fears. Lear has, after all, failed, and one can imagine him contemplating his last chance. Judging by observations thus far and the opinion of the Fool on the matter, Goneril and Regan are of like mind. The Fool's honesty is no reassurance when he says, "She will taste as like this as a crab does to a crab." In his preoccupation, Lear seems unmoved by the Fool's comments as he ruminates about Cordelia. "I did her wrong" is reminiscent of the previous scene where her faults seemed small compared to Goneril's.

Lear's illusory world is no longer intact, giving him new insights concerning the worth of his daughters and new perceptions of his own identity. In the previous scene he has begun to question that identity. "Who is it that can tell me who I am?" The Fool's painful metaphor suggests that he is a snail that has given his shell, or house, away to his daughters. He considers taking Goneril's half of the kingdom back again, but the Fool interjects with "Thou shouldst not have been old till thou hadst been wise." The intrusion of his reality leads him to invoke the heavens to "Keep me in temper, I would not be mad!" Here again, we see his belief in the natural order of things with a higher being in control of the universe.



***Study Questions***

1. Who is sent with a letter for Lear's daughter Regan?
2. How does the Fool expect Regan to receive her father?
3. How does Lear feel about Cordelia at this point in the play?
4. What does the Fool mean when he says that a snail has a house to put his "head in, not to give it away to his daughters"?
5. What does Lear want to do to Goneril because of her ingratitude?
6. In what way is Lear's illusory world disappearing?
7. What does the Fool mean when he says he is "old before his time?"
8. What evidence do we have that Lear believes in a higher being?
9. What is the purpose of the Fool in this scene?
10. What is the main purpose of this short scene?

***Answers***

1. Kent, the disguised servant of King Lear, is sent to the city of Gloucester with a letter for Regan.
2. The Fool thinks Regan will be exactly like her sister.
3. Lear feels he has not treated Cordelia properly.
4. The Fool is censuring Lear for giving his kingdom to his daughters. He feels it is an unnatural thing to do.
5. He would like to take Goneril's half of the kingdom back.
6. He has gained new insight regarding his daughter Cordelia.

7. The Fool means that Lear is "old before he is wise."
8. Lear invokes the heavens to keep him from going mad.
9. The Fool acts as an honest commentary on the King's fears.
10. This short scene reflects Lear's emotional state at this point in the play.

### *Suggested Essay Topics*

1. Lear has lived in a world of deception and illusion thus far in the play. Discuss Lear's illusory world in relation to his three daughters. Compare these illusions to the new insights he is gaining at the end of Act I. How does he feel about his daughter Cordelia at this point in the play? Cite examples from the play to support your answer.
2. Lear has made a decision to leave his daughter Goneril's palace and live with Regan instead. How do you think he feels as he contemplates this move? Does he feel sure Regan will welcome him? Discuss his guilt abut Cordelia. Explain your answer.

# SECTION THREE

# Act II

## Act II, Scene I (pages 31–35)

New Character:

**Curan:** *a courtier at Gloucester's castle*

***Summary***

Curan, the courtier, informs Edmund that the Duke of Cornwall and Regan will be coming to Gloucester's castle shortly. He also gives Edmund inside information about the likelihood of war between Cornwall and Albany. Seizing the opportunity to use the Duke of Cornwall's visit to his own advantage, Edmund immediately sets his plan into action. Calling his brother Edgar from his hiding place, he warns him to flee in haste before his father can capture him. He tells Edgar that Cornwall's unexpected visit might prove dangerous to him. In an attempt to stage a convincing escape, Edmund draws his sword and urges his brother to do the same, pretending to defend himself against Edmund. He is supposedly trying to capture Edgar and bring him to his father. After Edgar's escape, Edmund, aware that Gloucester has been watching from a distance, secretly wounds himself in the arm. The sight of blood, he thinks, will impress upon his father that he has, indeed, fought a hard fight.

Gloucester approaches, demanding to know the whereabouts of Edgar. He calls for the pursuit of the villain. Edmund tells his father that Edgar tried to persuade him of "the murther of your lordship." Ironically, Edmund has supposedly warned his brother that the revenging gods are opposed to parricide, and the child is "bound to th' father." Edmund continues his deceitful tirade, declaring how "loathly opposite" he stood to Edgar's opinion and "unnatural purpose." For all this Edmund received a wound from the fleeing Edgar. Gloucester reacts with rage, calling Edgar a "murderous coward" and declaring that he will catch him and bring him "to the stake." He will use the authority of the Duke of Cornwall to bring him to justice. Edmund also accuses Edgar of calling him an "unpossessing bastard" whose word would not stand up against his if he denied writing the letter. According to Edmund's account, Edgar told him that he could, in fact, easily blame the murder plot on Edmund. More determined than ever to find Edgar, Gloucester prepares to publish his picture throughout the kingdom. Calling Edmund his "loyal and natural boy," he promises to arrange to have him acknowledged as his legal heir.

Cornwall and Regan enter, having heard the shocking news about Edgar. Quick to accept Edmund's deceitful story, Regan promptly blames Edgar's behavior on his association with Lear's "riotous knights." Having been informed by Goneril of Lear's arrival, Cornwall and Regan have decided not to stay and wait for him. Cornwall invites Edmund into his service, commending him for his virtue and obedience. Explaining why they have come, Regan asks for Gloucester's counsel concerning Goneril's "differences" with her father.

***Analysis***

This scene, involving the subplot, is analogous to the first scene of the play. In the main plot, King Lear is duped by his older daughters into believing they love him "more than words can wield the matter." In the subplot, Edmund deceives Gloucester about his own devotion toward his father: "by no means he could... Persuade me to the murther of your lordship." Edmund's gain is necessarily Edgar's loss. In both cases, Lear and Gloucester, through their own lack of insight, must bear the loss of one of their children. W. R. Elton sees the double plot as a "developing metaphor" in which the action in these two parts "mirror each other." (W. R. Elton, "Double Plot in King Lear.") Gloucester's rage, triggered by the slender evidence against his son Edgar, is reminiscent of Lear's violent anger demonstrated toward Cordelia resulting in her banishment. The main plot and the subplot operate in contrapuntal fashion to render depth and a clearer perception of the play as a whole.

Curan's news about the rumored civil strife brewing between the Dukes of Albany and Cornwall is a foreshadowing of future strife in the kingdom. Edmund is an opportunist who wastes no time plotting against his brother Edgar when he hears of Albany's arrival at Gloucester's castle. He is a master at manipulating the minds of Regan and Albany and immediately gains favor in their sight.

The irony runs deep in this scene when Edmund criticizes Edgar, attributing to him the very vices that are second nature to himself. There seems to be a role reversal with Edmund being the "loyal and natural boy" instead of Edgar. The irony reaches its peak, however, when Edmund talks of warning Edgar that the gods will wreak their vengeance against parricides, and "the natural bond of child to father" must be honored. In view of Edmund's idea of nature, in which he rejects the hierarchical order in a previous scene, his fabricated story to his father is a masquerade. He is, indeed, a wolf in sheep's clothing. Gloucester's lack of insight leads him to seek the wrong villain when he asks, "Now, Edmund, where's the villain?"

Outwardly, Regan and Cornwall seem honest in administering justice in the case of Edgar. Regan, however, all too quickly links Edgar's alleged actions to her father's "riotous knights." Her decision to be gone when her father arrives at her house reveals her true character, linking her with her evil sister Goneril.

***Study Questions***

1. Why does Edmund ask Edgar to raise his sword against him?
2. Why is Edmund's arm bleeding in this scene?
3. What does Gloucester propose to do after Edgar's escape?
4. Who does Gloucester ask to help him find Edgar and bring him to justice?

5. Who does Regan blame for Edgar's alleged problem with his father?
6. What will the King find when he and his followers reach Regan's house?
7. Why have Cornwall and Regan come to Gloucester's castle? What do they wish to discuss with him?
8. Why does Cornwall commend Edmund?
9. Whom does Gloucester call his "loyal and natural boy"?
10. Why does Gloucester intend to publish Edgar's picture throughout the kingdom?

***Answers***

1. Edmund wants his father to see him attempting to prevent Edgar's escape.
2. Edmund gave himself a wound with his own sword to impress his father.
3. Gloucester says that Edgar shall not remain uncaught and proposes to send his picture throughout the kingdom.
4. Gloucester asks the Duke of Albany's help in finding Edgar and bringing him to justice.
5. Regan blames his association with the King's "riotous knights" who, she thinks, have put him up to it.
6. The King will find that Regan and her husband are not there.
7. Cornwall and Regan have come to ask for Gloucester's advice about the quarrel between Goneril and the King.
8. Cornwall commends Edmund for his virtue and obedience.
9. Edmund is called Gloucester's "loyal and natural boy."
10. Gloucester plans to publish Edgar's picture throughout the kingdom so that someone will report having seen him, which could help matters regarding his capture.

***Suggested Essay Topics***

1. The subplot often functions to give depth and a clearer perception of the characters and the action in the play. Compare this scene to the first scene of the play. In what way do Lear and his daughters compare to Gloucester and his sons? Discuss the analogy between Edgar and Cordelia. Cite examples from the play to support your argument.
2. Edmund's speeches in this scene are filled with irony. Discuss the irony in his account of his alleged conversation with Edgar. Why are these lines in opposition to Edgar's beliefs? Use examples from the play to support your answer.

## Act II, Scenes II and III (pages 36–42)

***Summary***

Oswald appears at Gloucester's castle, and Kent, Lear's courier, promptly recognizes him as Goneril's steward whom he had "tripp'd up by the heels" and beaten for his insolent behavior to the King only a few days before. Feigning innocence, Oswald pretends he has never seen Kent. Kent rebukes him harshly and then draws his sword, challenging Oswald to do the same. Edmund enters in response to Oswald's cries for help. Edmund's sword is drawn and Kent turns on him, but Cornwall, who has just appeared, orders them to "keep peace." Regan and Gloucester, following closely behind Cornwall, are appalled at the sight of weapons. Cornwall demands to hear an account of their differences. Continuing to rail at Oswald, Kent calls him a "cowardly rascal" whom "Nature disclaims," and who must, therefore, have been made by a tailor. Oswald defends his cowardice, telling Cornwall he has spared Kent's life because he was a "grey beard." Enraged by Oswald's outright lie and his patronizing attitude toward him, Kent rants on with irreverent expletives about this rogue "who wears no honesty."

Cornwall takes the part of Oswald, however, and calls for Kent to be put in the stocks. Kent reminds Cornwall that he serves the King, and this move will surely create ill feelings. Troubled by the effect it will have on the King, Gloucester too pleads with Cornwall to rescind his decision. Cornwall remains stoic, however, and Regan is determined to put her sister's feelings above her father's.

Left alone, Kent is optimistic about his time in the stocks. He will catch up on some much-needed sleep and the remainder of the time he will spend whistling. Before he sleeps, he finds comfort in reading a letter from Cordelia.

Edgar's soliloquy in Scene 3 portrays him as "poor Tom," a Bedlam beggar. He will disguise himself by griming his face with filth, tying his hair in knots, and covering his nakedness with only a blanket. Fleeing from the law, he has escaped capture by hiding in the hollow of a tree.

***Analysis***

On the surface, it would seem that Kent's scurrilous treatment of Oswald in the beginning of the scene is excessive and unjustified. Greeting Kent with courtesy and decorum, Oswald seems undeserving of his verbal abuse. Kent immediately recognizes him as Goneril's insolent steward, however, who behaved badly to the King only a few days earlier. Kent also realizes that Oswald comes with letters against the King taking "Vanity the puppet's part." The implication is that Vanity, a character in ancient morality plays, is, in this case, personified by Goneril. Oswald repeatedly denies knowing Kent, but later he relates to Cornwall the details of his recent experience with Kent and the King. It is this pretense that Kent, who is characteristically blunt and honest, cannot tolerate. For his inability to engage in flattery, Kent is now awarded time in the stocks just as it had brought him banishment earlier. In this sense, Kent's experience is analogous to Cordelia's. Disorder flourishes in the world of the play where the honest characters are castigated and the deceitful ones rewarded.

As was true in previous scenes, lack of respect for old people is a recurring theme in the play. Cornwall refers to Kent as a "stubborn ancient knave" whom he intends to teach a lesson by putting him in the stocks. Kent's satiric retort, "Sir, I am too old to learn," lends humor to the idea that with age comes wisdom, which is in keeping with the natural order of things.

Cornwall spends much time and effort getting at the truth of the quarrel between Kent and Oswald. It is noteworthy that his abrupt decision to "Fetch forth the stocks," catching Kent and Gloucester by complete surprise, comes in the wake of Oswald's account of the King's abusiveness toward him. Cornwall's sudden decision to place Kent in the stocks is an act of defiance against the King's authority. The Duke is unmoved by Kent's appeal for the respect of his master, the King. Regan too feels it would be worse to abuse her sister's servant. To Gloucester's appeal "the King must take it ill/ That he,.../ Should have him (Kent) thus restrained," comes Cornwall's curt reply, "I'll answer that." The Duke shows no visible remorse for his act of rebellion against the King.

Left alone in the stocks, Kent speaks in verse at the end of the scene, reverting back to his true character, the noble Earl of Kent. He looks forward to perusing a letter from Cordelia, who has fortunately been informed of his disguise and his situation as servant of the King.

Scene 3 is a short account of what has happened in Edgar's life since the betrayal of his half-brother, Edmund. In his soliloquy, Edgar tells us he has been living in the hollow of a tree, escaping "the hunt." Like Kent, Edgar will also take on a disguise to preserve his life. He plans to hide in the guise of a Bedlam beggar. Bedlam is another word for Bethlehem Hospital, a London madhouse of the sixteenth century. The madmen of that day who roamed the London streets begging for food became known as "poor Toms." "Edgar I nothing am," indicates his loss of identity as Edgar, son of the Earl of Gloucester.

***Study Questions***

1. Why is Kent violently angry at Oswald, Goneril's steward?
2. Does Oswald pretend that Kent is a total stranger to him? What proves him wrong?
3. Why is Kent placed in the stocks?
4. What does Regan think would be worse than putting her father's servant in the stocks?
5. What is Cornwall's response to Kent's statement that he serves the King?

6. How does Gloucester feel about Kent being placed in the stocks?
7. Why does Kent speak in verse when he is alone in the stocks and in prose earlier in the scene?
8. Whose letter does Kent read before he falls asleep?
9. Where has Edgar been living since he fled from his father's castle?
10. How will he disguise himself in order to save his life?

***Answers***

1. Kent is angry because Oswald comes with letters against the King and pretends he has never seen Kent.
2. Oswald pretends he has never met Kent, but later he tells Cornwall the entire story.
3. Kent is placed in the stocks because Cornwall takes Oswald's side against Kent's in the quarrel.
4. Regan feels it would be worse to have her sister's steward abused than to have her father's courier put in the stocks.
5. Cornwall remains stoic about putting Kent in the stocks.
6. Gloucester feels the King will "take it ill" when he sees him in this condition.
7. When he is alone he no longer needs to maintain his disguise.
8. Kent reads a letter from Cordelia.
9. Edgar has been living in the hollow of a tree.
10. Edgar will disguise himself as Tom o' Bedlam.

***Suggested Essay Topics***

1. Kent has been portrayed as an honest character thus far in the play. Discuss his honesty in the light of his banishment and his time in the stocks. Compare the honest characters to the deceitful characters in the play. Is Kent's blunt

honesty necessary? Cite examples from the play to support your answer.

2. Kent and Edgar both assume disguises in the play. Compare and contrast their reasons for the disguise. Discuss the differences in their physical disguises. How are their disguises alike? Is Edgar in greater danger than Kent? Explain your answer.

## Act II, Scene IV (pages 43–53)

***Summary***

Lear, his Fool, and his Gentleman arrive at Gloucester's castle. The King finds it puzzling that Cornwall and Regan have left their house on the night of his expected arrival without sending a message to explain. Kent who is still in the stocks, greets his master. Shocked to see his courier in this shameful condition, the King thinks it must be a joke. Kent tells Lear it was Regan and Cornwall who placed him there. In disbelief, Lear argues with Kent, bandying back and forth until the King finally faces the truth. He insists that they would not dare engage in such an act of disrespect toward the King through his messenger. Incensed by Cornwall and Regan's actions, Lear calls it a "violent outrage" that is "worse than murther." When asked for a reason by the King, Kent truthfully admits that he demonstrated "more man than wit," when he drew his sword on Oswald.

Commenting on the action, the Fool recites fanciful rhymes about Lear's problems with his daughters, observing that poor fathers "make their children blind" while rich fathers "see their children kind." Asking for his daughter's whereabouts, Lear is told she is within. Determined to rectify the situation with Kent, Lear presently enters the castle, asking the others to stay behind. Kent inquires about the King's decreased train of followers. The Fool tells him that it is a question deserving time in the stocks. When Kent asks why, the Fool answers in prose and verse alluding to the stormy times ahead.

Lear and Gloucester enter with the news that Cornwall and

Regan refuse to speak to Lear, giving the excuse that they are sick and weary from traveling all night. Lear requests a better answer from Gloucester, who discreetly reminds the King that the "fiery quality" of the Duke is at the heart of the problem. Lear's explosive reply calls for vengeance and death. He demands to speak with the Duke of Cornwall and Regan immediately, but Gloucester simply states that he has already informed them. The King's fury increases as he excoriates the "fiery Duke." His mood suddenly changes, however, when he considers that the Duke may not be well. When he is reminded of Kent's humiliation in the stocks, however, he is sure this act is a symbol of the death of his royal power as king. He again calls for the Duke and Regan to "come forth and hear me."

Gloucester enters with Cornwall and Regan. They both greet him with proper decorum, addressing him as "your Grace" and telling him they are glad to see him. Kent is set free. The King promptly begins his diatribe complaining about Goneril's depravity and her "Sharp-toothed unkindness," but Regan steps in to defend her sister. She asks him to return to Goneril and apologize for having "wrong'd her." Lear falls on his knees begging Regan to take him in. Annoyed, Regan tells him to stop his unsightly tricks and go back to Goneril's house. Cursing Goneril and swearing never to live with her again, he promises Regan that she will never have his curse.

The King asks Regan who put his man in the stocks, but is interrupted by Oswald's arrival. Recognizing him as Goneril's steward, Lear orders him out of his sight and again demands to know who stocked his servant. This time he is interrupted by Goneril's arrival. Seeing her, the King invokes the heavens to come down and take his part. Lear admonishes her for daring to face him, but she feigns innocence and justifies her past behavior. Cornwall finally admits having put Lear's man in the stocks.

Regan approaches Lear, trying to persuade him to return to her sister's for the remainder of the month, dismiss half his train, and then return to her after she has had time to make provisions for his arrival. Infuriated, Lear declares that he would rather "abjure all roofs" than give up 50 of his men. Goneril casually tells him it is his choice. Rebuffing her with contempt, he reminds her he can stay with Regan and keep his 100 knights. Regan's quick reply, "Not altogether so," is a reminder that she has not yet made preparations for him and his large train of followers. What's more, she decides to reduce his train further and allow him only 25 followers. Lear's painful outcry "I gave you all" is met with a cold response from Regan. After some thought, he decides to go with Goneril where he will at least be allowed 50 knights, but Goneril and Regan proceed to cut his entire train and only allow him the use of their own servants. Condemning his daughters as "unnatural hags," Lear swears he will go mad rather than succumb to weeping. In "high rage" the King wanders out into the impending storm while Goneril and Regan affirm their resolution to cut off the services of all his knights. Regan and Cornwall then implore Gloucester to "Shut up your doors" against the wild night and leave Lear to his own devices.

***Analysis***

Lear's Fool places himself in the middle of the action in this scene with a variety of poignant phrases that again expose the truth of Lear's folly in relation to his daughters.

> Fathers that wear rags
> Do make their children blind,
> But fathers that bear bags
> Shall see their children kind.

With his use of metaphor, the Fool satirizes Lear's foolishness in giving away his "bags" of money to his daughters. In only a matter of weeks, Goneril and Regan have changed from overt expressions of love and kindness before his division of the kingdom to a dogged blindness to their father's needs after they inherit all his money. When Kent is placed in the stocks by Cornwall and Regan, the Fool's comment, "Winter's not gone yet," bears the implication that the worst is not over. The Fool clearly recognizes the act of irreverence and rebellion to the King inherent in their actions toward Kent, his messenger.

In the opening part of the scene, the Fool thinks Kent has been remiss in delivering an answer to Lear's letter from Regan. According to the Fool, Kent, therefore, wears "cruel garters" made of wood because he has been "overlusty at legs," or, run from his duty instead of tending to the service of the King.

The Fool foreshadows the imminent storm at the end of this scene when he talks in rhyme about those who "serve and seek for gain." They will, the Fool says, "pack when it begins to rain,/ And leave thee in the storm." The image is clear, working on the literal as well as the symbolic level of the play. Lear is, indeed, left out in the storm as Regan counsels Gloucester to "Shut up your doors."

The Fool's advice to "set thee to school to an ant, to teach thee there's no laboring i' th' winter" alludes to the Bible and would have been readily understood by audiences of Shakespeare's day.

> Go to the ant, thou sluggard;
> consider her ways and be wise:
> Which having no guide, overseer, or ruler,
> Provideth her meat in the summer,
> and gathereth her food in the harvest.
>
> Proverbs 6: 6-8

Even the ant is wise enough to know there is no labor in the winter. Lear, in the winter of his life, is likened to a great wheel going downhill and finally deserted. But in the prophetic words of the Fool himself, "the Fool will tarry, the Fool will stay."

Lear's characteristic tendency to judge his daughters' love on a mathematical scale is readily apparent in this scene. In the first scene he promises to extend the "largest bounty" to the one who "loves us most." In the same mode, he refuses to live with Goneril after she dismisses 50 of his men. On the other hand, when Regan refuses to take him in unless he reduces his train of followers to 25, Lear suddenly decides to live with Goneril whose "fifty yet doth double five and twenty,/ And thou art twice her love." Ultimately, of course, both daughters decide they will receive the King "But not one follower." Devastated, Lear stumbles out into the storm in "high rage."

By admonishing Lear to apologize to Goneril, Regan commits an atrocity well recognized in Elizabethan England. The King would not, by the laws of society, ask the forgiveness of his daughter, nor would he be forced to beg, though ironically, for food and raiment. Lear invokes the gods to touch him with "noble anger."

He vows to avenge his daughters who are "unnatural hags." Some critics feel his behavior at this point in the play becomes almost childish. Hovering at the verge of a temper tantrum, he fights back "women's weapons, water-drops." The alliteration and rhythm forces a heavy emphasis on each word, creating a tone that demonstrates Lear's disdain for acting "womanish," and, thereby, destroying the natural order.

***Study Questions***

1. Why is the King puzzled when he arrives at Gloucester's castle?
2. Whom does the King see in the stocks? Why was he put in the stocks?
3. Which metaphor does the Fool use to foreshadow the storm?
4. What excuse do Cornwall and Regan give for not greeting the King when he arrives at Gloucester's castle?
5. Why has Lear come to Regan's house?
6. Why does Lear fall on his knees to Regan?
7. How many of Lear's men has Goneril dismissed when he arrives at Gloucester's castle?
8. How many men does Regan want him to have in his train?
9. Whom does Lear refer to as "unnatural hags"?
10. Where does Lear go after his daughters reduce his train of followers to nothing?

***Answers***

1. The King cannot understand the reason for Cornwall and Regan's absence on the night of his expected arrival.
2. The King sees Kent, his messenger, in the stocks. He has been placed there by Cornwall.
3. The Fool says that those who serve for gain "Will pack when it begins to rain,/ And leave thee in the storm."

4. Cornwall and Regan say they are tired and sick from traveling all night.
5. Lear and Goneril have quarreled, and he wants Regan to take him to live with her.
6. On his knees, Lear begs Regan to take him in.
7. Goneril has reduced Lear's train of followers by 50 men.
8. Regan thinks 25 in his train would be an ample amount.
9. Lear refers to his oldest two daughters as "unnatural hags."
10. Lear goes out into the storm and braves the "wild night."

***Suggested Essay Topics***

1. The Fool's purpose in the play is to comment on the action. Discuss the poem that begins "Fathers that wear rags." Explain the metaphors in this poem. How do they apply to Lear and his daughters? Cite examples from the play to support your answer.
2. Lear's daughters have usurped his power by depriving him of his entire train of followers by the end of the scene. Compare and contrast the characters of Goneril and Regan in this scene. How are they alike? How are they different? Why does the King call them "unnatural hags? Give examples from the play to support your answer.

# SECTION FOUR

## *Act III*

### Act III, Scene I (pages 55–57)

***Summary***

On the heath near Gloucester's castle, Kent, braving the storm, immediately recognizes the King's Gentleman. He informs Kent that the King is "contending with the fretfrul elements" with only his Fool to keep him company. The Gentleman reports that Lear roams bareheaded on the stormy heath, striving to "out-scorn...the wind and rain," as his loyal Fool desperately tries to comfort him.

Kent quickly realizes the Gentleman is one whom he can trust. He discloses to him rumors of a division between Albany and Cornwall, though it is still not out in the open. The King of France, Cordelia's husband, has sent his spies to attend the households of Cornwall and Albany as servants. Under their surveillance, quarrels and plots between the two houses have been reported and news of their abusiveness to the King has reached France. Kent thinks "something deeper" also may be brewing. France's secret invasion of England's "scattered" kingdom is imminent. Kent asks the Gentleman to go to Dover to disclose to its citizens the "unnatural" treatment of the King. Assuring the Gentleman of his noble birth, Kent gives him a ring to hand to Cordelia whom he will most likely find in Dover. He explains that she will confirm Kent's true identity. The two then part ways, searching for Lear in the storm and agreeing to give the signal when he is found.

***Analysis***

This scene functions to inform us of Lear's struggle against the elements on the stormy heath. The loyalty of the Fool who accompanies Lear is reminiscent of the previous scene where the Fool confirms his constancy and allegiance. When others "leave thee in the storm," he says, "I will tarry, the Fool will stay." Attempting to ease the King's sorrows, the Fool "labors to outjest/ His heart-strook injuries." If the fool's candid jesting about Lear's lack of good judgment as a father and a king has been annoying at times, one can only stand in awe of his loving care and devotion to the King in the worst of all possible situations, the storm on the heath.

In this scene we hear further rumors of the possibility of a war between the Dukes of Cornwall and Albany. Curan, a courtier in Gloucester's castle, has already predicted the conflict in his conversation with Edmund in Act II, Scene 1. It should be noted, however, that the dissension between the two households is likely to be led by Goneril rather than Albany.

In Cordelia's letter, read by Kent while he was in the stocks in Act II, Scene 2, she writes that she has been "inform'd/ Of my (Kent's) obscured course." In this scene, we learn that Cordelia's informers are, indeed, spies acting as servants in the houses of Cornwall and Albany. Kent informs the Gentleman that Cordelia will most likely be in Dover. Together with the French Army, she waits there to rectify her sisters' abuses toward her father, the King. In this scene, we are given a glimmer of hope that Cordelia will liberate her father from the hands of her self-seeking sisters. Certain that the recent events leading to the King's condition will anger his loyal citizens in Dover, Kent sends the Gentleman to spread the news.

***Study Questions***

1. Where is the King at this point in the play?
2. Who has stayed with the King to give him comfort?
3. What are the rumors concerning Cornwall and Albany?

4. Who are the spies sent to England by the King of France?
5. What news do France's spies bring regarding King Lear?
6. Where does Kent think Cordelia will be staying?
7. What does Kent tell the Gentleman to show Cordelia as proof of Kent's identity?
8. Before the Gentleman goes to Dover, what does he do?
9. What does the French Army intend to do in England?
10. What is Cordelia's purpose for her temporary stay in Dover?

***Answers***

1. Lear's Gentleman tells Kent that the King is in the storm on the heath outside of Gloucester's castle.
2. Only the Fool accompanies the King on the heath.
3. It is rumored that there is division between Cornwall and Albany, leading to civil strife in the kingdom.
4. The spies act as servants in the households of Cornwall and Albany.
5. The spies bring the news that King Lear has had to bear the abuses of Goneril and Regan, his daughters.
6. Kent thinks Cordelia is waiting in Dover.
7. Kent instructs the Gentleman to give Cordelia a ring as proof of Kent's identity.
8. The Gentleman helps to find Lear in the storm.
9. The French Army intends to stage a secret attack on England.
10. Cordelia waits, along with the French Army, to rectify her sisters' injustices to the King.

***Suggested Essay Topics***

1. The Fool has been censuring his master for his lack of judgment as a king but stays with him and helps alleviate his

suffering in the storm on the heath. Write an essay discussing the Fool's loyalty to the King in the storm. Why is he critical of the King? Why does he stay with him when others desert him? Cite examples from the play to prove your point.

2. Cordelia seems to be associated with Kent thus far in the play. Both have been banished, but she has stayed in touch with Kent. Compare and contrast the characters of Cordelia and Kent. How do they personify the good or evil inherent in the play? Explain your answer using examples from the play.



## Act III, Scene II (pages 57–60)

### *Summary*

The groundwork has already been laid by the Gentleman in the previous scene informing us of Lear's struggle against the fierce storm on the heath. As the scene opens, Lear fervently calls upon the winds to blow, the lightning to "Spit, fire," the rain to "drench the steeples," and the thunder to crack open "nature's moulds" and spill the seeds that make "ingrateful man." The Fool counsels Lear to submit to his daughters' authority over him and beg to be taken out of the storm. He reasons that it would be better to "court holy-water," or, in other words, flatter his daughters, than to continue braving the stormy night. Ignoring the Fool's pleas, he addresses the elements, telling them he will show them no unkindness since he never gave them his kingdom, and, therefore, they owe him nothing. His mood quickly swings, however, as he rails against the rain, wind, thunder, and lightning, suspecting that they are, after all, only the "servile ministers" of his "pernicious daughters" fighting a battle against him.

The Fool, continuing his jesting in rhyme, again censures the King, telling him that the person who has "a house to put 's head in" has a good brain. In a strained attempt to control his passions, Lear swears he will be the epitome of patience.

Kent enters with expressions of terror at the night sky that is unparalleled in his memory. Lear calls on the gods to wreak their stormy vengeance on criminals who have never been brought to justice. He considers himself above them, stating that he is "More sinn'd against than sinning." Kent gently guides the "bare-headed" Lear into a hovel that provides shelter from the storm. He talks of turning back to Gloucester's castle with the intention of forcing them to receive him.

Lear tells the Fool his wits are beginning to turn. For the first time he shows compassion for him, asking him whether he is cold. The Fool delays the end of the scene, quoting a long prophecy in rhymed verse.



***Analysis***

In the sixteenth century, the theaters were relatively devoid of stage props. Shakespeare's setting of the storm on the heath is, therefore, largely dependent upon the strong and vigorous imagery of Lear's language. Though the Fool disagrees, preferring a "dry house" to the stormy night, Lear calls upon the elements to wreak their vengeance on "ingrateful man." With metaphors, he paints an image of rain, wind, thunder, and lightning that provide the setting for the storm.

> Blow, winds, and crack your cheeks! rage, blow!
> You cataracts and hurricanoes, spout
> Till you have drench'd our steeples, (drown'd) the cocks!
> You sulph'rous and thought-executing fires,
> Vaunt-couriers of oak-cleaving thunderbolts,
> Singe my white head!

Personifying the elements, Lear sees them as "servile ministers" to his daughters who are engaging them in a battle to destroy him. Hence, the storm outside becomes analogous to Lear's inner struggle in his chaotic world where the political forces, who are now his daughters, threaten to destroy him. Having lost his powers when he gave away his kingdom, he is as vulnerable to his daughters' vengeance as he is to the all-encompassing storm when he roams bareheaded on the wild and barren heath.

Lear calls on the all-shaking thunder to "[c]rack nature's moulds" and spill the seeds that create "ingrateful man." J. F. Danby notes that the thunder acts as the King's agent that carries out the "King's desires in annihilating the corrupted world of man" (*Shakespeare's Doctrine of Nature,* p. 183). Lear, however, cannot, at this point in the drama, identify with that corruption. He still feels he is "More sinn'd against than sinning."

In ancient times people were in constant fear that they would, by some inadvertent act, anger the gods who would, in turn, threaten to destroy them. Though *King Lear* is set in pre-Christian times, Shakespeare's audience would have held similar views. The audience harbored a strong belief in the natural hierarchy of things, which creates a perfect harmony among all stages of being all the way down to inanimate objects. This intricate balance could be upset, however. If, for example, a king was dethroned, as is true in the case of King Lear, God might show his wrath through frightening storms. Shakespeare's *Julius Caesar* is comparable in that the storm is conjured up by the gods to avenge the impending assassination of Caesar. Casca trembles at the "scolding winds" attributing the storm to a world that has become "too saucy with the gods," incensing "them to send destruction" (*Julius Caesar,* Act I, Scene 3). Kent's misgivings about the storm are analogous to Casca's when Kent says that he has never seen "such sheets of fire, such bursts of horrid thunder" since he was a man. Casca echoes Kent's feelings when he makes claims to have seen unsettling storms in the past "But never till to-night, never till now,/ Did I go through a tempest dropping fire" (*Julius Caesar,* Act I, Scene 3).

Lear's indulgence in self-pity is all-pervading in this scene until the tone shifts suddenly with "My wits begin to turn." In a sudden flow of compassion, Lear remembers the humanity of his Fool, and, in fact, his own. "Come on, my boy. How dost, my boy? Art cold?/ I am cold myself." Lear's search for straw in order to warm himself humbles him as he realizes that necessity makes all human conditions relative.

The Fool's last speech delays his exit with a prophecy that seems to confuse time and place. His repeated use of the word "when" is anticipatory, though our immediate reaction to the first few lines is that these circumstances are not reserved for the future, but do, in fact, already reflect the evil world of the play.

Reaching no conclusion, the Fool tells us that he is simply predicting the prophecy of Merlin who has not yet been born. The audience realizes then that it has attempted to follow his nonsensical rhyme to no avail.

***Study Questions***

1. How does Lear set the scene at the beginning?
2. How does Lear compare his daughters to the elements?
3. What does the Fool beg Lear to do to get out of the storm?
4. Who later joins Lear and the Fool in the storm?
5. Where does Kent finally lead Lear to shelter him from the storm?
6. What does Kent plan to do after he finds shelter for Lear and the Fool?
7. How does Lear express his compassion for his Fool?
8. What does Lear wear on his head when he goes out into the storm?
9. Whose prophecy does the Fool recite?
10. According to the King, who has sent the terrible storm on the heath?

***Answers***

1. Lear uses imagery depicting the storm on the heath.
2. Lear personifies the elements as "servile ministers" of his daughters who are trying to destroy him.
3. The Fool begs Lear to ask his daughters' blessing so they will take him in.
4. Kent joins Lear and the Fool in the storm.
5. Kent leads Lear into a hovel to shelter him from the wind and the rain.
6. Kent plans to go back to Gloucester's castle to see whether he will receive him.

7. Lear feels sorry for the Fool, inviting him into his hovel and asking him whether he is cold.
8. Lear goes into the storm bare-headed.
9. The Fool recites the prophecy of Merlin who has not yet been born.
10. Lear thinks the gods have sent the storm to punish the secret crimes that have never been brought to justice.

***Suggested Essay Topics***

1. In Shakespeare's day, there were relatively few stage props in the theater. Discuss the way in which Shakespeare sets the scene through the character of King Lear. Discuss Lear's use of metaphorical language to depict the storm. Relate the outer storm to Lear's inner turmoil in this scene. Give examples to support your answer.
2. The storm on the heath is viewed by Lear as a punishment to the people for their wrongdoings. Write an essay analyzing the idea that storms were a punishment by God. Discuss the storm in relation to the loss of King Lear's power and the resulting chaos after he divided his kingdom between his two daughters. Cite illustrations from the play to support your view.



## Act III, Scene III (pages 60–61)

***Summary***

Taking Edmund into his confidence, Gloucester informs him that Cornwall and Regan have taken over the use of his castle, castigating him for attempting to help the King. They have forbidden Gloucester to seek any aid for the King and adamantly prohibit him to talk about him.

Edmund responds as his father expects him to, expressing surprise at such actions which are most "savage and unnatural." Gloucester tells Edmund there is division between the Duke of

Cornwall and the Duke of Albany. He asks Edmund not to divulge the dangerous contents of a letter he has received containing the news of a power ready to avenge the injuries done to the King. The letter is presently in Gloucester's closet under lock and key.

Instructing Edmund to cover for him at the castle in case Cornwall asks, Gloucester resolves to find the King and help relieve his misery. He tells Edmund that he has been threatened with death for taking the King's part and warns him to be careful.

Left alone, Edmund immediately decides to inform the Duke of Cornwall of all that his father has told him, including the contents of the letter. With his eye on his father's title as Duke of Gloucester, Edmund intends to expose him to Cornwall and, thereby, gain advantage over his own father.

***Analysis***

This short scene functions as an interim to the actions of Kent, Lear, and the Fool on the heath. It allows the trio enough time to reach the hovel in the next scene and keeps the audience abreast of the most recent developments in the subplot.

If there has been any doubt thus far in the play, this scene reveals Edmund's complete depravity. His cunning deception and betrayal of his father establishes him as an evil character in the play. Adept at covering his guilt, Edmund reacts appropriately to Gloucester's account of Cornwall and Regan's treatment of the King which is "Most savage and unnatural." But the minute Gloucester's back is turned, he decides to expose his father to Cornwall. Edmund is an opportunist and will stop at nothing, even the threat of death to his father, to gain power.

Gloucester has been caught in a precarious situation between his loyalty to his former master, the King, and his fear of offending Cornwall and Regan. In this scene, he finally takes a stand against the injuries imposed upon the King. It is not until Cornwall and Regan's harsh takeover of his castle, however, along with their directive to break all communication with the King, that he vows to side with Lear. The contents of the letter seemingly offer hope for some respite from the King's desperate situation. With the letter locked safely in his closet, Gloucester finally makes his death-defying decision to leave his castle and "incline to the King." We will later learn that the power that is "already footed" is that of the King of France and Cordelia, who are waiting on the shore near Dover with an army. For the first time since the division of the kingdom, there is hope that the tide will turn, restoring Lear's kingdom back to its natural order.

***Study Questions***

1. Why do Cornwall and Regan refuse to grant Gloucester the use of his own castle?
2. How does Edmund feel about the abusive treatment of the King?
3. What news does Gloucester's dangerous letter contain?
4. What powers are "already footed" in this scene according to Gloucester?
5. Where does Gloucester keep the letter?
6. What does Edmund decide to do about the news his father has given him?
7. Why does Edmund betray his father's trust in him?
8. What does Gloucester tell Edmund to say to Cornwall if he asks for him?
9. What will be the penalty if Cornwall discovers Gloucester's intentions?
10. In what way does this scene function as an interim scene?

***Answers***

1. Cornwall and Regan are punishing Gloucester for giving help to the King.
2. Edmund claims it is "savage and unnatural," but he feels otherwise.
3. We may assume that the letter talks of powers that are waiting to avenge the abusive treatment of the King.
4. The King of France and Cordelia, we will learn later, are waiting on the shore near Dover with an army.

5. Gloucester has locked the letter in the closet.
6. When Gloucester leaves, Edmund immediately decides to impart the information to Cornwall.
7. Edmund wants his father's title as Earl of Gloucester.
8. Gloucester asks Edmund to tell Cornwall he is sick in bed.
9. Gloucester has been threatened with death for associating with the King and offering him help in his time of need.
10. This scene functions as an interim scene, breaking the action of Lear, Kent, and the Fool on the heath.

***Suggested Essay Topics***

1. Edmund is seen as a depraved character throughout the play. Write an essay comparing his behavior in this scene to his first speech in Act I, Scene 2. What were his aspirations in this soliloquy? Is he beginning to fulfill his desires in life by Act III, Scene 3? Cite examples from the play to support your view.
2. Gloucester's actions are commendable in this scene. Discuss Gloucester's courage in defying Cornwall and Regan. Why is he courageous? What are his motives? Is he a loyal subject of the King? Explain your answer.



## Act III, Scene IV (pages 61–67)

***Summary***

Seeking shelter from the raging storm on the heath, Kent repeatedly prods Lear to enter the hovel. At first he rebuffs Kent, asking him to leave him alone, but the King finally replies that the storm invading his body is scarcely felt since the tempest in his mind is a "greater malady." Ranting on about "filial ingratitude," he reproachfully alludes to his daughters who, he thinks, "tear this hand" that feeds them. Vowing to refrain from weeping, he firmly resolves to endure, though his daughters have shut him out on a night like this. Calling their names through the din of the storm, he reminds them that he "gave all." He promptly checks himself, afraid he will go mad. He decides to shun that kind of talk. Kent responds positively and again urges him to enter the hovel. Lear finally agrees to go in, but asks Kent and his Fool to enter first. He promises to follow them after he has said a prayer. Praying with heartfelt compassion for the poor homeless and unfed wretches, he is remorseful for having taken "too little care of this."

As Lear ends his prayer, a strange voice is heard. Rushing out of the hovel, the Fool cautions Lear not to enter since there is a spirit inhabiting the shelter. Responding to Kent's command, Edgar, disguised as Tom o' Bedlam, appears from the hovel, muttering incoherent phrases about the "foul fiend" who is following him. Lear immediately perceives him as one who has been swindled by Goneril and Regan, but Kent informs Lear that this man has no daughters. Lear is not convinced. He is sure that nothing but "Those pelican daughters" could have brought the madman to this pass.

The disguised Edgar portrays himself as a former servingman who has lived a life of questionable morals. The King contrasts Edgar to the three sophisticates: Lear, Kent, and the Fool. He recognizes Edgar as "the thing itself," devoid of all the trappings that distinguish man from a "bare, fork'd animal." Identifying with Tom's madness, Lear tears at his own clothes that are only "lendings" from nature.

Gloucester enters with a torch. The disguised Edgar identifies him as the "foul (fiend) Flibbertigibbet" who roams the streets at night. Gloucester gives an account of the impossible situation with Lear's daughters, explaining their command to bar the doors of his castle, shutting Lear out in the storm. He assures the King that he has come to take him to an outbuilding near his castle where he will be given food to eat. Lear, in his madness, responds by requesting a word with the philosopher, Tom o' Bedlam. In his concern for the King whose "wits begin t' unsettle," Kent implores Gloucester to extend the offer of food and shelter once more.

Gloucester empathizes with the mad Lear whose "daughters seek his death." He tells the disguised Kent that he had a son who also sought his life, and it has "craz'd my wits." Ironically, he makes a positive reference to the banished Kent who had predicted this would happen. Gloucester finally convinces the King to take shelter in the hovel, but Lear will only go in if his philosopher, Tom o' Bedlam, will keep him company. Humoring the King, Kent and Gloucester usher all of them into the shelter. Tom o' Bedlam echoes a familiar English ballad as the scene closes.

***Analysis***

The storm on the heath is symbolic of the tempest in Lear's mind. He censures Kent for his excessive concern over bodily comforts as he repeatedly urges Lear to go into the hovel. "Thou think'st 'tis much that this contentious storm/ Invades us to the skin; so 'tis to thee." On the edge of madness, Lear is tormented by a "greater malady" bringing visions of his unkind daughters shutting him out on such a night. The storm outside is scarcely felt when it is met by a stronger affliction which is that of "Filial Ingratitude." Agonizing over his misfortunes, the tortured Lear can only see others' adversities in terms of his own. As he encounters Edgar, disguised as Tom o' Bedlam in the hovel, he repeatedly insists that it was Tom's daughters who brought him to this state of madness. "Didst thou give all to thy daughters? And/ art thou come to this?" When Kent interjects "He hath no daughters, sir," Lear threatens him with death, calling him a traitor for opposing his king.

The storm on the heath symbolizes not only Lear's emotional turmoil, but also the disorderly tumult pervading the entire kingdom. There are rumors of wars between the Dukes of Cornwall and Albany, and Edmund intends to join forces with them. Deceit runs rampant as children turn against their parents, and the honest characters, Kent and Edgar, must disguise themselves for their very survival.

Lear's self-centered obsession with his own difficulties, however, begins to turn as he prays for the "Poor naked wretches" out in the pitiless storm. Reflecting on the plight of the homeless and hungry left without shelter in the storm, he chides himself for having taken "Too little care of this!" L. C. Knights has observed that "This is pity, not self-pity; and condemnation of others momentarily gives way to self-condemnation." (*Shakespearean Themes*, p. 104) It is only momentary, however, and Lear again indulges in self-pity as he lashes out at his "pelican daughters."

Disguised as Tom o' Bedlam, Edgar's description of himself as a former servingman portrays the vision of a man who embodies all worldly vices: "False of heart, light of ear, bloody of hand; hog in sloth, fox in stealth, wolf in greediness, dog in madness, lion in prey." He has, in fact, descended from a human being to a "poor, bare, fork'd animal."

Lear's vision of Tom o' Bedlam as "the thing itself" stands in sharp contrast to the sophisticated three. Stripped of his power and rejected by his daughters, Lear lapses into a sudden visionary madness in which he longs for the natural state "unaccommodated man." In his incongruous endeavor to escape his true identity as a dignified king, he tears at his clothes, muttering "Off, off, you lendings." Edgar later becomes Lear's philosopher, whom he takes to a hovel as a companion. It is noteworthy that Lear, who usually speaks in verse, reverts to prose in this speech as he descends from sophisticated humanity into madness.

The main plot and the subplot are analogous in the scene when the feigned madness of Edgar is held in juxtaposition to the actual madness of Lear. Gloucester's heartbreak concerning his son, who allegedly sought his life echoes Lear's devastating situation with his daughters who also seek his death. Confiding in Kent about his own griefs, Gloucester compares them to the King's. "Thou sayest the King grows mad, I'll tell thee, friend,/ I am almost mad myself." Ironically, he talks of "good Kent," unaware it is, indeed, the loyal Kent whom he is addressing. It is a strange paradox that Kent must hide his true identity from the King, just as Edgar must disguise himself from his father, Gloucester. In both the main plot and the subplot, the "good" characters must disguise themselves while the evil ones parade about openly.

***Study Questions***

1. What does the storm on the heath symbolize?
2. Who is Edgar in disguise?
3. What type of clothing does Tom o' Bedlam wear?
4. According to Lear, who are the three sophisticated ones?
5. Who does Lear say is the "thing itself"?

6. Whom does Lear pity in his prayer on the heath?
7. What is Gloucester carrying as he enters the hovel?
8. What does Edgar call Gloucester when he approaches the hovel?
9. How does Gloucester's situation compare to Lear's?
10. Why has Gloucester come out into the storm?

***Answers***

1. The storm symbolizes Lear's tempest in his mind.
2. Edgar is disguised as Tom o' Bedlam, a madman.
3. Tom o' Bedlam wears only a blanket.
4. The three sophisticated persons are Lear, Kent, and the Fool.
5. Edgar in disguise is referred to as the "thing itself." He is natural, "unaccommodated" man.
6. Lear pities the homeless and hungry who have no place to go for shelter from the storm.
7. Gloucester is carrying a torch into the hovel.
8. Edgar calls him the foul fiend who walks the streets at night.
9. Gloucester and Lear both have children who seek their death.
10. Gloucester has come to find Lear and offer him food and shelter in an outbuilding near the castle.

***Suggested Essay Topics***

1. Lear's prayer is a turning point from self-pity to compassion for the "houseless heads" and "unfed sides" who are left to fend for themselves in the storm. Write an essay comparing and contrasting Lear's prayer with his speeches in the rest of the scene. Does he show compassion to others in this scene? If so, in what way? Cite examples from the play to support your view.

2. Lear sees Edgar, disguised as Tom o' Bedlam, representing "the thing itself; unaccommodated man." Write an essay explaining the meaning of these words in relation to the rest of the scene. Why does Lear wish to become like Edgar? Why does he tear off his clothes? Give examples from the play to defend your answer.

## Act III, Scene V (page 67)

### *Summary*

Acting as an informant against his father, Edmund convinces Cornwall that Gloucester is guilty of treason. Determined to have his revenge, Cornwall now reasons that Edgar's plot to kill his father was not entirely due to his brother's "evil disposition" but was, in fact, provoked by Gloucester himself. Bellying his evil motive, Edmund produces Gloucester's supposed letter as evidence that he has been supplying secret information to France. Edmund invokes the heavens to witness his regret that he should have detected his own father's treason. Cornwall rewards Edmund with his new title as Earl of Gloucester and urges him to find his father so that he can be apprehended. In an "aside" to the audience, Edmund voices his wish that he might find Gloucester "comforting the King," which would augment Cornwall's suspicions. He then turns to Cornwall, assuring him of his loyalty to the kingdom in spite of the conflict it will cause between him and his father. Confident that he can trust Edmund, Cornwall assures him that he will love him as his own son. (Better than Edmund's own father).

### *Analysis*

We again see the development of the subplot in this scene in which Edmund uses Gloucester's letter as evidence of his guilt. Unlike Edgar's, Edmund's disguise is spiritual, rather than physical, as he hides behind an innocent façade, hoping to gain undeserved power and wealth at others' expense. Cloaking his deception in glossy language, Edmund laments the fact that he must "repent to be just." The irony is clear as Cornwall puts his complete trust in Edmund, promising to help him bear the loss of his father by offering himself as "a (dearer) father."

Cornwall is obviously being gulled by Edmund which becomes even more apparent in his "aside" to the audience. In his depravity, Edmund guilefully demonstrates his disloyalty to both Cornwall and Gloucester. "If I find him comforting the King, it will stuff his suspicion more fully." Turning to Cornwall, he vows to persevere in his "course of loyalty," but he is, in fact, only loyal to his own ambition of becoming the Duke of Gloucester.

Edmund calls upon the heavens to look with pity on his adversity. "O heavens! that this treason were not; or not I the detector!" He is fully aware that his piety will impress Cornwall. We are, however, reminded of Edmund's renunciation of the supernatural in Act I, Scene 2 when he condemns those who are "sick in fortune" for blaming their plight on the heavens. Unknown to Cornwall, Edmund is only calling on the god of the natural world in view of his lack of belief in the supernatural.

Filled with a desire for revenge against Gloucester for taking the King's part against him, Cornwall, no less than Edgar, carries on an illusion of fairness and integrity throughout the scene. Reaching the height of all absurdity, he vows to replace Gloucester as a loving father to Edmund.

***Study Questions***

1. What does Edmund produce as evidence of Gloucester's treason?
2. What important information does the letter contain?
3. How does Cornwall reward Edmund for being his informant against Gloucester?
4. Why does Edmund call upon the heavens?
5. What will Cornwall do to Gloucester for his crime of treason?
6. What is Edmund's main ambition?
7. What does Cornwall think might have been the cause of Edgar's plot to murder his father?

8. What does Cornwall promise to do to replace the loss of Edmund's father?
9. What is Cornwall's attitude as a Duke in this scene?
10. How will Cornwall search for the Duke of Gloucester?

*Answers*

1. Edmund shows Cornwall the supposed letter that Gloucester received from France.
2. The letter, it can be assumed, contains news of France's impending invasion of England.
3. Cornwall rewards Edmund by giving him the new title of the Duke of Gloucester.
4. Edmund calls upon the heavens to pity him in his adversity.
5. Cornwall will apprehend Gloucester when he is found.
6. Edmund hopes to replace his father as Earl of Gloucester.
7. Cornwall thinks that Gloucester might have provoked Edgar to plot the death of his father.
8. Cornwall promises Edmund that he will love him even "dearer" than his own father would.
9. Cornwall pretends to possess the qualities of fairness and integrity and will see that justice is done.
10. Cornwall asks Edmund to bring his father back to him.

***Suggested Essay Topics***

1. Edmund is the epitome of deception, manipulating Cornwall for his own advantage. Write an essay demonstrating the irony of his relationship with Cornwall in this scene. How does Edmund deceive the Duke? Why is this deception ironic? What does Cornwall gain from his contact with Edmund? Cite examples from the drama to support your point.

2. Cornwall plans to avenge Gloucester for supplying secret information to the King of France. Discuss Gloucester's threat to Cornwall. Why has Cornwall forbade him to see King Lear? How would Gloucester's loyalty to Lear affect the new divided kingdom? Explain your answer.

## Act III, Scene VI (pages 68–71)

### *Summary*

In an outbuilding near his castle, Gloucester shelters Lear from the raging storm on the heath. Kent thanks Gloucester for his kindness, afraid that the King's "wits have given way to impatience." Promising his quick return, Gloucester leaves Kent, Edgar, and the Fool with Lear to find the necessary supplies for their comfort. Edgar, still disguised as Tom o' Bedlam, continues his chatter about the foul fiends that are plaguing him. Alluding to Chaucer's "Monk's Tale," he says that Frateretto tells him "Nero is an angler in the lake of darkness." He implores the Fool to pray and beware of the "foul fiend." The Fool continues his lighthearted humor, asking whether a madman is a yeoman or a gentleman, to which Lear quickly replies, "A king, a king."

Breaking into the middle of the Fool's continued jesting, the King suddenly decides to conduct a mock trial. Edgar will be his "learned justicer" and his wise Fool will assist him. He appoints Kent as one of the judges. His daughters, Goneril and Regan, are the "she-foxes" who are brought to trial, taking the form of joint stools.

Kent urges Lear to lie down and rest, but Lear ignores his pleas and decides that Goneril will be the first to be arraigned. Lear testifies that she "kick'd the poor king her father." Turning his thoughts to Regan, he rails at her for the corruption she has brought and censures the "false justicer" for letting her escape. Feeling deep sympathy for the King in his madness, Kent realizes Lear's wits are failing. Edgar also tells us that his tears for the King make his disguise and buffoonery difficult to maintain. Kent finally convinces the King to lie down and rest.

Gloucester enters, asking for Lear but is told by Kent that his "wits are gone." Gloucester instructs Kent to put him in a litter and quickly drive him to Dover because his life is in danger. He warns Kent that within a half hour the King and everyone associated with him will be killed if they stay in this place. Making sure the Fool is not left behind, Kent orders him to help lift his master, who is now asleep.

Left alone, Edgar, again speaking in verse, drops his disguise as Tom o' Bedlam and decides he will disclose his true identity and get involved in the recent events of the kingdom. After seeing the King's suffering, he decides that his pain is light by contrast. He ends by wishing the King a safe escape.

***Analysis***

Lear's mock trial of his daughters, the "she-foxes," is closely associated with grotesque comedy. Bordering on the absurd, Lear, in his madness, appoints Tom o' Bedlam as his "robed man of justice" which is, of course, a pun on his sole article of clothing, a blanket. The incongruity of the Fool acting as a "yoke-fellow of equity," a legal partner of Tom o' Bedlam, is utterly preposterous. Two joint-stools are set up representing Lear's daughters, the defendants. The Fool immediately mistakes Goneril for a joint-stool and all the while Edgar is muttering about the foul fiend who persecutes him. Goneril has committed the crime of kicking "the poor king her father," and even the household dogs bark at him. Lear has, in his madness, turned his tragedy into an undignified farce, arousing our pity, but not our reverence and awe.

Kent's deep concern for the King's welfare, consistent throughout the scene and the play as a whole, lends dignity to Lear. "O pity! Sir, where is the patience now/ That you so oft have boasted to retain?" Edgar, too, breaks down, almost unable to go on, as he sees the King slip further into madness. Even Lear himself, still seeking for an answer to his tragic situation, wishes to "anatomize Regan" so he can get at the cause of her hard heart. This is only temporary, however, as he quickly turns to Edgar, ready to refashion his garments, and we are back to absurdity again.

This is the last appearance of the Fool in the play. His affinity with Cordelia is noteworthy. When we first meet him, he is yearning for Cordelia who has been banished by the King, and he disappears from the action before she reappears. In Act V, Scene 3, Lear, holding the dead Cordelia in his arms, talks of his poor fool being hanged. There has been much controversy over this passage since the Fool has not been seen in the play since Act III. Some critics say that "Fool" is an affectionate name for Cordelia and others simply admit to confusion. The Fool has acted as Lear's conscience, functioning to disturb him with truths about his erroneous choices regarding the division of his kingdom and the resultant effects they have had on his life. The wise sayings of the Fool have sometimes been disguised as paradoxical truths. Overall, his wisdom and insight have usually been cloaked in riddles and humorous verse bordering on the grotesque.

Edgar's last speech is spoken in verse as he sheds his disguise as Tom o' Bedlam to follow the rumored events between France and England. "Tom away!/ Mark the high noises, and thyself bewray." Edgar's opportunity to share in Lear's suffering has made his own pain seem "light and portable." The next time we see Edgar he will again need to disguise himself as Tom o' Bedlam as he leads his blind father to Dover. The motive for his disguise will no longer be fear of Gloucester but one of love and concern for him instead.

***Study Questions***

1. Who are the defendants in Lear's mock trial?
2. Who is chosen by Lear as the "justicer" in the mock trial?
3. Why does Lear refer to Edgar as a "robed man of justice"?
4. What is the Fool's position in the mock trial?
5. How does Kent respond to his position as one of the judges?
6. Whom does the King arraign first in the mock trial?
7. What is Goneril's crime in the trial?
8. What does the King wish to do to Regan?
9. What does Gloucester tell Kent to do with the King? Why?
10. What is significant about Edgar's actions at the end of the scene?

***Answers***

1. Goneril and Regan are the defendants in Lear's mock trial.
2. Lear chooses Edgar, disguised as Tom o' Bedlam, as his "justicer."
3. The blanket Edgar wears is considered a robe by Lear.
4. The Fool is Edgar's "yoke-fellow of equity" or legal partner.
5. Kent feels only pity for the King and says very little.
6. The King arraigns Goneril first.
7. Goneril's crime is kicking "the poor king her father."
8. The King would like to "anatomize Regan" to find the cause of her "hard heart."
9. Gloucester tells Kent to take the King to Dover in a litter. Gloucester is afraid for the King's life.
10. Edgar's pain has become "light and portable" and he feels restored.

***Suggested Essay Topics***

1. The Fool is considered to be Lear's conscience in the play. Write an essay explaining this concept. In what ways does he represent Lear's conscience? How does he use paradox to bring out truth in the play? What forms do his wisdom usually take? Why are the Fool's methods an effective way of exposing the truth? Use examples from the play to explain your answer.
2. Lear's mock trial reveals the incongruity of his actions as a king. Write an essay explaining the way in which the mock trial is incongruous behavior for a king. How do the supposed legal titles of Edgar and the Fool add to that incongruity? Cite examples from the play to support your argument.

## Act III, Scene VII (pages 72–75)

New Characters:

**Servant #1:** *Cornwall's servant who stabs him and is fatally wounded by Regan*

**Servants #2 and #3:** *they follow Gloucester to Dover and soothe his bleeding eyes.*

### *Summary*

Cornwall instructs Goneril to bring Albany a letter containing the news that France's army has landed. He then orders his servants to find the traitor Gloucester and bring him back. Regan wants him hanged immediately, and Goneril calls for his eyes to be plucked out. Assuring them he will take care of things, Cornwall advises Edmund to accompany Goneril since their revengeful act toward his father will not be fit for his eyes. Cornwall asks Goneril to encourage the Duke of Albany to send an answer back as quickly as possible. He bids Goneril and Edmund goodbye, addressing him as "my Lord of Gloucester." Oswald enters with reports that Lear is being conveyed to Dover by the Lord of Gloucester accompanied by about 36 of the King's knights. He has also heard they will all be under the protection of well-armed friends in Dover. Oswald then prepares the horses for his mistress Goneril, and she and Edmund begin their journey.

Cornwall's servants quickly bring Gloucester back to his castle where he is immediately bound to a chair and cross-examined. Addressing them as guests, Gloucester begs them not to involve him in any foul play. Plucking his beard, Regan calls him an "ingrateful fox" and a "filthy traitor." Gloucester rebukes Regan for her unkind treatment of her host. Continuing their inquiry with harsh invectives against the so-called traitor, Cornwall and Regan question him about the letter from France and about the "lunatic" King. Gloucester admits the King is on his way to Dover where he will be protected from Regan and Goneril's cruel treatment of him. Lashing out at them for leaving Lear out in the storm, Gloucester calls for swift vengeance from heaven to overtake the

King's children. In response, Cornwall promptly gouges out one of his eyes. As Gloucester cries for help, Regan coldly prods Cornwall to pluck out the other eye, too. In defense of Gloucester, Cornwall's lifelong servant draws his sword and orders Cornwall to stop tormenting the old Duke. Cornwall is wounded and Regan grabs a sword, stabbing the servant in the back and killing him. Cornwall immediately gouges out Gloucester's other eye. Calling for his son Edmund to "quit this horrid act," Gloucester is told it was Edmund who disclosed his father's act of treason. Invoking the gods to forgive him for his foolishness in trusting Edmund, Gloucester blesses Edgar and hopes he will prosper. Regan orders Gloucester thrust out to "smell/ His way to Dover." As Regan leads her wounded husband by the arm, Cornwall orders the dead servant thrown on the dunghill.

Left alone with Gloucester, two of the servants decide to follow him to Dover with the hope of engaging the help of Tom o' Bedlam to lead the blind Duke. But first they apply a soothing remedy to his bleeding face.

***Analysis***

In this scene we see the most overt expression of cruelty anywhere in the play, and, perhaps, in all of Shakespeare's works. Cornwall unmercifully gouges out Gloucester's eyes, which is shocking to our human sensibilities and has contributed to the difficulty producers have long had in staging this scene. Some critics have perceived Cornwall's deed as an awe-inspiring act of terror designed to satisfy the human desire for sensationalism in Shakespeare's sixteenth-century theater. This view does not consider, however, the symbolism of the blinding of Gloucester and its relation to the play as a whole. Ironically, it is not until Gloucester has literally suffered the loss of his eyes that he is able to realize how little he saw when he actually had eyes. As soon as his sight is gone, Gloucester immediately sees the villainy of Edmund, who has informed on him. Promptly recognizing his folly regarding Edgar, he asks the gods to forgive him. Stanley Cavell has observed that these three actions take only 20 syllables. Gloucester's "complete acquiescence" to his sudden fate is, according to Cavell, attributed to the Duke's realization that his blindness is a retribution for past deeds, "forcing him to an insight about his life as a whole" (Stanley Cavell, "The Avoidance of Love: A Reading of King Lear, 1987). He has misjudged both of his children and must now pay a heavy price.

It is notable that all of the evil characters in the play, Cornwall, Regan, Goneril, Edmund, and Oswald are gathered together in one place, Gloucester's castle. Ironically, Gloucester has literally been evicted from his own castle where "robber's hands" have taken control. Besides Gloucester, the only characters in this scene with any compassion and human decency are the three servants. Fearless in his valor, one of the servants stands up with his sword against Cornwall's brutality. He pays for his actions with his life which stands in stark contrast to the cruel and unprincipled Cornwall. The other servants also show concern as they care for Gloucester. "I'll never care what wickedness I do,/ If this man comes to good." They apply "flax and whites of eggs," a household remedy for his bleeding eyes, before they guide him to Dover.

On the surface, Gloucester's only crime is in befriending the King. To Cornwall and Regan, however, the King represents a threat to their own power in the kingdom. That threat becomes even more imminent as the armies of France hover along England's shores, ready to restore the kingdom back to its natural order. Although Gloucester is the victim of cruel and barbaric treatment, Cornwall and Regan's actions seem to be indirectly pointed toward the King. Except for his friendship with the King and his followers, Gloucester would pose little threat to them. "And what confederacy have you with the traitors/ Late footed in the kingdom?" asks Cornwall. Regan demands to know "To whose hands you have sent the lunatic king." They associate Gloucester with the King's potential political power. Regan also condemns his age and parenthood by plucking his gray beard and making condescending remarks about his age. "So white, and such a traitor?" They also support and identify with Edmund, who has double-crossed his own father.

Images of sight pervade this scene, moving the action forward. Gloucester echoes Goneril's words in her desire to "pluck out" Gloucester's eyes. As his reason for sending the King to Dover, Gloucester tells Regan he "would not see" her "Pluck out his poor old eyes." Threatening to "see" vengeance done to Lear's children, Gloucester's challenge is met by Cornwall with "See't shalt thou never" as he plucks out the old Duke's eye. Ready for the other eye, he responds to Regan's urging with "If you see vengeance," but is stopped by his servant. As Cornwall's servant dies in defense of Gloucester, he cries out, "My lord, you have one eye left/ To see some mischief on him." As if the servant has given him the cue, Cornwall continues the business at hand. He gouges out the other eye "lest it see more...Out, vile jelly!" Darkness then falls on Gloucester who has, at last, been prevented from seeing the evil so prevalent in this scene. Ironically, his insight improves as he "smells his way to Dover."



***Study Questions***

1. Who accompanies Goneril on her way to see her husband, the Duke of Albany?
2. What news does Oswald bring to Cornwall and Regan?
3. Why does Cornwall advise Edmund to leave?
4. What happens to Gloucester after the servants bring him back?
5. Where does this scene take place?
6. Why does Gloucester say he took the King to Dover?
7. Who gouges out both of Gloucester's eyes? Who encourages him?
8. Who draws his sword on Cornwall and wounds him?
9. Who kills the servant of Cornwall by stabbing him in the back?
10. Which characters appear to be the only good ones in this scene?

***Answers***

1. Goneril is accompanied by Edmund.
2. Oswald tells Cornwall and Regan that the King and 36 of his knights are on their way to Dover.

3. Cornwall says that it is not wise for Edmund to observe the revenge they will take upon his traitorous father.
4. Gloucester is bound to a chair and cross-examined.
5. Ironically, the scene takes place in Gloucester's own castle.
6. Gloucester tells Regan he took the King to Dover so she would not pluck out his eyes with her nails.
7. The Duke of Cornwall, Regan's husband, gouges out Gloucester's eyes in his own castle. Regan encourages him.
8. Cornwall's servant draws a sword in defense of Gloucester. He receives a fatal wound for it.
9. Regan stabs the servant in the back and kills him.
10. Besides Gloucester, the servants appear to be the only good characters in this scene. Full of compassion, they are unable to bear the cruel treatment of Gloucester.

***Suggested Essay Topics***

1. In this scene, we see one of the most shocking expressions of cruelty in all of Shakespeare's plays. Write an essay discussing the purpose it serves. Do you think Shakespeare resorts to sensationalism for the entertainment of the audience? Relate Shakespeare's purpose to the symbolism of sight in this scene. Use examples from the play to support your argument.
2. This scene portrays the evil characters as they meet at Gloucester's castle. Compare and contrast the "evil" characters with the "good" characters in this scene. What virtues do the good characters possess? What vices do the evil characters portray? Are they entirely evil? Cite examples from the play to explain your answer.

# SECTION FIVE

# Act IV

## Act IV, Scene I (pages 77–79)

New Character:

**Old Man:** *Gloucester's tenant who leads him after he is blinded*

### *Summary*

Alone on the heath, Edgar reasons that things can only improve since fortune has already imposed the very worst on him. Confident in the belief that he has paid his dues and now "Owes nothing" more, he begins on a positive note until he sees Gloucester. Edgar's mood quickly changes as he watches his blinded father led by an old man, a former tenant. Concerned about the old man's safety, Gloucester urges him to leave since the old man can do nothing for him. Troubled about Gloucester's inability to see his way, the old man is persistent. Gloucester tells him he has no way and, therefore, needs no eyes since he "stumbled" when he saw. Lamenting the loss of his "dear son Edgar," Gloucester wishes for a chance to touch him once more. Edgar is soon recognized by the old man as "poor mad Tom." Seeing his blind father has caused Edgar to feel his life is worse than ever. Gloucester recalls meeting a madman and a beggar in last night's storm. He remembers that seeing him brought his son Edgar to mind though they were not yet friends.

Edgar then greets his master and is immediately recognized by Gloucester as the "naked fellow." The blind Duke orders the man to bring some clothes for Edgar and meet them a mile or two down the road to Dover. Gloucester says he will allow Edgar to lead him to Dover. The man exclaims that Edgar is mad, but Gloucester says it is a sign of the times "when madmen lead the blind." Determined to find the very best apparel for Edgar, the old man leaves.

Edgar is afraid he will be unable to continue his disguise, but he decides he must. He looks sadly into his father's bleeding eyes as he assumes the role of poor Tom who is haunted by the foul fiends. He assures the blind Duke that he knows the way to Dover. Gloucester then entrusts him with his purse as he confirms his belief in a more equitable distribution of wealth so that all men can have a sufficient amount. Gloucester describes a cliff near Dover where he wishes to go. After that he will need poor Tom no more. Edgar takes the blind Duke's arm and the strange pair begin their trek to Dover.



***Analysis***

In his opening soliloquy, Edgar expresses genuine hope that his situation will now improve since he has seen the worst. He decides the worst can only return to laughter. A reversal of circumstances in which he sees his blinded father immediately changes his perspective, however. He decides that the worst is, after all, a relative condition.

> O Gods! Who is't can say, "I am at the worst"?
> I am worse than e'er I was.
> ..............................................
> And worse I may be yet: the worst is not
> So long as we can say, "This is the worst."

The degree of suffering is relative to our own experience, and, therefore, we can never say "This is the worst." As is the case with Edgar, the characters in the play are repeatedly led to the brink, believing relief from suffering is in sight, but are again thrust into an even more difficult situation. This is particularly true of Lear and Gloucester. Lear's madness continues in subsequent scenes and his suffering does not end even after he meets Cordelia. Gloucester too has suffered the sting of mistaken loyalties, lost his castle and title, and now even his eyes. Metaphorically, he voices his futility:

"As flies to wanton boys are we to th' gods." This is, in Edgar's words, not the worst, however, for he still has the image of his "dear son Edgar," and he lives to "see thee (Edgar) in my touch."

As Gloucester meets Edgar in this scene, he remembers a madman and a beggar whom he met in the storm the night before. He refers to Tom o' Bedlam "Which made me think a man a worm." Shakespeare's audience would have been familiar with this concept from the Bible. It appears in Job 25:6. Bildad is speaking to Job regarding man's position relative to God. "How much less man, that is a worm? and the son of man, which is a worm?"

Commentators have often compared the suffering of Lear to the prolonged afflictions of Job. It seems no accident that Biblical imagery, also from the book of Job, is alluded to as Gloucester asks the man to find "some covering for this naked soul." In his worship Job declares, "Naked came I out of my mother's womb, and naked shall I return thither." (Job 1:21) Nakedness in Edgar is akin to "the thing itself" which is "unaccomodated man." It is man stripped of all his illusions. Ironically, it is not until Gloucester has lost his sight that he gains his capacity to feel for poor naked Tom. He orders a covering for his nakedness which would raise him above a mere worm or a common animal.

Gloucester reprimands the "superfluous and lust-dieted man," who has no insight regarding his excesses because he has no feeling for the poor. Advocating equal distribution of wealth, Gloucester's speech echoes Lear's prayer in Act III, Scene 4 when the King prays for the poor, naked wretches without a roof over their heads or food to eat. Before they experienced their own suffering, Lear and Gloucester had both "taken too little care of this." Gloucester himself admits he stumbled when he saw. Shakespeare's audience, anchored in the Christian tradition, would have seen Lear and Gloucester's new concern for the poor as a sign of the beginnings of a moral regeneration that has come about through suffering.

***Study Questions***

1. Who is leading the blind Duke as the scene opens?
2. Who leads Gloucester to Dover?

3. What is Edgar's mood in his soliloquy?
4. How does Edgar feel when he sees his blind father?
5. What does Gloucester tell the old man to bring for Edgar?
6. How does the old man respond to Gloucester's request for clothes?
7. Why is it difficult for Edgar to keep up his disguise?
8. Why does Gloucester give Edgar his purse?
9. In this scene how does Gloucester feel about the distribution of wealth?
10. Where does Gloucester want Edgar to lead him near Dover?

***Answers***

1. The old man, a former tenant, leads the blind Gloucester.
2. Edgar, still disguised as Tom o' Bedlam, leads Gloucester to Dover.
3. Edgar feels encouraged, thinking that the worst is over.
4. Edgar feels he is worse than he ever was, now that he sees his blinded father.
5. Gloucester tells the old man to bring Edgar, disguised as poor Tom, some clothes to wear.
6. The old man says he will bring the best apparel that he has.
7. It is difficult for Edgar to look at his father's condition and still keep up his madman's disguise.
8. Gloucester gives Edgar his purse because he trusts him. He is blind and cannot handle his own money.
9. Gloucester feels each person should have enough.
10. Gloucester wants Edgar to lead him to a cliff near Dover.

***Suggested Essay Topics***

1. In Edgar's soliloquy, he feels that his fortune can only get better because he has seen the worst. Write an essay

explaining the concept that things cannot get any worse because they are now at their worst. Why is this idea relative? How does it apply to Edgar? How does it apply to people in general? Cite examples from the play to support your answer.

2. Gloucester states, "I stumbled when I saw." Explicate this passage in the light of Gloucester's renewed insight. Why did his blindness contribute to his moral regeneration? How has his suffering changed him? In what ways has he changed? Draw your examples from the play to support your idea.

## Act IV, Scene II (pages 80–83)

New Character:

**Messenger:** *brings news of the death of Cornwall*

***Summary***

Goneril and Edmund arrive at the Duke of Albany's palace. As Oswald enters, Goneril inquires about Albany and is told he is altogether changed. Puzzled by the Duke's behavior, Oswald reports that Albany smiled when he was told the French had landed, showed annoyance when he heard his wife was coming, and called him a sot when he told him of Gloucester's treason and Edmund's loyalty to the kingdom. Albany's attitude is the direct opposite of Oswald's expectations. Goneril promptly attributes his changed disposition to his cowardice. Afraid that Edmund will not be welcomed by Albany, Goneril advises him to go back to Cornwall and aid him in assembling an army against France. She tells Edmund she will take charge at home, switching roles with her "mild husband" and handing her duties over to him. She assures him that Oswald, her trusty steward, will keep them both abreast of the latest news. She then kisses Edmund, promising that he may find a mistress dispatching his commands. Edmund leaves in high spirits.

Reflecting on his manliness, Goneril refers to Edmund as

"Gloucester" and compares him to the fool who "usurps my (bed)." Albany enters, immediately chastising her for what she has done to her father, the King. He tells her she is not "worth the dust which the rude wind/ Blows" in her face. He calls Goneril and Regan "Tigers, not daughters," as he engages in a long diatribe concerning her degenerate and unnatural behavior. Ignoring his anger, she tells him his words are foolish, coming from a "Milk-liver'd man" who pities villains that are justifiably punished before they can do any harm. She tells him France is, at this very moment, ready to invade their military troops while he wastes his time moralizing. Unmoved by the news, Albany tells her she is a devil disguised as a woman, and he finds it difficult to keep from striking her.

A messenger enters with news of the death of the Duke of Cornwall. He informs them that the Duke has been killed by his own lifelong servant who opposed the act of plucking out Gloucester's eyes. He tells them that before the servant died, he wounded Cornwall who has since succumbed to the injuries he received. Overcome with empathy for Gloucester, Albany is promptly convinced that a higher power exists that has avenged Cornwall's crime.

In an aside, Goneril expresses ambivalence about Cornwall's death which would, on the one hand, give her complete power. Regan, being widowed, would, however, have free access to Edmund. The messenger continues the gruesome tale of the blinding of Gloucester. Albany, grateful for Gloucester's kind treatment of the King, calls for revenge.

***Analysis***

In reference to Goneril's cruel treatment of her father, Albany censures her for the nature in which she holds contempt for her origins. With the use of imagery representing a family tree, he chides Goneril for slivering and disbranching or, in other words, cutting herself off from "her material sap." He tells her that surely such a tree will wither and die. Referring to Lear as "A father, and a gracious aged man," he reminds her of the reverence she owes him. Albany is certain that if the heavens do not show their powers soon to vindicate the good and punish the evil in the kingdom, chaos will be the result.

> It will come
> Humanity must perforce prey on itself,
> Like monsters of the deep.

When daughter turns against father and no respect is shown for age or origins, we are left with Edmund's unnatural world where power is bought at any price, even the blinding of one's own father. Conversely, Albany is the proponent of an orderly respect between child and parent where kings are awarded the reverence that is their due. This is not only Albany speaking but Shakespeare as well. Compare the famous speech on degree in *Troilus and Cressida* (Act I, Scene 3).

> Take but degree away, untune that string
> And hark what discord follows,
> ...........................................................................
> And the rude son should strike his father dead,
> Force should be right, or rather, right and wrong
> (Between whose endless jar justice resides)
> Should lose their names, and so should justice too!
> Then everything include itself in power
> Power into will, will into appetite,
> And appetite, an universal wolf
> (So doubly seconded with will and power),
> Must make perforce an universal prey
> And last eat up himself.

Shakespeare's sixteenth-century audience understood the natural law of degree. Bestial humanity, only strong in its "vild offenses," could not long endure, for it would "prey on itself,/ Like monsters of the deep" and finally destroy itself. It is already happening with the death of Cornwall which Albany perceives as divine justice for his "nether crimes." When Regan is widowed, Goneril shows signs of jealousy over Edmund which will culminate in the sisters' murder and suicide in Act V.

We last saw Albany in Act I, Scene 4 when Goneril had just stripped the King of 50 of his knights. Albany, in that scene, demonstrated a rather mild-mannered position regarding Goneril's aggressive behavior toward the King. In view of Albany's image so far in the play, Oswald's words describing him as a "man so chang'd" seem entirely credible. In this scene, we see Albany as the new exponent of moral goodness who rails at Goneril for injustices done to her father. Ironically, Goneril, whose evil deeds have just been scrupulously exposed by Albany, still thinks of her husband as a "milk-liver'd man." Albany's forceful denunciation of the unnatural acts committed against Lear and Gloucester, and his determination to avenge the injustices done to them give us hope that their horrible fate will finally be reversed.

Goneril's attraction to Edmund is simply another link in the chain of events leading to her downfall. Edmund is a master of deceit and comes across as a cavalier in the service of his lady. "Yours in the ranks of death," he utters with grace and charm. Through Goneril he sees his opportunity to achieve the luxury and splendor of the political position as Earl of Gloucester that he has relished for so long.

***Study Questions***

1. Why does Goneril send Edmund away when they arrive at Albany's palace?
2. In what ways has Albany's disposition changed?
3. To what does Goneril attribute Albany's change?
4. What does Albany accuse Goneril of doing?
5. What news does Goneril bring to her husband, Albany?
6. In what way does Goneril compare Edmund with Albany?
7. How does Albany describe Goneril's personality?
8. What important news does a messenger bring to Goneril and Albany?
9. What is Goneril's reaction to Cornwall's death?
10. Why does Albany want revenge?

***Answers***

1. Goneril sends Edmund back to her sister because she does not think he would be welcomed by the changed Albany.

2. Albany smiles when told the French army has landed, he does not welcome his wife upon her arrival, and calls Oswald a "sot" for telling him of Gloucester's traitorous activities.
3. Goneril feels Albany is cowardly and, therefore, he wishes to avoid the recent events that have taken place in the kingdom.
4. Albany accuses Goneril of cruel treatment of her father, the King.
5. Goneril brings news of the impending invasion by France.
6. Goneril sees Edmund's manliness as superior to Albany's.
7. Albany describes Goneril as a devil disguised in a woman's body.
8. The messenger brings news of the Duke of Cornwall's death.
9. Goneril has mixed feelings about Cornwall's death. She delights in the power she has gained but is afraid that her sister might strike up a new relationship with Edmund.
10. Albany wishes to avenge the recent sufferings of Gloucester, who had his eyes gouged out.

***Suggested Essay Topics***

1. Albany invokes the heavens to vindicate the good and punish the evil. Write an essay discussing the possible results of Albany's prediction that "Humanity must perforce prey on itself." Explicate the passage, relating it to the views prevalent in Shakespeare's day. What was their view of an orderly society? What did Shakespeare's audience believe was the cause of chaos in society? Cite examples from the play to support your argument.
2. In this scene, Albany is not portrayed as the "milk-liver'd man" Goneril perceives him to be. Contrast his character in previous scenes to the changed Albany in this scene. How does his change lend hope for the future of the other characters in the play as a whole. Use examples from the play to support your answer.

## Act IV, Scene III (pages 84–85)

New Character:

**Gentleman:** *brings news to Kent of Cordelia and the King of France*

### *Summary*

This scene takes place in the French encampment near Dover. Explaining the reason for the King of France's sudden departure from the camp, a Gentleman tells Kent that the King was called back to France on urgent business that, in his absence, could prove dangerous to the state. He has left Monsieur La Far, his marshal, in charge while he is away. Kent inquires about the letters he has written to Cordelia concerning Goneril and Regan's cruel treatment of their father. The Gentleman explains that often a tear would trickle down her cheeks as she fought to control her passion while she was reading the letters. He describes her queenly dignity and patience, and the way she covered her tears with smiles. Musing about the contrast between Cordelia and her sisters, Kent wonders how one parent could produce such different offspring. He concludes it is "The stars above us, that govern our conditions."

Kent informs the Gentleman that Lear is in town, but, when in his right mind, has refused to speak to Cordelia out of guilt and shame for what he has done to her. Kent tells of the things that sting the King's mind. He has stripped Cordelia of his blessing, given her rights to her "dog-hearted" sisters, and turned her out to foreigners. His shame detains him from seeing her.

Kent then tells the Gentleman that Albany and Cornwall have raised an army, but he has already heard. Apprising the Gentleman of some secret business, Kent invites him to come with him to see the King to whom the Gentleman will attend until Kent returns.

### *Analysis*

In this scene, Cordelia stands in juxtaposition to Goneril, who in the previous scene, according to her husband, is "not worth the dust which the rude wind/ Blows" in her face. Cordelia, by contrast, is "queen/ Over her passion." This is reminiscent of the first scene in which Cordelia, by calmly telling her father that she loves him "according to my bond" refuses to resort to the flattery in which Goneril engages. We again meet Cordelia in the next scene, 20 scenes after her last appearance. The conversation between Kent and the Gentleman portrays Cordelia as Lear's ideal daughter.

The *First Folio*, published in 1620, does not include this scene. It was, perhaps, thought to be unessential for moving the action along. For the most part, the scene functions to inform. Expounding on the moral goodness of Cordelia, it signals her return to the play in the next scene. The Gentleman discloses the news of the return of the King of France called back to attend to urgent business. This scene also provides information about King Lear's condition and his feelings toward Cordelia since he has arrived in Dover.

In his effort to understand how Lear could have fathered the virtuous and loyal Cordelia and her self-seeking sisters as well, Kent attributes the mystery to the stars. His belief that the stars "govern our conditions" echoes that of Gloucester in Act I, Scene 2. Gloucester blames the "late eclipses of the sun and moon" for all the societal ills in the kingdom. Edmund scoffs at his father and all others who subscribe to the idea that the stars control our destiny. "I should have been that I am, had the maidenl'est star in the firmanent twinkled on my bastardizing." John F. Danby feels that Shakespeare's sympathy is with Edmund. "Edmund is the new man... Edmund is the last great expression in Shakespeare of that side of Renaissance individualism which has made a positive addition to the heritage of the West." Kent and Gloucester embrace the orthodox view which is already becoming old-fashioned in the sixteenth century. Perhaps this is why Edmund's view is more readily understood by people in our modern society.

The Gentleman's description of Cordelia presents an image of the conflicting feelings of simultaneous smiles and tears. Pearls become a metaphor for her tears and diamonds represent her eyes. She is always the literal and symbolic "queen over her passions." The Gentleman, explaining to Kent how "she shook/ The holy water from her heavenly eyes," metaphorically, capitalizes on the effects of alliteration as he draws his divine image of her. In his poetic description of Cordelia, he has made his point. Cordelia represents the "better way" in her love and grief for her lonely and dejected father, the King.

***Study Questions***

1. Where has the King of France gone?
2. What letters does Kent ask the Gentleman about?
3. What is Cordelia's reaction to Kent's letters about her father?
4. What reason does Kent give for the differences in Lear's daughters?
5. Why does Lear refuse to see his daughter Cordelia?
6. Who will watch over the King in Kent's absence?
7. Is Kent aware that Cornwall has died?
8. What does the "holy water" represent in this scene?
9. Who are the "dog-hearted daughters" whom Kent refers to?
10. Where is Lear in this scene?

***Answers***

1. The King of France has gone back to France to take care of business that could, in his absence, prove dangerous to the state.
2. Kent asks the Gentleman about the letters written to Cordelia containing news of her father's suffering.
3. Cordelia reacts with sorrow and love for her father.
4. Kent thinks the answer is given in the stars that "govern our conditions."
5. Lear is filled with guilt and shame for what he has done to her, and, therefore, refuses to see her.
6. The Gentleman will watch Lear while Kent is gone.

7. Kent speaks of Albany and Cornwall's powers so we can assume he thinks Cornwall is still alive.
8. The "holy water" is a metaphor for Cordelia's tears.
9. The "dog-hearted daughters" are Goneril and Regan.
10. Lear has been taken to Dover where he will be safe from his older daughters.

***Suggested Essay Topics***

1. Cordelia is portrayed as a vision of queenly goodness. Write an essay characterizing her in relation to her sister Goneril. Compare the sisters' attitudes toward their father. Why do you think Cordelia has forgiven her father for banishing her? Use examples from the play to support your opinion.
2. King Lear refuses to communicate with Cordelia in this scene. Write an essay explaining the reasons for his attitude. Is the King still angry at Cordelia for refusing to please him with flattering words of love in the first scene of the play? Has he had a change of heart? Explain your answer.

## Act IV, Scene IV (pages 86–87)

New Characters:

**Doctor:** *Cordelia's physician brought to heal the mad King*

**Messenger:** *brings news of England's armed troops*

***Summary***

In the French camp, Cordelia speaks of her mad father who has been seen wandering around in the fields, wearing the weeds that grow among the corn as a crown on his head. She orders the officer to scour every acre of the fields until they find him. She then asks the doctor whether medical knowledge can do anything to heal the King's mind. The doctor assures her that rest, brought about with the aid of medicinal herbs that grow in the countryside, will be an effective treatment to cure the King's madness. Cordelia calls upon the rare healing herbs of the earth to grow as they are watered by her tears. Afraid the King may die, she feels an urgency in her request.

A messenger enters, telling Cordelia that the British powers will soon invade the French army. Cordelia has officially taken command of the French troops in the absence of her husband. She wants it understood, however, that it is not her own ambition for power that moves her army to fight. She declares that her motive is solely to defend her father's rights so unjustly taken over by Goneril and Regan.

***Analysis***

After Lear falls asleep in the shelter during the storm, we do not hear from him again for almost 500 lines. His next appearance will be in the countryside near Dover where he meets the blind Gloucester who is led by Edgar. In this scene, Cordelia prepares us for his reappearance by describing his condition, which has steadily declined into madness. Singing loudly, Lear wears a crown made of weeds and flowers that grow in the cultivated fields. The gruesome picture Cordelia paints is a far cry from the image of the King in royal robes that she remembers. In view of this contrast, it is no wonder that she is moved to tears.

The "idle weeds" that the King has shaped into a crown for his head is, ironically, an incongruous symbol of his kingship. Hemlock, immediately associated with Socrates' death, is a poisonous plant with a disagreeable odor, and nettle is an herb with stinging bristles. Cordelia's aversion to this pathetic image of her father promptly leads her to send out an officer to search for him.

Cordelia does not accept the King's fortune as one that is governed by the stars as Kent and Gloucester would, nor does she invoke the gods to free her father of evil spirits. In her grief, she turns to the doctor to heal the King. Stephen Greenblatt has noted that "Lear's madness has no supernatural origin; it is linked, as in Harsnett, to... exposure to the elements, and extreme anguish, and its cure comes at the hands not of an exorcist but of a doctor" (Shakespeare and the Exorcists, 1988, p. 282). Greenblatt attributes this idea to Shakespeare's source, Harsnett's *Declaration of Egregious Popish Impostures* (1603). The doctor prescribes only sedated rest, brought about by medicinal herbs.

Our foster-nurse of nature is repose,
The which he lacks; that to provoke in him
Are many simples operative, whose power
Will close the eye of anguish.

Symbolically, Cordelia's tears are called upon to water the rare herbs that will aid the King in his "repose." If rest is, indeed, the cure for her father's illness, her tears, symbolic of her love, will be a remedy for his distress, allowing him to rest peacefully.

France's invasion of Britain is sanctioned by Cordelia as an act of pity for her father, the King. It is his business that she is transacting. In view of Cordelia's self-assured integrity, there can be no doubt that she is fighting to protect her "ag'd father's right."

***Study Questions***

1. As Cordelia enters, what has she heard regarding the King?
2. What does Cordelia instruct her officer to do?
3. Who does Cordelia depend on to heal her ailing father?
4. What will the doctor use in his treatment of the King?
5. What kind of treatment does the doctor prescribe?
6. In what way will Cordelia's tears aid the King's treatment?
7. Why is Cordelia anxious to find her father very soon?
8. Why does Cordelia's army invade Britain?
9. What is this scene's main function?
10. What was the King wearing when Cordelia last saw him?

***Answers***

1. Cordelia has heard that the King is singing loudly and wears a crown of weeds on his head.
2. Cordelia instructs her officer to search for the King until he finds him.
3. Cordelia depends on the Doctor to heal her father.
4. The Doctor will use medicinal herbs to treat the King.
5. The Doctor prescribes sedated rest for the King.

6. Cordelia's tears will water the rare herbs that will remediate her father's distress.
7. She is afraid he will die if he goes on much longer.
8. Cordelia says the French army is there to defend her "ag'd father's right."
9. This scene functions to give us background on the King's condition before he reappears.
10. The King was dressed in his royal regalia when Cordelia was banished in Act I.

***Suggested Essay Topics***

1. Cordelia does not invoke the gods nor call on the stars to relieve the King's distress. Write an essay contrasting her view to that of Kent and Gloucester in previous scenes. Does she feel the stars "govern our conditions?" Who does she call on for help in curing her father? Cite examples from the play to support your view.
2. Cordelia justifies France's invasion of Britain as an act of love toward her father. Write an essay explaining her attempt to justify the invasion. Is it right for her to invade her homeland? How would Shakespeare's audience have felt about it? Use examples from the play to support your answer.

## Act IV, Scene V (pages 87–88)

***Summary***

Back in Gloucester's castle, Oswald informs Regan that Albany, after much fretting ("much ado"), has reluctantly agreed to raise an army against France. He adds that Goneril is a better soldier than her husband, Albany. Oswald has come to deliver Goneril's letter to Edmund. Referring to him as "Lord Edmund," Regan questions the contents of the letter, but Oswald claims he does not know. Expressing regret about letting the blinded Gloucester live, Regan is sure that sympathy for the old man will turn people against them. She thinks Edmund is on a mission to murder his father and, thereby, strengthen their cause.

Oswald is determined to find Edmund, but Regan urges him to go with the troops the next day since the way is dangerous. Oswald apprises her of his duty to his mistress, Goneril. Suspicious of her sister, Regan questions her secrecy, wondering why she is not sending her message by word-of-mouth instead of by a letter. Promising to make it worth his while, she asks Oswald's permission to unseal the letter. Oswald protests, but Regan tells him that she has observed her sister approach Edmund with amorous looks, and she knows Oswald is in Goneril's confidence. Oswald feigns innocence, but Regan confidently reaffirms her belief that he knows the truth. She tells him that she and Edmund have already agreed that she would be a more convenient wife for him than Goneril since she is now a widow. She promises a reward if Oswald will find Edmund and present him with a token from her. She tells Oswald to warn her sister about their conversation concerning Edmund. Promising Oswald a promotion, she asks him to find the blind Gloucester and kill him. He agrees to do what she asks and, in this way, prove what political party he favors.

***Analysis***

Only a few scenes earlier, Albany predicts what will happen if Regan and Goneril's "vile offenses" are not tamed (Act IV, Scene 2). His prophetic words have come to fruition in this scene where evil is beginning to "prey on itself." In their sinister attempts to satisfy their appetites for power, the sisters have worked well together. They have turned their father out in the storm, stripping him of all dignity and title, and have blinded Gloucester, who stood by the King in his time of need. But now we finally see the evil results of their licentious behavior turn in on themselves. Goneril has already apprised us of her fear of Regan's competition for Edmund's attentions at the time of Cornwall's death. Now Regan makes it clear that, as a widow, she is the logical woman for Edmund's hand in marriage. Edmund is an opportunist who cares for neither of the sisters, but sees them as a means toward his own ends.

Kent, in an earlier scene, has already expressed his opinion of Oswald and has been thrown in the stocks for it. Oswald had, in that case, only done the will of his mistress Goneril who instructed him to be rude to the King. In this scene, we again see Oswald obeying Goneril's commands. Even Regan's bribery does not tempt him to let her unseal Goneril's letter to Edmund. His stoicism in denying any knowledge of Goneril's relationship to Edmund is also reminiscent of his denial in Act II, Scene 2 where he pretends to be a complete stranger to Kent. As a result, Kent abhors him because he "wears no honesty." Oswald is, nevertheless, faithful to the shrewd and manipulative Goneril. Perhaps his loyalty to her is his only redeeming quality, though he is, in fact, loyal to an evil cause.

Goneril, Regan, and Edmund have all aimed their vicious cruelty at their own fathers, making their wickedness seem more atrocious than that of the other evil characters in the play. Regan speaks of Edmund, who has gone out to kill his father as if it is a trifling matter. It is the expedient thing to do in order to assuage "The strength of the enemy." Evil deeds have become second nature to Regan, who stops at nothing to get what she wants. The outcome of the sisters' rivalry over Edmund remains to be seen.

***Study Questions***

1. Has Albany raised an army to fight France?
2. Who is a better soldier than Albany? Why?
3. What does Regan think Edmund has set out to do?
4. Why does Regan want Gloucester out of the way?
5. Who sent Oswald with a letter for Edmund?
6. Why does Regan want to read Goneril's letter to Edmund?
7. Does Oswald know what the letter contains?
8. According to Regan, what are the obvious signs of Goneril's love for Edmund?
9. What does Regan ask Oswald to do to Gloucester?
10. How does Oswald feel about his instructions to kill Gloucester?

***Answers***

1. Albany has raised an army, but only with much persuasion.
2. Goneril, Albany's wife, is a better soldier than he because she has ambition for her own power.
3. Regan thinks Edmund plans to murder his father.
4. Regan wants Gloucester killed because sympathy for his blindness will turn people against her.
5. Goneril sent Oswald with a letter for Edmund.
6. Regan wants to read Goneril's letter because she sees her sister as her rival for Edmund's attentions.
7. Oswald probably does not know the contents of the letter.
8. Goneril has been gazing amorously at Edmund.
9. Regan wants Gloucester to be killed.
10. Oswald will do anything as long as he can get a promotion for doing it.

***Suggested Essay Topics***

1. Regan and Goneril have become involved in a bitter rivalry for Edmund's love. Write an essay explaining the way in which this rivalry is indicative of the evil characters preying on each other. What do you think this rivalry will eventually do to them? Cite examples from the play to support your view.
2. Oswald remains stoic in his encounter with Regan in this scene. Write an essay comparing Oswald in this scene to Oswald in Act II, Scene 2 where he claims to be a stranger to Kent. In what way does his attitude stay the same in both scenes? Why do you think he is considered an evil character in the play? To support your argument, use examples from the play.

## Act IV, Scene VI (pages 89–98)

***Summary***

Edgar, dressed as a peasant, is supposedly leading the blind Gloucester to the precipice near Dover where the Duke plans to end his life. In an effort to dissuade him, Edgar tries to mislead his father by telling him they are nearing the steep cliff. Though they are on flat ground, Edgar talks of the sounds of the roaring sea and the ascent of the rising terrain that is leading them to the hill. Gloucester insists the ground is even, but Edgar replies that losing his sight must have affected his other senses.

His father perceives a change in Edgar's improved speech, but Edgar flatly denies it. When they arrive at "the place," Edgar gives a lengthy description of the view below with its people who appear dwarfed from such dizzying heights. Gloucester hands Edgar a purse with a valuable jewel and bids him farewell. In an aside, Edgar explains that his motive for his actions is to cure his father's despair. Before he jumps, Gloucester prays to the "mighty gods" and renounces the world whose afflictions he can no longer bear. He blesses Edgar if he is still alive and then falls to the ground. Edgar then calls out to Gloucester, but he tells him to leave him alone and let him die. Pretending to be a passing bystander who has observed him from the bottom of the precipice, Edgar tells Gloucester his life is a miracle since he has survived a dangerous fall from the high, chalky cliff. Edgar lifts the disappointed Duke to his feet, and asks him about the fiend he had seen with him on top of the hill. Confused, Gloucester replies that he had taken him for a man. Edgar reminds his father that the gods, who deserve our reverence, have miraculously saved his life.

Lear enters, wearing a crown of weeds and flowers on his head and mumbling incoherently. Edgar is stunned at the sight of the mad Lear, and Gloucester promptly recognizes the King's voice. Lear, in his madness, identifies Gloucester as "Goneril with a white beard." Gloucester insists it must be the King. Lear replies, "Ay, every inch a king" and continues a long tirade defending adultery and denouncing cold, chaste women who feign virtue but are Centaurs from the waist down.

Asking Lear whether he recognizes him, the blind Gloucester laments that Lear, in his condition, is a "ruin'd piece of nature." Referring to him as blind Cupid, Lear asks Gloucester how he sees the world without eyes, and he replies that he sees "it feelingly." Lear reasons that he must look with his ears since he is left without eyes. The King again engages in a long diatribe, railing against the official who administers punishment by whipping the whore when he, in fact, should be whipped for using her in that way. He adds that "Robes and furr'd gowns hide all," as sin is plated with gold, while those wearing rags are quickly brought to justice. Edgar observes that Lear's talk reflects "Reason in madness." Finally calling Gloucester by name, Lear preaches him a sermon on birth when all come to "this great stage of fools."

A Gentleman enters who has been sent by Cordelia to rescue the King and bring him back to her, but the mad Lear runs away from them, challenging them to come after him. The Gentleman informs Edgar that any hour now, Albany's army will be advancing toward the French at Dover.

Gloucester's tone has changed as he calls on the "ever-gentle gods" to keep the evil spirit from tempting him to take his own life. With pity for Gloucester, Edgar takes him by the hand, leading him to a shelter. As Oswald enters, he promptly claims the blind Gloucester as his "prize" that will increase his good fortune. He draws his sword on Gloucester, but Edgar politely interrupts, asking Oswald to let them pass. Oswald challenges the audacity of a poor slave who would defend a traitor. Edgar slays him, and, as he is dying, Oswald requests that Edmund receive the letter he was sent to deliver to him. Edgar reads Goneril's letter to Edmund in which she asks him to murder her husband, Albany, in order to win her hand in marriage. Drums are heard in the distance as Edgar leads his father to lodge with a friend.

***Analysis***

The subplot and the main plot have been staged in contrapuntal fashion throughout the play so far. Both remaining faithful to their fathers, Edgar, in the subplot, is Cordelia's counterpart in the main plot. Lear's wicked daughters, Goneril and Regan, correspond to Gloucester's evil son, Edmund. Thematically, both plots have dealt with parent-child relationships. In this scene, the two plots are merged in the actions of Lear, Gloucester, and Edgar. The anguish that each father has suffered at the hands of his children, though it is different, runs parallel to the other. Gloucester suffers physical agony while Lear suffers mental torment.

Gloucester's absurd attempt at suicide has set the scene for Lear's equally preposterous image as he enters, bedecked with a crown of weeds and flowers, declaring he is the "King himself." An incongruous and humorous figure for a king, to be sure, but at this point we can only feel pity. Equally incongruous is the image of the blind Gloucester who has been rendered powerless even to accomplish his own suicide. "Is wretchedness depriv'd that benefit,/ To end itself by death?" His ludicrous actions as he falls on the flat ground prepare us for the comic madness of Lear. We are not, however, moved to laughter but only compassion and tears.

It is Edgar who observes that Lear reaches "Reason in madness." Lear reasons that even "a dog's obey'd in office." He has learned profound truths through his suffering. "Robes and furr'd gowns hide all. (Plate sin) with gold," but if that same sin is found on one wearing rags, he will be quickly punished by the law. He has learned the difference between appearance and reality. Ironically, Gloucester must lose his sight before he learns to see. Regarding Edmund's betrayal and Edgar's loyalty, Gloucester himself has already declared previously that "I stumbled when I saw" (Act IV, Scene 1). When Lear wonders how Gloucester can see the way the world goes, he replies, "I see it feelingly." Gloucester has learned to "feel" both literally and emotionally, but Lear adds another dimension. He advises Gloucester to "Look with thine ears." If he listens, Lear says, he will find it difficult to distinguish the "justice" from the "thief."

Lear complains that his daughters "flatter'd me like a dog... To say 'ay' and 'no' to everything that I said! 'Ay' and 'no' too, was no good divinity." In these lines, Shakespeare alludes to the Biblical passage regarding advice against the swearing of oaths. It is found in James 5:12. "... but let your yea be yea; and your nay, nay; lest ye fall into condemnation." Lear now understands the mortality even of the king. He knows he is not "ague proof" as his daughters had led him to believe.

In his short sermon to Gloucester, Lear describes life as a "great stage of fools." When we are born, he says, we come into the world crying. Stanley Cavell notes that "Lear is there feeling like a child, after the rebirth of his senses...and feeling that the world is an unnatural habitat for man" (Stanley Cavell, "The Avoidance of Love: A Reading of King Lear" 1987, p. 250). Lear had been unaware of injustice and the plight of the poor, however, while he was still the King. He is now being forced into a new level of human sensibility, and he cries out in protest like a newborn baby.

Edgar's disguises change throughout the play as he slowly progresses closer to his own true identity. Tom o' Bedlam serves his purpose as long as he is escaping from his father's wrath. After Gloucester's sight is gone, Edgar leads him to Dover as Poor Tom, fully clothed but still haunted by fiends. It is not until the fiends are gone, and he emerges as a peasant with altered speech that he calls Gloucester "father" for the first time since he fled his castle. Though unrecognized by Gloucester, Edgar refers to him as "father" four times in this scene. It is not until the end of the play, however, that he makes his true identity known to his father.

Lear's speech, in which he denounces women who pretend to be chaste and virtuous but are actually fiends, is reminiscent of his reference to Regan's dead mother in an earlier passage. Regan has just told the King she is glad to see him.

> If thou shouldst not be glad,
> I would divorce me from thy mother's tomb,
> Sepulchring an adultress
>
> (p. 47)

The implication is clear. If Regan, too, would turn him away as Goneril has just done, Lear would think they were not his natural daughters.

Kent has, in an earlier scene, denounced Oswald, calling him a coward and declaring that "a tailor made thee." An opportunist, Oswald sees the blind Gloucester only as a "proclaim'd prize" with a price on his head. Oswald is insulted by the advances of Edgar, a lowly peasant who would dare to protect a villainous traitor. He remains true to his mistress, Goneril, to his dying moment, however, requesting that Edgar deliver her letter to Edmund.

Oswald is nothing but a "serviceable villain" who does his duty, carrying out the vices of his mistress without question. He has, in this case, entrusted the letter to an enemy. In his rigid attempt at being a dutiful steward, he has inadvertently divulged the contents of the letter to Edgar. Ironically, Goneril and Edmund's secret love affair and their plot to murder Albany has been exposed because of Oswald's strict adherence to duty.

***Study Questions***

1. How is Edgar dressed in this scene?
2. Where is Gloucester standing when Edgar tells him he is at the edge of the cliff?
3. Who does Gloucester think has saved him when he supposedly jumped off the cliff?
4. What does Edgar call Gloucester after he has jumped?
5. How does Gloucester say that he can see without eyes?
6. What is the "great stage of fools"?
7. Who is Oswald's "proclaimed prize"?
8. Who kills Oswald to protect Gloucester?
9. What are Goneril and Edmund plotting against Albany?
10. What is the Gentleman's news to Edgar about the war with France?

***Answers***

1. Edgar is dressed as a peasant in this scene.
2. Gloucester is standing on flat ground far from the roaring sea.
3. Gloucester thinks that the gods have saved his life.
4. Edgar calls Gloucester father for the first time since his escape from Gloucester's castle when he fled for his life.
5. Gloucester says that he sees "feelingly."
6. The "great stage of fools" is the world that all of us come to when we are born.

7. Oswald sees the blind Gloucester as a prize since Regan has put a price on his head.
8. Edgar kills Oswald to protect Gloucester from being killed.
9. Goneril and Edmund are plotting Albany's death.
10. The Gentleman tells Edgar that Albany's army will arrive to fight the French.

***Suggested Essay Topics***

1. Through Lear, Shakespeare espouses the theme of appearance versus reality. Analyze Lear's words, "Robes and furr'd gowns hide all" and explain how this entire passage supports the theme. How does the "great image of authority" apply to this theme? Support your opinion with examples from the play.
2. Lear says that we are born into "this great stage of fools." Write an essay explaining the symbolism of these words. What does the cry of the newborn baby represent in this passage? How does it explain Lear's rebirth? Use examples from the play to support your view.

## Act IV, Scene VII (pages 99–102)

***Summary***

Kent has divulged his true identity to Cordelia though he is still dressed as Caius. With heartfelt gratitude, Cordelia tells Kent she will not live long enough to adequately repay him for what he has done for her father, the King. Kent assures her that acknowledgment of his services is, in fact, an overpayment. She asks him to change his attire so they can put behind them all reminders of the "worser hours" he has spent with the King on the heath. But Kent tells her he is not ready to reveal his identity yet. To do so would cut his purpose short. She promptly concedes, turning to the doctor to inquire about the King. He tells her the King is still asleep. Calling upon the "kind gods," she asks them to cure the "great breach" in his nature and tune up the discord in his life brought about by his children.

The doctor then asks permission to awaken the King, and Cordelia leaves it up to his better judgment. She is assured by the Gentleman that they have dressed her father in fresh garments. Certain that the King will maintain his self-control, the doctor asks Cordelia to stay nearby when her father awakes. Lear is brought in on a chair carried by servants as soft music plays in the background. Cordelia kisses her father with the hope of repairing the harm done to the King by her sisters. With compassion, she gazes at his face, reflecting on the suffering forced upon him in the storm. She agonizes over his necessity of finding shelter with the swine and lowly rogues.

When the King stirs, Cordelia is the first to speak with him. Thinking he has died, Lear sees her as a "soul in bliss." He imagines being bound to a "wheel of fire," however. Cordelia asks him whether he knows her and he replies that she is a spirit.

Confused, he does not know where he is now, nor where he spent the night. Cordelia asks him for his benediction, but he kneels to her instead. Realizing he is not in his "perfect mind," he begs them not to mock him. Cordelia is overcome with joy when he finally recognizes her as his child. He acknowledges the fact that she does not love him, adding that she has some cause, but her sisters have none. In a forgiving spirit, Cordelia declares she has "no cause." Questioning his whereabouts, Lear asks whether he is in France and is told he is in his own country. Observing that the "great rage is kill'd" in the King, the doctor suggests that he be left alone to avoid the danger of too much exertion.

After the King and his party leave, Kent informs the Gentleman that Cornwall has been slain, and Edmund has stepped in to take his place as the leader of his people. Unaware that he is speaking to the disguised Kent, the Gentleman apprises him of the latest news of Edgar and Kent who are rumored to be in Germany together. Left alone, Kent decides that the upcoming battle will determine his fate.



***Analysis***

When Lear awakens from his drugged sleep, "the great rage" has died in him, and he enters a world of awareness and insight he has never experienced before. Confused at first, his mind revives the mental sensibility of the suffering mad King. But he soon recognizes his "child Cordelia" and calls her by name. He has gained knowledge through his suffering and admits he is a "very foolish fond old man." There is no longer any need for hypocritical expressions of love from Cordelia as there had been when they last met in the first scene of the play. Through suffering, Lear has cast off that illusory world. L. C. Knights sees the action in this scene as "a moment of truth... the painful knowledge that has been won will reject anything that swerves a hair's breadth from absolute integrity" (L. C. Knights, *Shakespearean Themes*, 1960, p. 115). This truth has been arrived at through Lear's new capacity to feel. Like Gloucester, he now sees the world "feelingly." When he first sees Cordelia, he no longer makes demands on her.

> I know you do not love me, for your sisters
> Have (as I do remember) done me wrong:
> You have some cause, they have not.

Cordelia promptly responds to his unselfish sentiment with "No cause, no cause."

Thinking he has come out of the grave, Lear immediately recognizes Cordelia as "a soul in bliss." He remains hopelessly bound to a "wheel of fire," however. It seems quite clear that the soul that is in bliss would represent one who has gone to his eternal reward, but much controversy has centered around Lear's "wheel of fire," an image of hell. If Lear imagines himself in hell, there would be no souls in bliss. Mary Lascelles points out that Shakespeare uses this image to show that Lear is convinced that what he has done separates him from Cordelia forever (Mary Lascelles, "King Lear and Doomsday," p. 64). Lascelles continues by showing the torture of the wheel as the punishment of pride. This is accomplished through the account of the pains of hell as shown in the Biblical parable of the rich man and Lazarus. In any case, we can assume that the contrasting heaven/hell image puts Lear on a different level than Cordelia. He has been bound to the wheel of pride while she is free of the deceptive, illusory world so characteristic of not only Lear but of Goneril and Regan as well.

Kent's loyalty to the King does not go unnoticed by Cordelia. Her acknowledgment of his services to her father, though important, is not his chief motive for his fidelity. Kent belongs to the generation that reveres not only King Lear but the very office of the king. He serves his master because he believes in the King's authority. When that authority is challenged, as it was by Oswald in an earlier scene (p. 20), Kent is moved to violent wrath. Oswald, whom Kent abhors, calls him a "grey beard." Kent is no longer a young man, and he realizes it at the end of this scene when he considers that his labors for the King are coming to an end.

> My point and period will be thoroughly wrought,
> Or well or ill, as this day's battle's fought.

Even if he survives and the powers of good are victorious, he is cognizant of the possibility that this will be his last battle.

***Study Questions***

1. Why does Kent prefer not to reveal his true identity to anyone except Cordelia?
2. In what way has the King's attire been changed?
3. Why is the King able to sleep so well?
4. How long has it been since Cordelia has seen her father?
5. When Lear awakens, where does he think he has been?
6. Is Lear angry at Cordelia in this scene?
7. How does Cordelia feel when her father finally recognizes her as his daughter?
8. Why does the doctor want Cordelia and the others to leave the King alone after they have spoken with him for a while?
9. What news does the Gentleman tell the disguised Kent about Edgar and Kent?
10. Who has taken the former Duke of Cornwall's place as the leader of the people?

***Answers***

1. Kent is not ready to reveal his identity because at this point in the play his purpose for the disguise has not been completely fulfilled.
2. The King's clothes have been changed from the ragged attire that he wore in the storm to "fresh garments."
3. The King has been given a drug to help him sleep.
4. Cordelia has not seen her father since she was banished in the first scene of the play.
5. Lear thinks he has been taken him out of the grave.
6. Lear is not angry at Cordelia but tells her she has cause to hate him.
7. Cordelia is overjoyed when her father identifies her as his daughter.
8. The doctor does not want to risk the overexertion of the King.
9. Ironically, the Gentleman tells the disguised Kent that Edgar and Kent are rumored to be residing in Germany.
10. Edmund has taken Cornwall's place after his death.

***Suggested Essay Topics***

1. Through suffering, King Lear has gained knowledge and insights he did not have before. Write an essay in which you discuss those insights in relation to Cordelia, his daughter. What do Lear's feelings have to do with his new perception of reality? What has happened to his illusory world regarding his role as the king? Cite examples from the play to support your answer.
2. Lear sees himself bound to the "wheel of fire" as he views Cordelia as a "soul in bliss." Write an essay explaining the validity of this incongruous image. How does the image symbolize Lear's condition in life? What is meant by Cordelia's bliss? Give examples from the play to support your opinion.

# SECTION SIX

# Act V

## Act V, Scenes I and II (pages 103–106)

### *Summary*

Among the regalia of drum and colors, Regan and Edmund, accompanied by their soldiers, enter the British camp near Dover. Edmund shows concern regarding Albany's absence. He wonders whether Albany has made a firm decision to fight the French in view of their support of King Lear. Regan is sure Albany has met with some misfortune and Edmund agrees. Jealous of her sister, Regan begins to question Edmund about his relationship with her. Edmund swears that he holds only an "honor'd love" for her and that he has never enjoyed her sexual favors. He assures Regan she need not fear that he will become too "familiar" with Goneril.

Albany and Goneril enter with drum, color, and soldiers. At first sight of Regan and Edmund, Goneril, in an aside, declares that she would go as far as to lose the battle rather than relinquish Edmund to her sister. Albany greets Regan and Edmund formally and politely. He informs them that in view of the fact that the King has many followers who have defected to France because of the cruelties suffered under the new rule, the honorable thing to do would be to fight only the imposing army of France. His quarrel is not with the King and his followers. Edmund commends his statement as nobly spoken, and Goneril agrees that domestic strife is "not the question here."

Albany then invites Edmund to join him and his most

experienced soldiers in his tent to determine the proceedings of the battle. To prevent her sister from spending time alone with Edmund, Regan insists that she go with her. Just as the entire party leaves, Edgar enters with an urgent letter for Albany. Insisting that Albany read it before he goes into battle, Edgar promptly leaves though Albany coaxes him to stay until he has read the letter.

Left alone, Edmund ponders over his dilemma. He has "sworn his love" to both the sisters and agonizes over which one to "enjoy" without offending the other. He reasons that he cannot take Goneril as long as her husband is alive and finally concludes that he will use Albany for the battle and then allow Goneril to devise a method of getting rid of him. With Albany out of the way, Edmund will be in power, and he decides he will never grant mercy to Lear and Cordelia as Albany intends to do.

In Scene 2, the alarm sounds as Cordelia and the King, marching with drum and colors, accompany the French army across the field between the French and English camps. Edgar leads Gloucester to the shade of a nearby tree where he will be comfortable until Edgar returns. He prays that the "right may thrive," and leaves his father with a blessing. Soon after Edgar leaves, the alarum sounds within and Edgar rushes to his father's rescue, informing him that King Lear has lost the battle, and Cordelia has been captured. Taking him by the hand, he urges Gloucester to flee from danger. Gloucester balks at Edgar's demands, insisting that he wishes to go no further but would rather die in the field. Edgar reminds him that he must continue to endure but be ready for death when it finally comes. Gloucester agrees that this is true.

### *Analysis*

As the scene opens, we are aware of the Duke of Albany's dilemma in fighting Cordelia's army. He is "full of alteration and self-reproving." His decision has become even more crucial after the death of the Duke of Cornwall, for now he is the top official in charge of the state. On the one hand, he does not wish to fight the King and his supporters, but, on the other hand, he must prove his loyalty to Britain. Shakespeare's audience would not have tolerated Britain's defeat at the hands of the French even though it would be in the best interests of the King and Cordelia. To resolve his dilemma, Albany justifies his actions against the King by rationalizing it as a separate issue. "For this business,/ It touches us as France invades our land,/ Not bolds the King." Goneril is quick to agree that "these domestic and particular broils/ Are not the question here." He goes into battle with confidence that his cause is just, and he fully expects to grant mercy to Lear and Cordelia if the French are defeated.

When Edmund acknowledges the fact that "To both these sisters have I sworn my love" and yet "Neither can be enjoy'd/ If both remain alive," we can readily see love corrupted to mere lust. Cloaking his deceit in the language of respectability, Edmund speaks to Regan with phrases like "honor'd love" and "by mine honor, madam." Always the opportunist, Edmund realizes that whether he marries Goneril or Regan, he will be the victor. Unwilling to take chances, he pledges his love to both and, in this way, assures his future. He is content to use them to further his own ambition. Goneril is, perhaps, the better choice since she is already plotting her husband's murder. "Let her who would be rid of him devise/ His speedy taking off." With Albany out of the way, Edmund can reach his ultimate goal. Unknown to Edmund, however, Edgar exposes the murder plot by delivering Goneril's letter, intended for Edmund, into Albany's hands. The letter has been found by Edgar on Oswald's dead body, and its repercussions remain to be seen.

In Scene 2, Edgar's reproof of Gloucester's unwillingness to continue in the face of further adversity demonstrates a central idea prevalent in the seventeenth-century Jacobean period. When Gloucester wishes to die, Edgar admonishes him for his thoughts.

> Men must endure
> Their going hence even as their coming hither,
> Ripeness is all.

In these words, Edgar espouses the belief that one should maintain a stoical acceptance of the turn of fortune or loss of reputation characterized by an unflinching endurance in the face of pain. It is essentially a pagan philosophy that Gloucester himself expresses earlier in the play. "As flies to wanton boys are we to the gods,/ They kill us for their sport" (p. 78). There is a lack of justice in this fatalistic view where even the gods offer no comfort in the face of suffering. Of prime importance is the fact that one must accept whatever comes, be that death or suffering, stoically and with no hope of reward. To accept the will of the gods is the one virtue. Edgar taught Gloucester earlier that he must endure and that suicide is opposed to "ripeness." Gloucester has been duped into thinking the ever-gentle gods have saved his life, and he later prays to the gods that he will not be tempted again to "die before you please" (p. 96).

Edgar carefully situates Gloucester safely in the shadow of a tree. There is no doubt about his anxiety concerning his father's safety as he urges him to come away with him after the battle has been lost. Edgar's diligent attendance upon his father is constant and loyal after he has been cruelly blinded by Cornwall. But Edgar repeatedly chooses not to reveal himself to Gloucester as his son. In Act IV, Scene 1, he seems to have reached the perfect opportunity to drop his disguise in response to his father's lament, "O dear son Edgar... Might I but live to see thee in my touch,/ I'd say I had eyes again." Gloucester has just had his eyes plucked out, but Edgar remains cruelly silent. It is not until the last act of the play that he reveals his true identity, but it is too late. Too weak to bear the news, Gloucester dies. It is only then that Edgar finally confesses his error. "Never (O fault!) reveal'd myself unto him." To the very end, Edgar is not sure whether his father will actually give him his blessing.

***Study Questions***

1. Why is Albany concerned about the battle with France?
2. How does Albany finally resolve his dilemma about fighting the French?
3. To which sister has Edmund sworn his love?
4. Who joins Albany in the tent to talk about the upcoming battle with France?

5. Who delivers Goneril's letter to Albany?
6. What information does the letter contain?
7. Why is Goneril the better choice of mate for Edmund?
8. How does Edmund plan to treat Lear and Cordelia if Britain wins the battle with France?
9. Where does Edgar place his father during the battle?
10. What does Edgar tell his father when he does not want to flee to safety after the battle?

***Answers***

1. Albany is concerned about fighting his own father-in-law, the King.
2. Albany decides that the war with France is a separate issue from the domestic quarrels with Lear and Cordelia.
3. Edmund has sworn his love to both Goneril and Regan.
4. Edmund and the oldest and most experienced officers join Albany in his tent.
5. Edgar delivers Goneril's letter to Albany.
6. The letter, intended for Edmund, contains a plot to kill Goneril's husband, Albany.
7. Goneril plans to kill Albany, which would put Edmund in the top position in the kingdom if he married Goneril.
8. Edmund plans to show no mercy to Lear and Cordelia.
9. Edgar places his blind father safely in the shadow of a tree.
10. Edgar tells him that "Men must endure."

***Suggested Essay Topics***

1. Edgar states that he has sworn his love to both Goneril and Regan. Write an essay explaining Edmund's motive for his actions concerning the two sisters. Why does Edmund decide to choose Goneril in spite of the fact that Regan is a widow and free to marry? What does Edmund hope to gain

from his relationship with Goneril? Give examples from the play to support your view.

2. Albany faces a serious dilemma in Act V, Scene 1. Write an essay explaining Albany's resolution to his conflict. How does he justify fighting against the King with whom he has no quarrel? What will he do with the King and Cordelia if Britain wins the battle? Cite examples from the play to support your opinion.

## Act V, Scene III (pages 107–118)

### *Summary*

In military triumph over France, Edmund enters with Lear and Cordelia whom he has taken captive. Cordelia assures the King that they are not the first who have lost their fortunes in spite of good intentions. Her concern is for her father, but he is perfectly content to be confined with Cordelia "like birds i' th' cage." Edmund then instructs his soldiers to take them away to prison where they will be kept until they can be arraigned. He slips the captain a private note, promising him an advancement if he carries out the devious scheme he has outlined for him. The captain quickly agrees to the scheme.

Albany enters with Goneril, Regan, and their soldiers. Formally commending Edmund for his valiant efforts in battle, Albany promptly demands to see the captives that have been taken in the day's combat. Hesitantly, Edmund delays the Duke by telling him he has seen fit to send the King and Cordelia into confinement. He reasons that the King's title and influence could tempt Albany's soldiers to waver in their loyalties and cause them to turn against him. He advises Albany to wait until a more appropriate time and place when the sweat and blood of the battle will no longer be fresh in their minds. They can then settle the question of what will be done with the captives. Albany promptly questions Edmund's audacity in making such major decisions, thereby considering himself an equal to the Duke. Regan immediately speaks up in Edmund's defense, claiming that Edmund had been commissioned to take her place in the battle. Goneril rebukes her sister, maintaining that Edmund has noble qualities by his own merit. The sisters throw insults at each other and an argument ensues.

Regan complains that she is not well which keeps her from airing her full-blown anger. She makes it known, however, that Edmund is her proposed "lord and master." Goneril objects, but Albany tells her there is nothing she can do to prevent it. As Edmund enters into the argument, Albany promptly arrests him, along with Goneril, on charges of "capital treason." With bitter satire, Albany informs Regan that Edmund is betrothed to Goneril, Albany's own wife, and if Regan wants to marry, she will need to regard him as a possible mate.

Albany calls for the trumpet to sound, challenging any man of quality or degree to declare that Edmund is a traitor. Dropping his glove, Albany is ready to fight in case no man appears at the sound of the third trumpet. Accepting the challenge, Edmund drops his glove in the same fashion, swearing to defend his "truth and honor firmly." In the midst of it all, Regan, who has been poisoned by Goneril, becomes increasingly ill and must be led away.

The first trumpet sounds and the Herald reads the legal document calling for any man in the army of quality or degree to appear, declaring Edmund a traitor. At the sound of the third trumpet, Edgar arrives. In reply to the Herald's questioning, Edgar informs him that his name has been lost but swears he is of noble birth. He testifies that Edmund is his adversary and a false traitor to the gods, his father, and his brother. Calling him a toad-spotted traitor, Edgar lifts his sword, ready for action. Edmund resists Edgar's accusations and challenges him to fight. There is a skirmish and Edmund is immediately wounded. Goneril protests that Edmund has been duped with trickery, but Albany sternly reprimands her, showing her the letter she has written to Edmund in which she plots the Duke's murder. Defiantly, she challenges Albany to arraign her, knowing full well she is immune to the law. She leaves in a fit of anger, and Albany, concerned about her desperate state of mind, sends his soldiers after her. Aware that he is dying, Edmund confesses his guilt to Albany. Turning to Edgar, he forgives him for slaying him if he is, indeed, noble. Edgar then reveals his true identity to Edmund. Agreeing with Edgar that the gods are just, Edmund declares that the wheel has come full circle and he is back where he started.

Upon Albany's request, Edgar relates his "brief tale" of his difficulties with the blind Gloucester, his father. He regrets that only one-half hour ago he revealed himself to Gloucester as his son, Edgar. The news was too much for his father's already "flaw'd heart" and it "burst smilingly." Edmund urges him to keep talking, but Albany is afraid he can take no more. Edgar apprises them of the whereabouts of the banished Kent and his "piteous tale of Lear" whom he has been serving in the capacity of a slave. The Gentleman enters, crying for help with a bloody knife in his hand. He informs Albany that he found it on the body of his lady Goneril. Before she died, she confessed to the Gentleman that it was she who poisoned Regan, and then she killed herself. With irony, Edmund notes that he was contracted to both of them and now they will all be married in death. Albany orders the Gentleman to bring in the bodies whether dead or alive.

At this moment, Kent enters, requesting to see the King so he might bid him goodnight. Engaged in Edgar's story, Albany has completely forgotten the incarceration of Cordelia and Lear. He questions Edmund, but is interrupted as the bodies of Goneril and Regan are brought in. As Edmund "pants for life," he hurriedly decides to do some good in the world by rescinding his orders against the lives of Lear and Cordelia. He hands Edgar his sword to give to the captain as a token of reprieve, but it is too late. Lear enters in a few minutes with the dead Cordelia in his arms. In his agony, Lear knows she is "dead as earth," but tries to find some life. Horror-stricken, Kent attempts to comfort the King by kneeling to him and identifying himself as Lear's friend, the noble Kent. But Lear shouts back in desperation, calling them all murderers and traitors. The King feels some comfort in the fact that he killed the slave who was hanging Cordelia.

Lear then recognizes Kent but asks about his servant Caius. Kent tells him he is the same man as Caius who has followed the King since the time his fortunes began to decline. Kent informs the King his oldest daughters have died by their own hands (which is only true of Goneril). Lear takes the news without emotion which leads Albany to conclude that he is not in his right mind.

A messenger enters, announcing Edmund's death, but Albany replies simply, "That's but a trifle here." Addressing the "lords and noble friends" who are present, Albany recognizes the King as the "absolute power" for as long as he lives. He grants honor to the virtuous and punishment for his foes.

Lear again cries out that his "poor fool is hang'd." As he gazes on the dead Cordelia's face and lips, he dies. Edgar thinks he has fainted and coaxes him to "look up," but Kent admonishes him to let the King pass. Albany instructs Kent and Edgar to rule the state jointly, but Kent declines the offer. He says he must soon follow his master. Only Edgar is left to restore order in the state.

***Analysis***

This final scene, the Catastrophe, represents the falling action of the play. It winds up the plot and, because it is a tragedy, involves the death of the tragic hero. Today, denouement is a term more commonly used though it is not limited to tragedy. In *King Lear*, it includes the clearing up of mistaken identities and disguises, as in the case of Kent and Edgar. The villain, who is Edmund, is also exposed and brought to justice in the last scene. The reunion of father and child is demonstrated in the main plot through Lear and Cordelia, as they are led away to prison, and in the subplot through Edgar and Gloucester. When Edgar makes himself known to Gloucester, his mixed emotions of joy and grief cause his heart to "burst smilingly." Though father and son are momentarily reunited, the meeting ends tragically with the death of Gloucester. Representing the tragic hero of the subplot, it is essential that Gloucester should die before Lear. Echoing Gloucester's death in the subplot, Lear dies in somewhat the same manner. As Kent implies, the King dies of a broken heart. "Break heart, I prithee break!"

One of the central themes of the play is the education and transformation of Lear. He has gained new insights and knowledge through suffering brought about by his own folly. Humiliated by his older daughters, he has come to realize that their flattery meant nothing, for he found he was not "ague proof." High position was of no use to him in the raging storm. Slowly he has been stripped not only of wealth and power, but of pride and deception. Now all that is left for him are the bare realities. In this scene, as he goes away to prison with Cordelia, they will "sing like birds i' th' cage." Purged of the outward trappings of pride that were once so important to him, he will make up for lost time as he and Cordelia

> ...laugh
> At gilded butterflies, and hear poor rogues
> Talk of court news; and we'll talk with them too—
> Who loses and who wins; who's in, who's out—
> And take upon's the mystery of things
> As if we were God's spies;

He now sees himself as a mere impartial observer of the trivial life of the royal court. With new insight he rejects his past life and his past beliefs. L. C. Knights states "For what takes place in *King Lear* we can find no other word than renewal."

The subplot intensifies the theme as it runs parallel to the main plot. Gloucester too begins to see after he is blinded. His lack of insight regarding Edmund's deception has, ironically, cost him his eyes.

Albany's earlier prediction that "Humanity must perforce prey on itself,/ Like monsters of the deep" (p. 81) has reached its final climax in this scene. In this reference he pointed to Goneril and Regan's cruel treatment of their father, and his fear that chaos and anarchy would be the result. As Albany anticipated, Goneril and Regan, involved in a love triangle with Edmund, have finally turned their hatred on each other as Goneril poisons Regan and then kills herself. Edmund is stabbed by Edgar because of his traitorous attempt on Albany's life. Edmund is a Shakespearean villain whose wheel has now come full circle, for, as Edgar says, "The gods are just," and Edmund is back where he began.

The "noble Kent" who has served his master, the King, so selflessly throughout the play, is growing old. We are led to believe he will shortly follow the King in death. "I have a journey, sir, shortly to go:/ My master calls me, I must not say no." Devoted to the King, Kent is of a different time when Lear's name was still revered. After the death of Lear, he recognizes that his time will soon come and he is ready. When Kent comes "To bid my king and master aye good night," we can clearly see the symbolism as being that of death, not only Lear's but also his own. This is true particularly in the light of his last speech in the play.

After Lear's death, Kent's comment, "The wonder is he hath endur'd so long," echoes Cordelia's words spoken earlier. She has just heard the account of her father's night in the storm where he was sheltered in a hovel with the common beasts. "Tis wonder that thy life and wits at once/ Had not concluded all" (p. 100). Lear seems to survive the most dire circumstances, and when he finally dies, Edgar, still unbelieving, wants him to "look up."

An understanding of the play must necessarily include an adequate perception of the Elizabethan view of order. Harry Levin, in the Introduction to *The Riverside Shakespeare* describes this divine order.

The age-old conception of a "great chain of being," extending from God through the angels toward mankind and downward to beasts, plants, and inanimate matter, links together all created things.

This idea has been reviewed elsewhere in the text, but it bears repeating in the light of Kent's comment as he sees Lear enter with the dead Cordelia in his arms. "Is this the promis'd end?" Kent asks, and Edgar adds "Or image of that horror?" John Holloway notes that "the king's end is like the end of the world: not the Day of Judgement, but the universal cataclysm which was to precede it" (John Holloway, "King Lear," 1961). For the Elizabethans then, any breakdown in the natural universal order could be a potential for a collapse into world chaos. Their belief that the end of the world was imminent was an integral part of their fears. Though set in pre-Christian Britain, this is, nevertheless, the world of *King Lear*, beginning with Lear's unnatural division of the kingdom and ending with Edgar's almost impossible task of restoring some semblance of order to the "gor'd state."

***Study Questions***

1. Who has taken Lear and Cordelia captive after the French have lost the battle?
2. Who delivers Goneril's letter, intended for Edmund, to Albany?

3. Who answers the Herald's third trumpet sound?
4. How does Gloucester die?
5. How do Goneril and Regan die?
6. How does Edmund react to being stabbed by Edgar?
7. What have Goneril and Edmund planned to do to Albany?
8. How does Lear feel about going to prison with Cordelia?
9. What becomes of Cordelia in prison?
10. Who is left to rule the kingdom at the end of the play?

***Answers***

1. Lear and Cordelia have been taken captive by Edmund.
2. Edgar delivers Goneril's letter to Albany.
3. Edgar appears on the call of the third trumpet to expose his half-brother Edmund as a villainous traitor.
4. His heart bursts when Edgar reveals himself as his true son.
5. Goneril poisons Regan and then kills herself with a knife.
6. Edmund forgives Edgar for killing him as long as he proves to be noble.
7. Goneril and Edmund have planned to kill Albany.
8. Lear is happy to be in prison with his long-lost daughter. In prison, they will sing and discuss the matters of the court.
9. Edmund has ordered that she be hanged. The order is rescinded by Edmund, but it is too late.
10. Albany appoints Edgar and Kent. Kent declines and leaves only Edgar to restore the kingdom to order.

***Suggested Essay Topics***

1. Lear has gained new insights and knowledge through suffering. Write an essay discussing the experiences that have led to Lear's realization that vain deception leads to one's downfall. In what way had he deceived himself? What has

been stripped away from Lear by the end of the play? Cite examples from the play to support your argument.

2. Kent is shocked at the death of Cordelia, thinking it might prove to be the "promis'd end." Write an essay explicating this statement. How does it explain the beliefs of the Elizabethans and the way they saw the world? Relate this passage to their attitudes concerning the hierarchy of all beings. Give examples from the play to support your view.

# SECTION SEVEN

# Bibliography



***Primary Sources***

Shakespeare, William. *The Riverside Shakespeare*, ed. G. Blakemore Evans. Boston: Houghton Mifflin Company, 1974.

*The First Folio of Shakespeare, The Norton Facsimile*, ed. Charlton Hinman. New York: W. W. Norton and Co., Inc., 1968.

***Secondary Sources***

Adelman, Janet. ed. *Twentieth Century Interpretations of King Lear*. Englewood Cliffs, New Jersey: Prentice-Hall, Inc., 1978.

Booth, Stephen. *King Lear, Macbeth, Indefinition, and Tragedy.* New Haven: Yale University Press, 1983.

Bradley, A. C. *Shakespearean Tragedy*, New York: St. Martin's Press, Inc., 1992.

Danby, John F. *Shakespeare's Doctrine of Nature*. London: Faber and Faber Ltd., 1951.

*Holy Bible, King James Version*. New York: Collins' Clear-type Press, 1956.

Kermode, Frank, ed. *Shakespeare: King Lear. London:* The Macmillan Press Ltd., 1992. An invaluable source for seventeenth, eighteenth, and nineteenth century commentary and criticism on *King Lear,* and for twentieth-century studies.

Kernan, Alvin B., ed. *Modern Shakespearean Criticism*. New York: Harcourt, Brace and World, Inc., 1970.

Knights, L. C. *Some Shakespearean Themes*. Stanford, California: Stanford University Press, 1960.

Lovejoy, Arthur O. *The Great Chain of Being*. Cambridge, Massachusetts: Harvard University Press, 1950.

Muir, Kenneth and Wells, Stanley. *Aspects of King Lear.* New York: Cambridge University Press, 1982.

# DOVER · THRIFT · EDITIONS

## FICTION

# DOVER · THRIFT · EDITIONS

## FICTION

THE WORLD'S GREATEST SHORT STORIES, Edited by James Daley. (0-486-44716-2)

THE AGE OF INNOCENCE, Edith Wharton. (0-486-29803-5)

AGNES GREY, Anne Brontë. (0-486-45121-6)

AT FAULT, Kate Chopin. (0-486-46133-5)

THE AUTOBIOGRAPHY OF AN EX-COLORED MAN, James Weldon Johnson. (0-486-28512-X)

BARTLEBY AND BENITO CERENO, Herman Melville. (0-486-26473-4)

BEOWULF, Translated by R. K. Gordon. (0-486-27264-8)

CIVIL WAR STORIES, Ambrose Bierce. (0-486-28038-1)

A CONNECTICUT YANKEE IN KING ARTHUR'S COURT, Mark Twain. (0-486-41591-0)

THE DEERSLAYER, James Fenimore Cooper. (0-486-46136-X)

DEMIAN, Hermann Hesse. (0-486-41413-2)

FAR FROM THE MADDING CROWD, Thomas Hardy. (0-486-45684-6)

FAVORITE FATHER BROWN STORIES, G. K. Chesterton. (0-486-27545-0)

GREAT HORROR STORIES, Edited by John Grafton. Introduction by Mike Ashley. (0-486-46143-2)

GREAT RUSSIAN SHORT STORIES, Edited by Paul Negri. (0-486-42992-X)

GREAT SHORT STORIES BY AMERICAN WOMEN, Edited by Candace Ward. (0-486-28776-9)

GRIMM'S FAIRY TALES, Jacob and Wilhelm Grimm. (0-486-45656-0)

HUMOROUS STORIES AND SKETCHES, Mark Twain. (0-486-29279-7)

THE HUNCHBACK OF NOTRE DAME, Victor Hugo. Translated by A. L. Alger. (0-486-45242-5)

THE INVISIBLE MAN, H. G. Wells. (0-486-27071-8)

THE ISLAND OF DR. MOREAU, H. G. Wells. (0-486-29027-1)

A JOURNAL OF THE PLAGUE YEAR, Daniel Defoe. (0-486-41919-3)

JOURNEY TO THE CENTER OF THE EARTH, Jules Verne. (0-486-44088-5)

KIM, Rudyard Kipling. (0-486-44508-9)

THE LAST OF THE MOHICANS, James Fenimore Cooper. (0-486-42678-5)

THE LEGEND OF SLEEPY HOLLOW AND OTHER STORIES, Washington Irving. (0-486-46658-2)

LILACS AND OTHER STORIES, Kate Chopin. (0-486-44095-8)

MANSFIELD PARK, Jane Austen. (0-486-41585-6)

## DOVER · THRIFT · EDITIONS

### NONFICTION

## DOVER · THRIFT · EDITIONS

### NONFICTION

THE REPUBLIC, Plato. (0-486-41121-4)

POETICS, Aristotle. (0-486-29577-X)

THE DEVIL'S DICTIONARY, Ambrose Bierce. (0-486-27542-6)

NARRATIVE OF THE LIFE OF FREDERICK DOUGLASS, Frederick Douglass. (0-486-28499-9)

GREAT ENGLISH ESSAYS, Edited by Bob Blaisdell. (0-486-44082-6)

THE KORAN, Translated by J. M. Rodwell. (0-486-44569-0)

28 GREAT INAUGURAL ADDRESSES, Edited by John Grafton and James Daley. (0-486-44621-2)

WHEN I WAS A SLAVE, Edited by Norman R. Yetman. (0-486-42070-1)

THE IMITATION OF CHRIST, Thomas à Kempis. Translated by Aloysius Croft and Harold Bolton. (0-486-43185-1)

### PLAYS

ANTIGONE, Sophocles. (0-486-27804-2)

AS YOU LIKE IT, William Shakespeare. (0-486-40432-3)

CYRANO DE BERGERAC, Edmond Rostand. (0-486-41119-2)

A DOLL'S HOUSE, Henrik Ibsen. (0-486-27062-9)

DR. FAUSTUS, Christopher Marlowe. (0-486-28208-2)

FIVE COMIC ONE-ACT PLAYS, Anton Chekhov. (0-486-40887-6)

FIVE GREAT COMEDIES, William Shakespeare. (0-486-44086-9)

FIVE GREAT GREEK TRAGEDIES, Sophocles, Euripides and Aeschylus. (0-486-43620-9)

FOUR GREAT HISTORIES, William Shakespeare. (0-486-44629-8)

FOUR GREAT RUSSIAN PLAYS, Anton Chekhov, Nikolai Gogol, Maxim Gorky, and Ivan Turgenev. (0-486-43472-9)

FOUR GREAT TRAGEDIES, William Shakespeare. (0-486-44083-4)

GHOSTS, Henrik Ibsen. (0-486-29852-3)

HAMLET, William Shakespeare. (0-486-27278-8)

HENRY V, William Shakespeare. (0-486-42887-7)

AN IDEAL HUSBAND, Oscar Wilde. (0-486-41423-X)

THE IMPORTANCE OF BEING EARNEST, Oscar Wilde. (0-486-26478-5)

JULIUS CAESAR, William Shakespeare. (0-486-26876-4)

KING LEAR, William Shakespeare. (0-486-28058-6)